I Ha[illegible]ou,
Now Kiss Me

What Reviewers Say About Kimberly Cooper Griffin's Work

Tides of Love

"This was such a sweet story about coming to terms with change, assessing wants and desires over morals, and putting yourself first. …Just a lovely story with lots of heart and sentiment. Great to explore reflecting and resetting everything while being true to yourself."—*LESBIreviewed*

No Experience Required

"*No Experience Required* is full of realistic, multidimensional characters. …I liked the honest and straightforward way that bipolar disorder was discussed, and I feel like I understand how those with the disorder feel a little bit more than I had before. I think that so much of this book is relatable to readers in different ways, and can help us all stop and think about others and the bigger picture a bit more. Even if readers do not know anyone with bipolar disorder, or are not in a same sex relationship, the matters at the heart of the story are universal. …*No Experience Required* is a well written and engaging book. I thought the issues of dating advice and mental health were very well handled, and I honestly would love to see more from all the characters in the book. I will be reading more from the author."—*Sharon the Librarian*

"The author does a thorough job of explaining Izzy's condition, her internal workings, hopes and fears. …This book straddles a space between a being a romcom and something more serious (given that the protagonists are dealing with a mental disorder and paternal homophobic physical violence). One of the best things about the book is that at the end we feel that this couple will really be happy together because they seem to have got their shot together and have learnt how to be a couple that communicates and cares for each other."—*Best Lesfic Reviews*

Can't Leave Love

"Sometimes you just need a romance that will melt your heart, bring a tear to your eyes at least once or twice, and leave you with a warm, happy feeling at the end. Add a couple of the cutest dogs, and you have a wonderful story. That is exactly what I found in *Can't Leave Love* by Kimberly Cooper Griffin. Besides being a beautiful love story, this book deals with some serious issues which is where the occasional teary eyes may happen. …This is a well-written romance with well-developed characters (both human and canine), set in a lovely small town, with just the right amount of angst to make the story interesting. It is exactly the type of romantic tale that I love to read. In fact, I think I've found a new author to add to my list of favorite romance writers. I will definitely be looking for more from this author."—*Rainbow Reflections*

In the Cards

"Both main characters are very well developed and easy to connect with. The secondary characters are also well-written, especially Marnie, Daria's younger sister who is autistic. As the mother of an autistic son, I can tell you that Marnie is realistically written. The romance is fairly lighthearted and uplifting though the two mains do have several hurdles to overcome. They get a bit of a paranormal/magical push to help them find and fall in love with each other. …I truly enjoyed this book."—*Rainbow Reflections*

Visit us at www.boldstrokesbooks.com

By the Author

No Experience Required

In the Cards

Sol Cycle

Can’t Leave Love

Tides of Love

Sweet Spot

Lost Harbor

Exposure (with Nicole Disney)

Accidentally in Love

I Hate You Now Kiss Me

I Hate You, Now Kiss Me

by

Kimberly Cooper Griffin

BOLD STROKES BOOKS

2026

I HATE YOU, NOW KISS ME

ISBN 13: 978-1-63679-995-7

This Trade Paperback Original Is Published By
Bold Strokes Books, Inc.
P.O. Box 249
Valley Falls, NY 12185

First Edition: April 2026

Credits
Editors: Ashley Tillman and Cindy Cresap
Production Design: Susan Ramundo
Cover Design By Inkspiral Design

Acknowledgments

A world of thanks to all of the hardworking and dedicated people at Bold Strokes Books who keep putting out books so we can see ourselves and show others we exist. Thank you for letting me be a part of your very important world.

Thank you, Alicia, for your feedback, thoughts, and spending countless hours on Zoom with me while this book came to life one painful word at a time. It's always a wild time, writing silently in our little square video boxes, watching each other slam the backspace key.

Ashley! I'm not mad at you anymore for making me cut ten thousand words. You redeemed yourself by saving me the embarrassment of having my character tell someone they "can suck a bag of dicks," when the correct way to say it is "eat a bag of dicks." For that, I will be eternally grateful.

Most of all, thank you, dear readers, for buying and reading my books. Eight-year-old me is laughing in the face of my third-grade teacher who said I'd never be a writer with my messy cursive writing. Joke's on her!

Dedication

To Summer, the best part of me.

Chapter One

2012 Just Before Junior Year

Andy Phillips clenched her teeth, walking as normally as possible, praying to any entity listening she didn't look like a dork. Her toe pads screamed, raw from the newly applied slip tape covering the pool deck at the rec center. Danny, the rec center manager, and former World Cup of Surfing champion, had gone a little overboard with the gritty tape after Willa Shaffer slipped and knocked herself unconscious the week before. To be fair, she'd been running so it was her own fault, but Danny's MO was "safety first." He'd bubble wrap the entire facility if it protected the kids he oversaw. Only two weeks into the season, and Willa hadn't been the first to slip. She wouldn't be the last.

Andy respected Danny's precaution even if her toes didn't appreciate it. She'd walk across broken glass if it kept Lena Holmes off her ass. Lena's insults had been the soundtrack of her life the last five and a half years. This year, she'd hoped to at least minimize it by moving into a higher level, but Lena had moved up, too. So, she'd joined the diving team, something Lena wouldn't do, being afraid of heights. Although Andy would never reveal her secret. But Lena was on the bleachers, even though she never stayed after practice. Try as Andy may, she just couldn't get away from her. Even worse, Lena occasionally claimed Andy was stalking her. Lena wished.

Finally, things seemed a little better after taking her best friend Talia's advice to ignore her. It'd been hard at first, given they had half their classes together, and while she disregarded Lena outwardly, inside was a different story. Her awareness of Lena, no matter where she was, taunted her all the time. She didn't think she'd ever get over Lena breaking up their friendship at the end of fifth grade. Pathetic. Five and a half years. She should have gotten over it five and five-sixths years ago. It didn't help that Lena hadn't let it go, either. But ignoring her, and not giving her the response she expected, drastically reduced the incidents.

Lena being at the pool was suspicious. Swim practice had ended half an hour ago. Yet, there she was on the bleachers near the diving boards, hanging out with Crystal Peters, supposedly watching their boyfriends practice water polo. But they were at the other end of the pool. Yep. Lena was there just to effing mess with her.

No one pushed her buttons more than Lena Holmes, even after five freaking years of hating each other. Andy was tired of crying in bathroom stalls. Tired of looking over her shoulder. Tired of missing her former best friend. Ignoring her didn't work a hundred percent, obviously. Thus, her presence near the diving boards, probably thinking she looked all sexy in the bikini she'd changed into, knowing Andy would feel like an underdeveloped cretin in comparison. Of course, she kept it to herself.

The sensation of Lena watching her, waiting for an opportunity to embarrass her, still made Andy uncomfortable. Not that she'd let on. No way was Lena going to see her react. They were mortal enemies. She hated herself for caring.

"Your butt's hanging out of your suit like usual, Andrea!"

And there it was. Lena knew she hated being called Andrea, too. Only four more weeks and the rest of her summer would be Lena-free. She could ignore her that long. Probably.

Climbing the diving platform ladder, she started her routine, clearing her mind. Something about throwing herself from high places exhilarated her. It was like dropping into a big wave when surfing. She missed mornings at the beach while she was at swim camp. But it would still be there in four weeks. The euphoria in the pit of her stomach from diving was worth the wait. Coach called her a natural.

Naturally, swimming was her thing. Pools were her father's business. The beach was only a few blocks from her house. Diving was new. Inspired by visiting her aunt and cousin in Colorado during spring break. They'd gone to Casa Bonita, and while their moms visited and drank margaritas, she and Gabby went down to watch the cliff divers. Standing near the indoor waterfall, eyes trained upward, she watched enthralled, as one-by-one, they plunged headfirst into the sparkling blue pool. Gabby had drooled over the six-pack abs on the guys, while Andy couldn't keep her eyes off the only woman. The diver's long brown hair cascaded down her muscled back, while Andy watched breathlessly as she performed dive after dive. Each time she climbed out of the pool, a tingle spread through Andy. The way the woman squeezed the water from her dripping hair, the tiny hoop in her bellybutton glinting, made Andy ache. She was the second prettiest woman Andy had ever seen.

She already knew she liked girls. It was because her stomach flipped over the diver, she knew it wasn't just one particular girl. Which was a relief.

Now, standing atop the ten-meter platform, the sting of her raw feet and the noise all around faded into the background. She still felt Lena staring, she always did, but she focused on the forward twisting dive she'd learned that morning, mentally going through the motions.

"What are you waiting for, Andy? An invitation from the mayor?"

The teasing voice of Mitch broke her focus. Ignoring him, she inhaled, shutting everything but Lena out again. The first running steps activated her muscle memory. Leaping forward, she twisted her torso, bending forward in an airborne somersault, while extending her arms, and unfolding her body. Perfectly vertical in a head-down dive, she plunged like a knife into the water.

Everything felt good about that dive. She smiled as she took a few strokes toward the ladder and straightened the bottom of her one-piece suit before she climbed out of the pool. Intentionally projecting disaffectedness, she pulled her hair over her shoulder to squeeze the water out, secretly hoping that people had noticed her perfect execution. By people, she meant Lena. Most of the time, she hated attention, even when it came to academics or sports. After nailing the dive, Lena didn't have a reason to—

"Show off!"

Hiding the sting she knew all too well, she headed for the locker room. She should have known better.

❖

Lena wanted to go home. Practice had been brutal. The rest of the team was so much better, and she'd had to kill herself to keep up. She should have stayed at the level she belonged, but she couldn't accept being a level behind Andy. She'd always kept up. Sure, she had to train harder. But she had no choice. She didn't care if Andy was better. She liked how her presence made Andy uncomfortable. Which was her primary goal in life.

"Have you two even kissed?" Crystal asked. She studied the ends of her hair.

Lena nearly choked on her own spit. "What?"

"Have you kissed Bronson yet?" Bronson practiced water polo with Crystal's boyfriend, Kyle. Lena couldn't stand either, but Crystal thought she and Bronson looked cute together. He was the best-looking guy in their grade, but Lena would rather kiss a snake, and she was terrified of snakes.

"It's not going to happen."

Crystal dropped the lock of hair. "Already? What about the double date? We've been talking about it for weeks."

For one week, actually, but Crystal wasn't listening. Her eyes were back on Kyle already.

Lena was trying not to be obvious about watching Andy. She wondered what she thought about up there on the platform.

Andy pushed her soft auburn hair back and shook out her arms before taking a running start. Lena's stomach lurched when she jumped. Long thick hair whipped around as Andy bent herself into geometric angles before she dove head-first into the water. It was over in seconds. Lena looked away as soon as Andy hit the water. She told herself not to turn back, pretending to watch the water polo team bob around in their ridiculous speedos and stupid swim caps. In her peripheral vision, she saw that Andy climbed out of the pool. She was even good at that. She was good at everything.

Before she could stop herself, she shouted at Andy about her butt hanging out of her suit, even though it wasn't. Why? It was probably more embarrassing to admit she noticed, than it was for Andy. At least Crystal didn't say anything about her being obsessed again. For once, she was glad Andy didn't glance her way. Well, mostly.

"Give it some time. He's so into you."

Crystal needed to stop.

"Do you have a thing for him?" Lena was an expert at deflection. "It sounds like you do."

"As if. Kyle and I just hit six months. I'm not into anyone but him." Crystal pushed Lena's shoulder. "Let's do a double date before you decide. It's a free dinner at least."

Lena rolled her eyes. "Burrito Haven isn't much of an incentive. Besides, my mother said not until I'm sixteen. That's months away." It was a lie. Her mother didn't say it. Or notice. Or care. But her friends didn't know it, and she worked hard to keep it that way. Especially from Andy, with her perfect parents and family dinner nights. Blech.

"Stay at my house. Tell her we're going to the movies. Just you and me."

Lena's stomach churned. She didn't want to. She'd given up sleepovers in grade school.

"I'm just not feeling it." Acting above everything usually worked. Not that she was conceited, but being pretty came with some benefits.

Crystal rolled her eyes. "How many guys have you broken up with?" Lena glared. Crystal was smart enough to back down. "I know. I know."

Guys were stupid. Her dating-obsessed friends were stupid. And she was stupid to play along. She didn't want to talk to guys, let alone date them.

"Whatever. Do what you want. You always do," Crystal said. Her attention was on the guys in the water again, which gave Lena the opportunity to watch Andy, who was on the platform again. She pretended to watch the lifeguard. It's not like she cared. It was basically her full-time job waiting for Andy to do something stupid. It got tiring sometimes, but it was second nature after five years.

Andy ran down the platform and did the same dive she'd been doing all practice. How did Andy make diving look so easy? Like it was no big thing. And the little pop when she hit the water? Hardly making a splash. It was sort of amazing, but boring. Lena huffed and coughed to cover it up. She didn't need Crystal's commentary. Of course she was obsessed. She and Andy had hated each other since fifth grade. And there she was, getting out of the pool like she thought she was some diving star. Walking all cocky and smug toward the bench, pulling her hair over her shoulder, effortlessly gorgeous, acting like she didn't know it.

"Show off!" she yelled. It was weak. She wanted to shrink away, embarrassed. Irritatingly, Andy didn't even look. Lena didn't care. Not really.

Chapter Two

"It's called global warming, Lance. Look it up. Weather patterns across the globe are changing. No meteorologist is getting it right all the time." Lena tried to keep her voice even.

For the third time in as many weeks, Lance had sought her out with his whiney voice and unkept fingernails, which she couldn't help noticing when he pointed his finger at her. She was going to break it one day. The finger, not the fingernail. Lance had no business being a producer at Insight Phoenix, the dominant television and digital network in Arizona. It had twice as many subscribers as the next largest news network in the region, more than half having signed up since she'd started working there three years ago. And Lance had the audacity to tell her she needed to up her game? She laughed at the little turd. She was the station's highest-rated anchor ever. Lance could eat shit, but cannibalism was against the law. She laughed at her silent joke.

Most of their new subscribers came from her personal channels, where she geeked out over meteorology, talking about anything that interested her. She could display her acerbic wit without getting her producers all up in a twist about "keeping with the brand." Her subscribers loved it. They were loyal and steadily increasing because she made them feel like insiders. She could live off the sponsorship money she pulled in on her personal channels, but she truly loved being on-air. Therefore, Lance's repetitive declarations about how she was causing the network to bleed subscribers was a joke. And getting old. Every meteorologist was struggling to read the unpredictable patterns. Yet, she still had a higher rate of accuracy than the overall average. Did Lena like when she got it wrong? No. But her subscribers understood. They loved hearing the reasons why the variations occurred. Lance could eat a bag of dicks. She sighed. It wasn't worth the energy.

Lance waved his hand dismissively. "The global warming bullshit again? Only gullible idiots believe it."

"Did you just call me an idiot?" The iciness in her voice gave even her the chills. He blanched. She enjoyed how much she intimidated him.

"I called you gullible. It's ludicrous anyone believes such an obviously contrived theory. Spreading liberal propaganda and all that woke BS meant to distract from real issues."

"Strike two, Larry." She intentionally said the wrong name. He squirmed. "It's science. Do you believe the Earth is flat, too?"

Arizona as a state was concerned with global warming but still had some deniers. Unfortunately, they were louder in their stupidity, which appealed to the less intelligent, less informed viewers who wouldn't change their minds even if they were drowning in infallible scientific proof. Not surprisingly, Lance was one of those less intelligent, less informed viewers who should buy himself some arm floaties. Why was she even engaging with him? It had to be the feeling of unease she'd awoken with. Plus, it wasn't yet seven in the morning, and she hadn't had her coffee.

"Science is subjective. Results are results. This is the third time you've been off with the forecast in the last month. If it happens again, well, you know."

She tilted her head. His voice trailed off. She was at least two inches taller even when she didn't have her heels on. It gave her pleasure. A little kid with a paunch and a receding hairline. She didn't appreciate his not-so-veiled threat. Loosening her shoulders to appear calmer than she felt, she managed a smile.

"I know, what?" she asked.

"Well, consequences." He puffed out his chest in a display of what? Not intimidation, that was for sure. He couldn't even meet her eyes.

"Such as?" She smiled. He didn't have the authority to issue consequences. He was an assistant producer. The general manager was the one who wielded that power. She had it on good authority Mike barely tolerated Lance. She wasn't worried.

"I guess you'll find out the next time 'scattered showers' turns out to be torrents of flooding rain," he said.

"I guess I will, then," she said.

The overhead lights switched on with a thunk, as if to signal the conversation was over. Lance was a gnat, she reminded herself. A gnat related to the assistant general manager. But Mike was the boss. Lance was just swinging his inflated ego around. She sighed again. Insecurity brought out the worst in people.

Three misses? She'd had one miss in the last three months. It had been mostly hot and dry with a few scattered showers. Nothing difficult to forecast. There'd been the low-pressure system triggering a haboob last week, but while predicting rainfall was tricky, Lena had developed an algorithm she used in conjunction with the National Weather Service data that resulted in a more reliable forecast, and she'd nailed it when all the others hadn't. Of course, Lance had nothing to say about that. He also didn't mention her two percent above average prediction accuracy over the industry average.

❖

Halfway through the afternoon, she needed coffee, but just before entering the break room, she heard her name.

"Rory's going to quit if he doesn't get night anchor," Lance said in his peevish voice.

That was her spot. Rory was a friend. They shared an office. Why hadn't he said something?

"We already have the best in the business. Have you tried offering him the usual perks?" As general manager, Mike was fair and rational, and thought Lance was a douche, too.

"Lena's lost her touch. We're bleeding subscribers because of her." Again, with the lie. "Rory props her up. He gets more fan mail. People trust his forecasts more."

Lance was a lying bastard on every count, and she almost stormed in to say so. She did the forecasting for the entire station, including Rory. They'd all be off the mark if she was. Mike would set Lance straight.

"Look." Lena heard papers shuffling. "She was off three times in the last month, when Rory has remained within the acceptable margins."

Lying sack!

"What does Rory want?" Mike asked.

"The night slot and ten percent. I think it's reasonable. It's less than what Lena makes by twenty percent."

"I don't love these numbers. It's not Lena's normal. I'll get back to you by end of day."

What the fuck? Why hadn't Mike thrown the report back in Lance's face? Gripping her coffee cup tightly enough to crack it, she had visions of stuffing the report up Lance's ass. But she was a professional.

The wind began to blow.

Rory beamed his gorgeous smile when she sat down across from him in their office. "Good morning, sunshine," he said even though it was afternoon. It was his trademark greeting to his audience every morning.

"Did you tell Lance you were going to quit?" she asked without preamble.

His smile dimmed. "Not exactly."

"Exactly what, then?"

"I was going to—"

"Quit if you don't get the evening spot?"

His brow creased as much as it could with all the Botox. "That's your spot."

"What did you ask for?"

"Five percent and an extended contract. That's all."

That lying shit!

"You deserve it. The evening spot, too." She opened her laptop, feeling the wind at her back. She could easily retain her position, but the storm had picked up strength. She typed a short note and hit the factory reset. At the office door, she turned. "Take care of Bombo." She glanced at the corn plant situated at the end of their desks. It was a small office, but she'd been happy here.

"Please tell me you're just taking the day off."

"I just told Mike and Lance to go fuck themselves."

"Whoa. Did one of them do something inappropriate?"

She laughed. "Mike didn't do anything. That's the problem. Lance would be coyote food if he did. Maybe I'll tell you over beer sometime." She'd done this before. Just once. They deserved it, though. But she usually didn't burn bridges. This time, she wanted the bridge burnt to embers. So there was no going back. Besides, she'd been feeling the need to run growing stronger. This time it didn't feel so much like running away. More like running to. Shoot the flaming arrow and don't turn back. "And, Rory? Don't settle for less than twenty percent."

She closed the door behind her without saying goodbye to anyone else.

❖

The rattle of Andy's cell phone against the stainless-steel countertop reverberated loudly for the third time in less than fifteen minutes, disturbing the scientists working in or near the simulated tide pools at Mary Hubbard Marine Laboratories in Monterey, California. Andy was certain she'd set it to do not disturb before she'd slipped into the shallow water to record the progress of the newest mollusks in their breeding collection.

The fourth time the phone vibrated, Andy sighed but continued to ignore it. Heidi, one of the second-year grad students, looked up from an experiment. She'd been stealing glances at Andy all morning, which irritated her, but wasn't new.

"Want me to bring it, Andy Candy?" Heidi asked.

God, Andy hated Heidi's nicknames.

"First, please stop with the candy thing. Second, I'll get it when I get out." She hated being so terse with Heidi, but she'd been warned once already.

"You got it, boss." Heidi gave her a wink.

Andy gently returned the specimen to its previous spot. All the interruptions were annoying. It didn't help that she'd been feeling anxious all morning for no reason she could identify.

After exiting the pool, she removed her gear. When she finally looked at her phone, Heidi was watching with curiosity. Andy headed toward the door.

Indeed, it was on do not disturb. Only three numbers could circumvent the setting. Her mom, her dad, and her doggie daycare. It was probably the latter. Billie, her seven-pound, sweet chiweenie, was on her final warning for bullying Todd, the Doberman, who literally handed over his tennis ball every morning as soon as Billie strolled in. At home, all she did was nap, preferably in a lap. If it was about Billie, she'd be isolated like the reactive dogs. In a single occupant dog run, she'd cry inconsolably. It was a torture Andy wouldn't subject on her worst enemy, and even Lena Holmes probably couldn't handle it. What? Where had that come from?

Puffing out a breath, she saw it was her mother. Was a scammer with an unlisted number after her life savings? Granted, her mother had fallen for one years earlier and had given them her credit card number, but they'd caught it quickly and canceled the card. She'd been hypervigilant ever since. Hence the call. Normally, she called after work hours, though.

Her mother answered on the first ring. "You know I hate calling during your workday." The hair on Andy's body stood up. "Your father is in the hospital."

Andy's stomach dropped. He was only in his early fifties. "What happened?"

"He fell into an empty pool at a job site."

"Is he okay?" Andy's heart pounded in her ears. Of course he wasn't. He was in the hospital. She made some calculations. It was ten a.m. Her father lived seven hours away. She'd arrive at five p.m. Damn. LA rush hour. Add two hours. If she left immediately, she could be there by seven, eight at the latest. But she had to pick up Billie and pack a bag. She had to call Talia to have her watch the house. Someone needed to cover her classes. Who—

"Andy?" Her mom's voice yanked her out of her head.

"Sorry, Mom. I'm here."

"He's getting x-rays and they're testing him for a brain injury."

"Fuck," Andy said, blowing out a breath, then remembered who she was talking to. "Sorry, Mom."

"Fuck, indeed. The situation warrants it."

Despite the almost flippant response, her mother sounded upset. Her parents had been divorced for over a decade, but they still cared about each other. Her mom had remarried. But her dad hadn't. She worried he was lonely, but he insisted he liked living alone. Her grandma lived close, and he had friends, but he needed his family. They talked on the phone a lot, but she hadn't visited in three years. A pang of guilt hit her. Phone calls weren't enough. Her mother was still on a tangent about workplace safety. She had to interrupt her.

"How did you find out?"

"Robert called right after it happened. He asked me to tell you."

"Robert Holmes?" She'd almost forgotten her dad was friends with Lena's dad.

"Yes. Can you go?" Her mother wanted to go out to see him, but she had summer school this year.

"I'm already thinking about logistics." The mention of Robert Holmes reminded her why she didn't visit. Not him. His daughter. Too many bad memories and possible sightings. No, thank you. "I can work remotely for a few days if needed." She had interns she could offload work to.

"Call me when you get there?"

"Sure, Mom. Give Lydia a hug for me," Andy said, already planning what clothes to bring.

She was going back to Oceanside, California, the hometown in which she'd spent the worst years of her life. Yay.

Chapter Three

2013—Junior year

Things were bustling at the San Diego County science fair, where Lena had submitted what she was certain would be the first-place project. This year, she'd really gotten into meteorology, which showed in the project she'd chosen. Most years prior, she'd submitted various projects as her interests changed. She'd placed first in her category several times. She had an aptitude for science. In most subjects, really. She was smart and she owned it. But science was her thing, even if the science fair itself wasn't. The event was highly competitive, but Lena wasn't.

When Andy competed in the same category, however, she made a concerted effort to win. Andy was her only real competition in academics. While she would never admit it, Lena enjoyed the rivalry, and when it came to Andy, losing to her in science was like Medieval torture. It wasn't merely a disappointment, it was a mortal blow, complete and utter devastation. But, when she won, she felt invincible.

Lena competed in the science fair every year. It was a way to exercise her mind during summer vacation, given she'd already completed any concurrent college classes she could take before she started actual college. To Lena's frustration, Andy had taken the same college courses, but she only participated when her summer sports schedule allowed. This year, it did, and she'd entered the same category. The gloves were off, and Lena had come up with a concept far more interesting, unique, and complex than any of her previous projects. In her opinion, way better than any of Andy's previous projects, too.

The last day of the fair was judging day. As confident as she was, Lena's anxiety increased as the day progressed. Half an hour before the announcements were made, she was so jittery, she had to take a break. Science projects from all over the county were displayed in the large space. When judges began to attach ribbons in other exhibits, she made her way back to her project, still anxious. Andy always caused her anxiety. Not that she would admit to it to anyone.

Her project was a demonstration of a concept she'd been following in science journals. Obviously, weather forecasting wasn't an experiment she could physically reproduce. So, she'd put together a visual demonstration using fiber optics and stop-motion animation, with a paper proving that solar flares increased radiation in the Earth's atmosphere by micro amounts, thus causing micro-changes in the weather. Andy's project about reef rehabilitation was interesting but nowhere near her unique topic. This was going to be her year.

Confusion washed over her when she approached her section. Displayed on the top podium was Andy's project, adorned with a blue ribbon. Her project hadn't even garnered an honorary mention. She didn't understand. It was still in the same spot it had been all week. She swallowed hard, trying to make sense of it. Looking for an explanation, she saw two judges across the display area. But they were talking to none other than Andy and her lapdog, Mitch. They made a few motions toward the projects on the winner's table and to where her project was located, obviously talking about her. She ducked behind a partition, embarrassed and even more anxious, and waited for an opportunity to approach the judges on her own. Her chance presented itself a few minutes later, after Andy and Mitch left the area.

"Excuse me. Can I please talk to you about a submission by Selena Holmes from Oceanside STEM Academy?" A small tremor sounded in her voice. Mortification swept through her about how close she was to crying. Losing was one thing, but crying about it was unthinkable.

"Was that the solar flare?" the taller one asked a shorter man who consulted a set of papers.

"That's it," Lena said.

"Impressive presentation, however, we had to deduct points for incorrect data," the shorter man said, referencing his notes. "It's a stellar project. If you'd presented it as a model of a theory, the oversight in the calculations wouldn't have factored in. I was aggrieved to mark it down. If the calculations had been correct, it would have assuredly been on the winner's table. Probably first place."

Lena, fighting to retain composure, couldn't breathe for a few seconds. Shaking, she found her voice.

"What oversight?" she asked, while What the actual fuck? wanted to roll off her tongue.

"The calculation of the pulse speed from the solar flare was incorrect. Another participant tried to argue its validity, but I verified it myself."

"That's impossible." Lena clenched and released her fists.

"Judging is over," the tall judge said. She hated his arrogant attitude.

"Please verify it again." Lena wasn't about to go down without a fight. Especially when it gave the win to Andy fucking Phillips. Besides, she'd verified the calculations several times. They were accurate.

"If you wish to contest the decision, I can provide information about how to do it." The judge was beginning to look impatient.

Lena certainly did want to contest it, but Andy had come over. Probably to gloat. Suddenly, Lena's confidence slipped. Were her calculations off? Why was she was doubting herself? This was bullshit.

"I'll get back to you," she said to the judges, not looking at Andy. It was all she could do to maintain a calm façade. She'd scream into her pillow later, when there was no one to hear.

❖

Impressed with Lena's composure and pissed about the error the judges refused to fix, Andy watched her leave. As much as she despised her, Andy wasn't into winning when she didn't deserve it. Lena's projects were always interesting. Not only were they scientifically advanced, but she also had a knack for making what could be dry information into an engaging display. Of course, she'd never tell Lena this. She wasn't a masochist.

When Lena's project hadn't even placed, she reviewed the judge's notes explaining the points deduction. She didn't have enough knowledge of the project. But she did understand advanced mathematics. After going over the calculations, Andy saw where the judge misinterpreted the order of operations, getting incorrect results. Andy could prove Lena's work was correct. She'd gone to the judges with the proof, but he repeated what he'd told Lena. Judging was closed.

She had no choice but to take it to the regional director of the science fair. Unlike the first judge, the director hadn't been dismissive and agreed the reason for the deduction was incorrect. Either way, it should have been verified with others before being applied. However, because judging was closed, it needed to go through the challenge process. Before they left, Andy submitted the challenge, and the director promised a review of the situation. If the challenge was correct, an update to the annual science fair statistics would be applied, if applicable. It didn't help Lena now, though, and Andy remained haunted by the look on Lena's face when she'd left.

"She deserves to win," she told Mitch when she returned to the display room. "Most of these projects are just models. They just report findings from other scientists. Hers was so much more. That judge couldn't admit he was wrong."

"Why do you care? I thought you hated Lena."

"How I feel about Lena is irrelevant. And hate is such a strong word, anyway."

"I'm just going with what you've said."

Andy winced. It sounded so harsh. "We have our differences, but what that judge did was wrong."

Mitch shook his head. "You're a better person than me."

Chapter Four

It was good to be out of the car. Seven hours had turned into twelve when an accident stopped traffic on the 5, right after the 210 Exchange. Lucky her, the delay was so long, she'd missed LA traffic. By the time she arrived at the hospital, her dad was asleep for the night. She still went up to his room to see him with her own eyes, and after seeing he was sleeping soundly, she gave him a kiss before taking herself and Billie to his house. The day hadn't been longer than any other day for her, but she was twice as tired than usual. Probably from the worry.

In her dad's driveway, she stretched next to the open door of her car, taking in the scent that infused all her childhood memories. She hadn't been back in three years, but she knew the tapestry of scents and the feel of the night air like she knew her own name. If her eyes had been covered, she would have still known it was early June. That's how distinct the smells and the heaviness of the air were in San Diego from season to season and time of day. People who grew up here were tuned into it with all five senses.

Billie continued to sleep on the passenger seat while she quietly removed her suitcase and computer bag from the back of her Subaru. She took them up to the house, which hadn't changed much at all. Inside and out, the house looked almost exactly how she'd left it when she'd gone to college twelve years ago. The Norman's house next door had been torn down, and a two-story behemoth had been built in its place since the last time she'd been home, making her dad's house look small in comparison. While it was being built, he'd kept her apprised of the "travesty in progress." Their house, with its four bedrooms, two baths, and two-car garage, had originally been among the biggest on the block. Now it wasn't even in the top ten.

"Andy Phillips is that you?" a familiar voice called out. Mrs. Rafferty from the house on the other side stood on her driveway, hand shielding her eyes as if it would help her see better in the soft glow of the nearby streetlight. A rolling garbage bin was next to her, explaining why she was outside at the late hour. Her housedress, one of several similar garments Andy was pretty sure she'd worn since before Andy was born, fluttered in the mild breeze coming in from the ocean.

Andy stood at the edge of her dad's driveway. "Hello, Mrs. Rafferty. How are you?"

"Fair to middlin', honey. Fair to middlin'. You here to see your father?"

"Yes, ma'am. Just got here."

"As I ascertained from the suitcase you rolled into the house. Also, your car hasn't been parked here, but five minutes."

"Fair point," Andy said with a chuckle. "I guess I don't need to tell you, Dad's in the hospital."

Mrs. Rafferty nodded. "With quite a few broken bones, I hear. One of his crew knocked him into an empty pool. In the deep end. Nasty fall. He'll be in the hospital for a few days, I imagine. I made a casserole. I'll heat it up and bring it over tomorrow for your supper. It's in the dish I borrowed just before Ella passed. You can give it to another neighbor sometime and we can call it the neighborhood casserole dish. But not to Gary on the corner. He keeps putting garbage in my bin without asking. That's why I roll it out so late."

Ella was Mrs. Norman, who used to live where the behemoth currently stood. She passed two years ago and that's when the developer bought the house, resulting in her dad's consternation. "That's very nice of you, Mrs. Rafferty."

"Well, I better get this situated and get back inside before I catch my death." Mrs. Rafferty flopped a hand at the garbage bin.

Andy doubted she'd catch anything in the perfectly mild seventy-two-degree weather as she closed the distance between them. "I'll take it the rest of the way down."

"Oh, you don't need to go to the trouble."

"I'd like to. You brought it this far. It's just a few feet." Andy rolled the bin the rest of the way down the driveway and aligned it with the sidewalk line and two inches from the curb in the precise way she remembered Mrs. Rafferty liked it.

"Just like my Bruce used to line the bin up. You never got to meet him, Andy. He passed forty-one years ago. He was an Army man. By the book and neat as a pin. He liked angles and folds and precise edges. Everything had a purpose and a place. But when he closed the bedroom door, I tell you, that man didn't give a whit about his hospital corners or bouncing a quarter on the covers. Whether it was just me or a few friends, he always had the bedding in disarray and the mattress askew by the end of the night. But everyone left the room more than satisfied, and as neat as they came in. That was my Bruce. He didn't do anything halfway. He would have loved to have you as a neighbor, Andy. I'll be by tomorrow."

And just like that, Andy was alone again, processing what she'd just heard and almost glad to be back. She'd missed Mrs. Rafferty, who always had a story to tell and a plate of cookies to share. Andy hadn't heard her tell a story quite like that, but she'd lived a long and interesting life, and she reminded Andy how nice it was to have good neighbors.

She'd always liked her neighborhood, aside from the traffic, but she had mixed emotions about growing up in Oceanside. Although she often glibly stated that the last half of her life in Oceanside had been the worst years of her life, they hadn't all been bad. She'd had a lot of good ones, too. It was just that the last six and a half years were spent longing for the best friend she'd lost, and fighting the enemy who'd taken her place. The hard part was they were one and the same.

Once she'd started, she couldn't help but think about Lena. Like it or not, she'd been the center of her life for nearly the entire time she'd lived in Oceanside, and good or bad, she was part of every memory.

Andy turned her thoughts to the reason why she was here. When she'd called the hospital, she'd caught the doctor on duty. Her dad was still sedated and sleeping. The doctor described the extent of his injuries, the worst being a severe concussion. In addition to that, both legs were broken, as well as a broken left arm and left clavicle. He also had a dislocated right shoulder, two broken ribs, multiple bruised ones, and several abrasions. She was thankful he'd avoided a TBI or a broken neck. Only the broken arm with the compound fracture had required surgery to insert two plates, multiple screws, and a rod. This meant he had casts or braces over much of his body ensuring he'd be immobile for eight to twelve weeks, after which he'd have several months of physical therapy. As it was, he'd need around-the-clock care, most of it attending to his lack of mobility. Aides would visit twice a day, leaving the rest up to someone who could stay with him. That someone probably meaning her. Her dad would be the decision-maker about it as soon as he was fully lucid again. But she already knew it would be her. Either way, she'd have to update her employer as soon as she had specific details.

So, it appeared she'd be here for several months. She pushed her fingers through her hair, needing to think things through. Not tonight, however. She needed sleep. Ultimately, it came down to getting her dad through this. Nothing else mattered.

Completely depleted, fully clothed, and not bothering to shut off the lights, she fell to the couch and immediately sank into a fitful sleep.

❖

Somewhere north of Calexico, Lena got the feeling that the derecho wasn't chasing her, but something else was pulling her to her destination. She couldn't imagine what it would be. After all, she'd spent the last third of her life avoiding the place. Equally mystifying was that her thoughts were leaning toward the things she missed, rather than the things she'd run from. Maybe it's why her thoughts turned toward a certain girl, and she forgot how dangerous it was to let those thoughts catch hold, especially when she didn't have anything to distract her from them. Fortunately, a billboard announced the world's best jerky, soft serve ice cream, and spotless restrooms all in one place in only two and a half miles. Hell yes, she could really go for all of those, plus a cup of coffee and a bag of sunflower seeds. Looking forward to the convenience of bulk junk food was the distraction she needed. So she changed the station on her satellite radio and tried to decide whether to go out on a limb and get the teriyaki jerky or the black pepper.

Right about the time she hit the desert town of Ocotillo, California, just over a hundred miles east of her hometown of Oceanside, California, Lena felt the atmosphere begin to change. That far from her destination, it was still desert. But it was Southern California desert, which was different than any other desert, including the Arizona desert she'd left five hours earlier. People who lived in the Arizona desert were people born of the desert life. They were part of the landscape, used to the climate, usually descended from generations of desert dwellers.

The people who live in the desert of eastern California, close to the Mexico border were people who seemed to live a tired life. Not enjoying their life in the hard scrap of arid badlands but not necessarily hating it either. Resigned was what the place felt like to Lena. It was definitely a California atmosphere. Just not one of the glamorous ones most people associated with California. This was where main characters had their cars break down and end up staying to learn the lesson written into their character arc before they could go home to the place they'd fled with a new kind of respect for it. It was one of the many drive-through towns along the 8, that were usually a beige blur on the way through to somewhere more interesting.

To Lena, it was one of her favorite places to stargaze. She didn't think about that as she passed through, however. She was thinking about a kiss that had changed her on a cellular level twelve years ago. It seemed so long ago, but it had remained a vivid memory for her, albeit one she tried not to think about much. Keyword, tried. If it hadn't been so fucking good, she might have succeeded. But it was good, which is why she might become one of those main characters with a broken-down car someday, with an arc written with a choice—accept it or stay and become a third-tier side character without a name, who people simply call the Meteorologist.

About an hour later, when Lena reached the 805 Interchange in Mission Valley, the smell of the ocean welcomed her, and her body reacted to her return home on a more visceral level. Mission Valley to her, was a boundary from San Diego proper and the rest of San Diego coastal county. More city than town. She always associated it with shopping. When a person came in from the east, it was where the coastal ambiance became more evident. If one came down the coast from either direction, it felt several steps from the ocean. Lena took this in because she had no choice since her body was programmed to detect the nuanced changes experienced by those moving from one distinct San Diego setting to another. Her mind was still preoccupied with that kiss, though, so it was her lizard brain where her location detection operated. That kiss required most of her conscious mind and was all-consuming when she allowed herself to ruminate on it. Her body remembered the impact of the life-changing experience, and she was in its thrall when she merged onto the 805, barely aware of her surroundings and fully focused on the memory of those lips.

It was when the 805 merged with the 5 that a true coastal San Diego vibe really hit, ripe with the cool ocean breezes, the smell of dank lagoons, eucalyptus, and highway oleander. The smells were an olfactory ambrosia, and it only added to the wistful memory of kissing Andy Phillips after their last swim meet before they left for separate colleges. Wistful turned to despair when she took the Cassidy Street exit into the neighborhoods of Oceanside, California, just to acknowledge that Andy didn't live here anymore, just like her. And if she did, she would still hate her, so memories of kisses or not, there wasn't a chance of take two of the kiss. It didn't keep her from reexperiencing it like it was yesterday, which was what she was doing right now.

The genius loci of Oceanside was a full body reset. Shedding the external shell made of the amalgamation of locations she'd traveled through or lived in over the last twelve years, her freshly revealed original skin was back in place and absorbing the special elixir only Oceanside possessed. Sure, most towns in California possessed their own miasma of sensory detail, but to Lena this was the blend that she called home. And it reminded her so much of Andy Phillips it made her ache. That's why she had to lock it away again and refuse to pull it out. Because allowing that particular memory of the perfect kiss to mingle with the scents and energy of the place where it had occurred, was a torture she couldn't endure. Especially when she looked forward to the agony of dealing with Helena Holmes for an indeterminate period of time. She refused to pollute her recollection of the best kiss of her life with new trauma she was sure to be afflicted with during this visit.

What kind of masochistic self-flagellation had she wrought upon herself?

She allowed herself a few more seconds of the memory as she coasted down her old street and tucked it away as she pulled into the driveway of the house she'd spent the worst years of her life in.

Welcome home, Lena!

Chapter Five

2013—Junior Year

According to rumors, Claire Esteban threw the best parties. This was the first one Andy had attended after Talia and Mitch had worn her down. Claire's mom, who was the lead singer of a well-known metal band, and her dad who played banjo in a bluegrass band, were always touring with their respective bands. When both were out of town, Claire usually invited a few friends over. This time, it looked like half the junior class had been invited. Talia had told her to be prepared for something wild and lit.

That's how Andy found herself standing in the foyer at Claire's house, on top of a hill, surrounded by avocado groves and kids milling around holding red Solo cups. She hadn't even reached the porch, before Mitch dashed off in search of his buddies. The front door was open, spilling music. A guy from her French class walked by, making a show of checking her out, before giving his friend a fist bump. Yuck.

"Hey, Andy." Claire handed her a drink before giving her a one-armed hug. She looked her up and down. This one made Andy's cheeks warm. "You look cute, as always. Welcome to the zoo." Claire swept a hand through the air. The drink smelled like rubbing alcohol and Andy tried not to choke after a polite sip.

"Half the school's here," Andy yelled over the music. Her throat continued to burn. The good news was she didn't see Lena.

Instead of moving on, as Andy would have predicted, Claire stood next to her, casually watching the crowd. Most of the kids held red cups, but no one danced on coffee tables or swung from light fixtures.

After Lena had ditched her, splitting their friend group in half, and although Claire chose Lena's group, she remained nice to Andy. They'd only drifted apart because Andy needed distance from Lena.

"Any plans for the summer?" Andy asked. Dad talk? Really?

Claire shrugged. "Surfing and shopping, probably. We go on our family vacation at some point. I think it's Bali this year. We're staying in one of those huts built over the water."

"That sounds amazing."

She shrugged again. "It's your last year, right? You're graduating early like Lena? A couple of brain banks." She raised her cup. "Cheers to escaping Osta," she said, using the nickname everyone called Oceanside STEM Academy.

"Thanks." She tapped her cup to Claire's, who didn't seem to notice she wasn't drinking it. Judging by Claire's glassy eyes and soft smile, she'd already had a cup or two. "This is wild."

"It's pretty tame, so far."

"I'd be too worried about death and destruction to relax if I were you."

"My parents would totally revoke my party privileges over any deaths, but a service will come tomorrow to clean up the destruction." Claire nodded. "Yeah, so no. The death part hasn't happened yet. Knock on wood."

Andy hadn't heard right. "Your parents let you do this?"

Claire put a finger against Andy's lips. "It's cool in Europe. Where do you think I get the alcohol?"

Claire looked past her just before a wall of cologne enveloped her. Sweaty hands covered her eyes.

"Are you glad you came?" She barely understood what Mitch said and ducked away. An empty plastic cup hung between his teeth. Had he already finished a whole cup?

"I'm going to find Josh. He's out there helping Logan make some sort of video," Claire said, giving them a four-finger wave. "Have fun. That's an order." She pointed at Andy before going to find her boyfriend.

Mitch moved to where Claire had just been. "Answer me, woman."

She gave a warning glare.

He bowed apologetically. "Sorry. May I perchance elicit a response to my query regarding the quality of time experienced by you, thus far, m'lady Andrea?"

"We've only been here fifteen minutes." She gave his empty cup a meaningful stare. "Give me your keys."

He fished them out of his pocket. "Everyone's here."

"Talia's around somewhere, so you don't have to babysit me."

"Maybe I like hanging out with you." He stepped closer.

"I'm going to find the bathroom," she said. When he followed, she pushed him back. "I'll find you. Now go." He was like a duckling that had imprinted on her. Finally, he gave her finger guns and headed into the kitchen. She had to tell him.

Abandoning her cup, she went to look for a bathroom she didn't need.

Talia nearly tackled her in the living room. "You're here!"

"I told you I'd be."

"You always say so and don't show."

"I always say maybe."

"Whatever. I'm glad you're here." Talia took her hand, pulling her outside through a set of glass doors.

A band was setting up in a gazebo at the edge of a sprawling lawn. Several people were in the pool. A few wearing clothes. Andy grimaced. What about their phones?

Josh held out an arm. "Kyle's throwing anyone in civvies into the pool. Did you bring the required uniform?"

Mitch had warned her, so Andy had her swimsuit on under her clothes. She'd finally dared to wear a bikini in public. So far, she'd only worn it under her wetsuit when she went surfing. Regardless, making everyone wear swimsuits seemed like a skeevy ploy to get people nearly naked. Talia was already pulling off her tank top and shorts, though, so she did the same. Thankfully, she'd worn board shorts over her bikini bottoms. Talia wore a barely-there two-piece. Andy wasn't attracted to her very straight best friend since fifth grade, but she admired the look.

"You look cute," Talia told her after they'd stashed their clothes and phones behind a giant planter. She grabbed Andy's hands and raised her arms appraisingly. "Your swim team suit doesn't do you justice. Girl, you've blossomed."

Andy yanked her hands away, laughing. "Perv." Never mind she'd silently done the same to Talia.

Talia leaned in. "Evil lurking at two o'clock. She's with Crystal."

Andy didn't turn. "Coming this way?"

"Sitting, but she's staring."

"Seriously, I don't care." She fought not to turn. Why would Lena's stare make her tingle?

"Is that so? 'Cuz there are two chairs right next to her."

"Stop it. What's she doing now?"

Talia smiled. "She seems to like your suit."

A group of their friends walked up, saving Andy from responding. Lena's gaze was hot on her back the whole time. It was exhausting, pretending she was unfazed. Finally, she took Talia's hand and pulled her toward the house. "I need something to drink."

"She wouldn't stop staring at you. It can't feel good carrying around all that negative energy," Talia said, trailing behind.

After they found un-spiked punch, they wandered, stopping to chat with people they knew. The party was more fun than she anticipated, despite wondering where Lena was at any given moment. Mitch's cologne enveloped her again, and she dodged his arm.

"Are you going swimming?" he asked, indicating her top. He shoved his hands into his pockets, failing at casual. She lifted a questioning eyebrow. He'd seen her in a swimsuit a million times. "You're the swimmer."

"Okay." She drew out the word. It got even weirder when he just stood there. "Something wrong?"

He shrugged, tossing his head to get the hair out of his eyes. "I wanna tell you something."

"Okay," she said again.

"It's too loud." He led her toward a hallway.

Talia rolled her eyes and walked away. Andy followed him apprehensively. This was the time to lay it on the line.

"You're acting weird." When he made to go into one of the rooms at the end of the hall, she stopped him. "What's up?"

He shifted his weight from foot to foot, pushing his hands into his pockets again, not meeting her gaze.

"What?" Her patience faded.

"Something happened."

"What?"

"Lena was just talking to me about five minutes ago."

She waited for more. "And?"

Red stained his cheeks. "Weird, huh?"

"I guess." She and Lena didn't talk to each other's friends, with a few exceptions. Mitch had never been one. Honestly, Andy didn't care if Lena talked to Mitch. Not much, anyway. It depended on why.

"Do you think she was flirting?" he asked.

"Do you think she was?" Lena flirting with anyone seemed weird.

"Maybe." He bit his thumbnail.

"Like how?" Was she bothered now? About Mitch? Or Lena?

"She asked if I wanted to do something sometime."

"She asked you out?"

"I think so." He didn't elaborate.

"What did you say?"

"I might have inferred we were, um, dating?"

She didn't love that, but she could see him panicking. "As an excuse?" she asked, giving him a little grace.

He peered through his lashes, looking like a scolded little boy. “Kinda?”

“I don’t mind being your excuse.”

“I mean, you know I like you, right?” he asked, the red covering way more than his cheeks now.

She barely stopped herself from sighing. “We’ve talked about it, yes.”

“Are you, you know, jealous?”

“You can hang out with anyone you want. Even her. We’ll still be friends. It won’t bother me.” Not bothering her wasn’t the entire truth, but she wasn’t in the mood for introspection right now.

His face fell.

Impatient or not, she didn’t like seeing him upset. “You wanted to see if I’d get jealous?”

“I guess. Yeah.”

“I’m gay.” Not how she wanted to tell him, or to come out for the first time, but it had to be said.

“Huh?” He stared at her.

“I like girls.”

He pulled his hands down his face. “I’m such a moron.”

She rested a hand on his arm. “I should have told you before now. I just wasn’t ready.”

“I’m so sorry,” he said. He really did sound remorseful.

“You don’t need to be.” She tried to make him look at her. He wouldn’t.

“I freakin’ pestered you. I thought if I just kept trying, I’d wear you down.”

“Okay, well, that isn’t great. I mean, no means no, right? Maybe don’t do that with anyone else?” He nodded. “Are you okay, though?” She tried to get him to look at her again. “This doesn’t have to screw anything up, right?”

“I’m just embarrassed. I won’t tell anyone. It’s your business.” He glanced down the hall, looking like he wanted nothing more than to escape. Andy didn’t blame him. She did, too.

“Hey, if it helps, I never told anyone you liked me. As far as they know, we’ve always been friends. Because it’s true.”

His laugh sounded uncomfortable. But he smiled, which was a relief.

❖

Lena held her breath standing in the dark bathroom. She let it go after they passed. She hadn't meant to eavesdrop. She'd been taking a moment to herself when Andy and Mitch entered the hallway. She stepped into the empty bathroom before they could see her. Once inside, she almost died thinking maybe they were trying to be alone, which made her stomach churn. Worse, she worried they might find her. Maybe even notice she'd been crying.

She wished Crystal hadn't finally talked her into coming to this stupid party. She wished she hadn't lied about spending the night and going to the movies. After all the worry, her mother only seemed relieved to have her out of the house. She never expected she'd feel like shit about that. And she was so uncomfortable here. She knew who she was at school. At this party, she was totally out of her element, sitting like a loser by the pool, hoping people thought she was bored.

Most of all, she was embarrassed about how she'd stared at Andy, watching as she removed her clothes, staring at how hot she looked in that bikini. Staring at her with all the people who got to talk to her, when she couldn't. And that bikini top and swim shorts. God. She'd stopped breathing. Andy was gorgeous. Lena hated how many guys noticed Andy. And she hated how jealous she was when she thought Andy might be noticing them.

Lena had known she was into girls for a while. She'd also known she was more than just into Andy. Which she absolutely hated herself for. Now, she hated how Andy probably thought she'd been trying to steal her boyfriend, who wasn't really her boyfriend she'd just found out. And she hated how she'd listened like a creeper to their conversation, wishing she was anywhere else but here. But she didn't want to be anywhere else, because she was able to watch Andy be Andy, and see how Andy was when she wasn't around her, because she loved watching Andy move and talk and do normal things. And now she knew Andy was gay. But, more than anything, she hated that she'd never be able to shake this thing she had with Andy Goddamn Phillips now that she knew.

She wanted to feel bad about spying, but she couldn't. Not when she was too busy feeling a gazillion other things about the discovery that, not only were Andy and Mitch just friends, but Andy liked girls. It felt like a bomb exploded in her chest. She should have known. And why was she so happy? She was supposed to hate Andy. Andy certainly hated her.

"There you are. I've been looking all over for you." Crystal interrupted her thoughts. How long had she been standing in the doorway of the bathroom? She felt like she was floating above her body.

"Hey," she managed to say.

"Claire needs us to mix up more of that vile punch shit. Gah. It makes me gag just smelling it. I gathered all the stuff, but I just can't deal. Can you help?" Crystal hugged her arm and batted her eyes. "I'll love you forever."

"Sure," she said, still trying to get her mind around what she'd learned. A tingle buzzed through her. What the fuck? She hated Andy. Hated her.

"Lena Holmes. Where are you right now?" Crystal's voice cut sharply through her thoughts.

Lena jerked her head up. They were in the living room, and she didn't know how they'd gotten there. Lost in her thoughts again, probably. Maybe she should talk to Crystal.

"I just overheard the most interesting conversation…"

Chapter Six

"How long will you stay?"

They were the first words out of Lena's mother's mouth. No hello. No hug. Not even a smile. Helena Holmes always cut to chase. There'd never been a kind word, a hug, or a smile for her. The hurt Lena didn't want to feel, but always did, made her want to return the icy reception to see if it could inflict as much pain on her mother as it did her. It wouldn't even faze her. It would only give her an excuse to make Lena feel like a pile of shit. Did wanting to make her mother feel that way make her like her mother? It was a fear lurking in her darkest soul.

"Hello, Mother. Would you like me to stay somewhere else?" Lena chose a middle ground. She never wanted to trigger her mother, whose tongue was sharper than a razor, and when turned on her, never failed to send her right back to being a toddler to hear she was unlovable and unwanted. Her mother had said worse things, but that was the first time she remembered wanting to disappear.

"Honestly, Selena. You take offense so easily. I'm making the grocery list and would like to know how much food to have delivered."

Lena sighed inwardly, not wanting to raise her mother's ire. This was her mother being nice. It was hard enough to take. "I thought I'd stay the week. Is that okay?"

"You may stay as long as you like. It's not often you visit, let alone stay here. I look forward to the company."

Passive-aggressive. Ambiguously polite. For her mother, it was a warm greeting.

"I'm sorry it's been so long."

"You must be busy with your internet hobby on top of your television job," her mother said dismissively. "Are you on vacation?"

"You could say that." Lena wasn't planning to tell her the real reason. That she'd left Phoenix because she couldn't stand the reminder that she was expendable. That, for the first time, when the derecho hit, her first compulsion was to go back home, somewhere she'd been running from, yet searching for, her entire adult life. The compulsion was stronger than it had ever been. Which scared her, but intrigued her, too.

She referred to this urge of hers to run as being chased by the derecho. In weather terms, a derecho is a sustained and extremely strong windstorm, potentially dangerous. When the feeling hit, she always envisioned herself trying to outrun the wind that could just as easily knock her down or propel her forward. For the first time, though, she'd decided to run before the wind came. What did that mean?

Either way, this time, the mere idea of the derecho chased her back to Oceanside. A place she'd never thought she'd visit again. It wasn't the town she'd fled, all those years ago, but the memories it held. It reminded her of how small her mother made her feel and how she didn't matter to her father. And then there was Andy Phillips, but that was too painful to think about, so she tried not to.

"Your father's looking forward to seeing you."

But she wasn't? Three steps out of her car. Three fucking steps. God, this was going to be fun, she told herself sardonically. Some things would never change. She should ignore it. It seemed to work for others. A specific gorgeous brunette came to mind unbidden. But she was trying not to think about Andy Phillips, right?

"Is he here?"

"He said he'd be here for dinner. But who knows with him? I certainly never do."

And there it was. A new record for how quickly her mother would bring up their horrible marriage and how Lena had been the cause of it. Why they stayed married had always been a mystery to her. Oh yes, this was going to be fun. Would he grace her with his presence this time? Or stay wherever it was he hid from her? She suspected his swanky office, but she hadn't been there since she was six or seven. She hoped he'd stay away this time, too.

As she retrieved her bags from the back of her red Mercedes, a brown older model Buick drove slowly down the street. A blast from the past, and not a good one. Andy Phillips had driven a car like it in high school.

She hadn't seen Andy since graduation, but memories were harder to avoid. Some were good. Some were bad. Some knocked her to her knees. The later ones came randomly, and she never knew what would trigger them. Most recently, she'd been on vacation, snorkeling near the Great Barrier Reef. It had been one of many places listed in her and Andy's World Travels notebook. They'd filled it with places they'd planned to explore together some day. Each page had a destination with facts and things to do. Andy had entered the reef as one of their first destinations. Interestingly, when Lena had planned her vacation, she'd come across an online article Andy had written on reef conservation. That one led to another, and another. Unsurprisingly, Andy had published several papers. It wasn't as if she had to like Andy to respect her work, so she'd read them all.

When the car drew near, she discovered it wasn't a Buick. It wasn't even brown. The man behind the wheel waved with a smile as he passed. Lena was frustrated by how let down she was. She hoped this visit wasn't going to be a series of bad memories, unexpected hopes, and inevitable disappointments. She'd had enough of those throughout the years.

She tried to shake herself from the moroseness of her arrival in the distance between her car and the front door and hadn't gone two steps into the house before a fluffy ball of energy was at her feet. It both snarled and wagged its tail. It wouldn't let her pet it, but it stood on its back paws, front paws batting at her leg. She couldn't help but compare it to her mother, who'd always withheld warmth, let alone affection, and only came close enough to bury a verbal knife into her soul, before withdrawing. The vicious animal was nicer.

"Who's this?" she asked.

"Lourdes." Her mom clicked her tongue and leaned down. Lourdes jumped into her arms. "She's my little sweetness," her mother crooned, letting Lourdes lick her face.

"I thought Dad was allergic," Lena said, absolutely dumbfounded by her mother's lavish attention.

"Why do you say that?"

"You wouldn't let me have a dog because of it."

Her mother looked legitimately puzzled. "I don't remember that." She led Lena to her old room. "You can sleep in the guest room."

So, now she was a guest. Even when it had been turned into the craft room, her mother had referred to the room as her old room. It shouldn't have bothered her. But it did.

❖

Completely wiped out, Andy dropped into the recliner at the house after visiting her completely-out-of-it father. She'd been in crisis mode since the call yesterday. Without worry and fear driving her, her adrenaline crashed hard. She could barely move, her mind was mush, and the space between her shoulder blades felt like someone had driven their heel into it. Falling asleep on the couch the night before hadn't helped.

She allowed herself half an hour of rest now, saying it would be okay if she dozed off. But she hadn't dozed off. Apparently, her mushy brain could still create lists of things she needed to do, so she reluctantly shifted Billie from her lap onto the recliner. Figuring out the logistics of being her dad's caretaker, figuring out how to work remotely, and keeping her dad's business running was all impossibly daunting. So, she started simple. She'd transfer her bags to her old bedroom. After which, she'd take a shower. Then she'd sleep. Beyond that, she'd have to figure out. Every long journey started with the first steps, right?

Hair still wet, she stepped around the bags she'd dropped just inside her room before taking a shower. It was obvious no one had been in her room for years, probably not since the last time she'd visited. Staleness hung in the air, and a thick layer of dust coated every surface. In contrast, the rest of the house was spotless. Not a dish in the sink, no laundry in the hamper, the windows freshly cleaned. Her dad was fastidious, something she had learned from him. She knew she needed to eat, but with so much to do, it became a lesser priority, and she decided her next task wasn't going to sleep, but to tackle her room. Her to do list was nothing if not flexible.

She opened the window to let in warm, but fresh air, while Billie took the supervisory position on the freshly stripped twin bed, where she promptly fell asleep. Andy just shook her head as she bundled up the bedding and went in search of a dust rag. On the way, she reacquainted herself with the house in which she'd grown up. Again, nothing much had changed. Aside from a few photographs of whales and seahorses she'd given him over the years hanging in the hallway, it was comfortingly familiar. Collecting a dust rag and furniture spray after throwing the bedding into the washer, she streamed music to fill the silence and got busy tidying the rest of her room. A few songs in, nostalgia swept through her as a song she'd loved in high school played. It reminded her of Lena. Pretty much like almost everything in this town. Still, she didn't skip it.

Hours later, after an early dinner of Mrs. Rafferty's delicious casserole, she and Billie retired to her refreshed bedroom. Billie wasted no time ignoring her dog bed and made a nest of the pillows on the bed, stretching her wiener dog body across them, all while Andy sat at the desk she'd spent hours at as a kid, but was now only used to gather dust and display a few Lego models from the first Star Wars collection.

Bored, but also curious, she opened one of the drawers to peek into the past. It contained a half dozen Rubik's Cubes, notebooks from long ago classes, and a sheaf of printer paper. Boring. The next drawer held her collection of Marvel and Star Wars figurines. Way more interesting. She skipped the third drawer without opening it. Just a bunch of boring words describing ugly emotions. Old news. She needed to throw the dozen or so journals away. The only interesting thing about them was the interstellar space pen she'd used to write in them. The pen was cool. Her dad's father, her grandfather, had given it to her dad, who'd then given it to her. She'd never met him, but her grandma still lived in town, and she'd already called to ask if she could come over.

The top center drawer was far more interesting. First, there was the interstellar pen, which she put in her laptop bag. Aside from other office paraphernalia, there were a surprising number of lip moisturizers, a tampon, a few fidget toys, and a pack of playing cards featuring naked women Mitch had given her after she came out. She put that in her bag, too, wishing he still lived in Oceanside. They exchanged the occasional DM, but the last time she'd seen him was at his wedding. He and his wife and kids lived in Rhode Island now.

She swiped her hand toward the back of the drawer to see if she'd missed anything. Aside from a few paperclips and a penny, there wasn't anything else. But she knew better. She ran her hand along the underside of the desktop, where she'd long ago taped an envelope. The tape was old, nearly disintegrating at her touch. Inside were several two-dollar bills; a picture of Louie, her dog in grade school; a completed collector's card for coins from her birth year; a small stack of letters from her pen pal in the Philippines; a dead Tamagotchi; several Silly Bandz; and a folded piece of notebook paper. The folded note in the shape of a small triangle with a corner tucked into a pocket had her name printed neatly on it. Without opening it, she knew exactly what it said. *People just grow apart, Andy. Get used to it.* The words had broken her heart once. Just thinking about it produced echoes of pain. Rubbing the center of her chest, she slid it back into the manila envelope and dropped it into the drawer.

She was tired now, ready to escape the ache, feeling stupid for letting the loss of a fifth-grade friendship make her want to cry.

She stole a pillow from Billie and crawled into bed, falling asleep quickly, but her dreams made for a restless night. When she woke once in the night, Billie had her head on Andy's shoulder, snoring in her ear. Andy drifted back into a dreamless sleep.

Chapter Seven

2013—Junior Year

"Good morning, ladies," Principal Moreno said. She didn't look angry, but Lena still worried she was in trouble.

"Good morning," they replied in unison.

"I want to talk to you about your role in the graduation ceremony."

It took a second to sink in. "I thought we didn't get to walk in the ceremony, since it's not our class," Lena said. She chanced a glance at Andy, whose focus remained on Ms. Moreno.

"Walking in graduation is a rite of passage, a solidifying of connections to one's school and peer group." Ms. Moreno looked down at her hands, lying flat on her desk, one atop the other. "That's why I wanted to talk to you. Given your impressive yet identical academic achievements, you would have undoubtedly been chosen as co-valedictorians had you graduated with your class next year. It doesn't seem right not to let you walk or acknowledge your achievements. We can at least offer the latter."

"Thank you," Lena said, relieved she wasn't in trouble. She couldn't care less about connections with her peers, though. She'd never felt that kind of friendship. At least not since fifth grade. Against her will, she stole another glance at Andy.

"I'd like you to give a speech at the beginning of the graduation ceremony. I'll say a few words, then turn it over to you for a five- to seven-minute speech."

"Five to seven minutes each? Or five to seven minutes in total?" Andy spoke for the first time.

"It would be mindful of time if you gave it together. Of course, you'd write the speech together."

Lena's stomach churned. A collaboration? They'd once done a project together in a larger group, but she didn't know how this would work. By the end of the meeting, they'd agreed to do the speech. How could they not?

"Andy. Hold up." Lena nearly had to run to keep up with her.

Andy turned, her face expressionless. Her eyes weren't, though. Pain, sadness, anger, and other emotions lived in them. For the millionth time, Lena was ashamed of being the cause of it. It was the first time in months she'd given Lena any indication she was aware of her. Lena couldn't express how much Andy's dismissal affected her. In a weird way, any interaction with Andy had been better than none. The void she felt had become cavernous in the past year.

The familiar uncertainty struck her. It always did with Andy, although she'd never reveal it. Normally, she would have reverted to saying something shitty about Andy not fucking things up or having to carry her load, for example. But she couldn't summon her arsenal of snark. "I'm as surprised as you are. Do you think we can put our differences aside for this?"

Andy scoffed. "That's up to you."

Lena didn't need to ask her what she meant. She knew, as the usual antagonist. Yes, Andy had sometimes started it. But most of it rested on Lena's shoulders. Another thing she knew.

"I mean, it's an honor they even asked us," she said.

"I agree."

"But I can't see us at the same table collaborating as if we don't hate each other," Lena said.

"For once we seem to agree on something."

"A collaboration document worked with the group project last year."

"Because you—never mind." Andy hesitated before leaving it, obviously holding something back. Lena sought to slide a retaliatory response into the chamber out of habit. If she could have formulated one, but she was still held hostage by what she saw in Andy's eyes. But Andy was back on track. "I'll create an outline of the topics Ms. Hernandez listed and send the link. We can go from there."

"Can we agree to be professional in any feedback or responses?"

Andy nodded. "I'll pretend you're someone I don't know. Like a pen pal or another gamer in an online gaming channel."

Lena's heart hurt at the pen pal reference. She remembered helping each other write their letters for the grade school project. Andy's pen pal had been way more interesting than hers. But that was all before everything had gone to shit.

"Sounds good," Lena said, less sharply than she intended. She headed in the opposite direction. Lena's class was in the same direction Andy had been headed, but she refused to walk with her, especially after the pen pal comment.

❖

On stage behind Ms. Hernandez, Andy struggled not to bounce her leg, while Lena portrayed serenity in the chair next to her. Andy couldn't remember being so nervous. She took long breaths like she'd learned for speech and debate, reminding herself she'd spoken before bigger audiences. Relaxing her shoulders, she made herself smile.

Ms. Hernandez introduced them, and they took the podium, with Andy taking the mic first, before the standing-room-only auditorium. She waved at the poor individuals standing against the back wall. "I hope those in the back are wearing comfortable shoes," she started, eliciting genuine laughter from the audience. The rest of it went perfectly and she and Lena left the stage to energetic applause.

Behind the curtained wings, a sigh of relief rolled out of her. To her surprise, Lena released a similar sigh. Taking a bottle of water from the refreshment table, Andy sat in a nearby chair. Without further purpose in the graduation, they'd been asked to stay to take pictures afterward. Andy prepared for a long wait, being stuck alone with Lena for who knew how long. To make things worse, with her pick of so many others, Lena chose a chair next to her. Knee bouncing again, a drop from the water bottle slid down her chin when she took a drink. She self-consciously wiped it away. As always, Andy's awareness of Lena's proximity unnerved her.

"You were staring at me out there." Lena continued to look forward when she said it.

Heat rose up Andy's neck. She'd faced her to listen. Exactly like in rehearsal. Sure, she'd noticed how beautiful Lena looked in the spotlight, with her blue green eyes sparkling. Sure, Andy's stomach had seemed to float as she watched Lena give her speech. But Lena couldn't know any of that.

"I was paying attention. You know. Being polite?"

"By looking at my boobs?"

"I was not!" She hadn't meant to yell. She knew for sure that wasn't true.

"And my mouth. You looked like you were going to kiss me. Right there on stage."

"You wish."

Andy stood. She needed distance, but Lena followed. Where was the door? Screw the pictures. Panicked, she found herself behind the far back curtains, effectively cornered.

"Admit it."

"Admit what?" She couldn't ignore Lena like this. Not with the smell of her magnolia shampoo everywhere.

"You're still obsessed with me. The way you used to follow me around. The notes. You were always staring at me."

Something inside Andy broke. Tears welled in her eyes. She refused to let them fall. She called on anger. "You'd been my best friend. My feelings were hurt."

"People say you like girls." The snarky tone was gone, replaced with something softer.

A net of tingles descended Andy's body. "What does that have to do with anything?"

"That's why you stare at me."

"If anything, I avoid looking at you." She met Lena's eyes. "I also avoid you and the shitty things you say. I try not to care about what you say behind my back. I'm tired of watching out for your stupid ass." Looking into Lena's eyes had been a mistake. The best friend she'd lost was looking out.

"So, you admit you like my ass?" Lena's voice was softer.

"Maybe you're obsessed with me. I mean, you go out of your way to spew insults. It's called projection." Lena's expression had gone blank. "Google it."

Andy felt brave now. She'd shut Lena up for once.

"Is it true? You like girls?" Lena asked after a pause.

What had she heard?

"Big deal. It has nothing to do with you." Andy had gone for a dismissive tone, but it came out softer than that.

Lena looked thoughtful. "I was right. You want to kiss me."

Did Lena sway closer? Hadn't she? There was no way. But she seemed closer. And her eyes were on Andy's lips. Less than an inch away and Andy held her breath. Lena's eyes flicked to hers as she shifted closer, a millimeter between them. When Andy's stomach plummeted like she was cresting the big drop on the Mind Eraser roller coaster, she pulled away, banging her shoulders on the cement wall behind her. She'd almost kissed Lena. She'd wanted to. She tried to ignore the disappointment of not getting to know what kissing her was like.

"You wish. I don't care what anyone thinks. Especially you." Andy's voice shook and she cleared her throat. "Go ahead. Tell people." Emotions played across Lena's face before landing on an unfamiliar expression Andy couldn't decipher.

"Were you just about to kiss me?" Lena asked. Her eyes were back on Andy's lips.

"Dream on." Fear and excitement flared in Andy.

"You were."

She hadn't taken her eyes off Lena this whole time. She couldn't look away. "And vomit? No thanks."

"Have you kissed a girl?" Lena moved in. Any closer and they'd be touching. "Do you like it?"

"Why? Are you interested?" Andy whispered.

"No," Lena said, the conviction of her previous statements gone.

"What would your friends think?" Was she hypnotized? It was the only explanation. Why was she lying to herself?

"I honestly don't care what they think. They don't really know me. No one does." Raw hurt clouded her eyes.

"Lena."

Lena blinked and it cleared. "No one needs to know you were the one I decided to kiss first."

"First? But your boyfriends."

"Can you shut up for a minute?" Lena inched closer. "I hate you. Now kiss me."

And Andy did.

It was quick, barely a touch of her lips against Lena's, but she'd done it. Before she could examine it, Lena leaned back in, and her warm mouth pressed against Andy's. This kiss was completely different. All Andy was aware of was how soft Lena's lips were. When Lena took her hands, intertwining their fingers, Andy sought a better angle. Their lips slid against each other. Her stomach fluttered. The skin around Lena's mouth was soft, too. So soft. A sigh escaped, as powerful feelings swept through her. She'd forgotten to breathe. It was too much. Gasping for air, Andy turned her head because she couldn't step back.

Lena yanked her hands away. They flew to her mouth. Eyes wide. Her expression dazed. She struggled for breath, too. Emotions played across her face. Andy wrapped her arms around herself, confused and scared, but the feeling of Lena's lips lingered on hers. How would Lena react? She'd be mad. She knew it.

She braced herself for the worst reaction. Unexpectedly, Lena's expression settled on something like wonder, and she had the softest of eyes. God, she was beautiful. A tide of warm tingles began at the base of Andy's neck, washing down her back. Lena's mask slid back into place then, replaced by the familiar distance Lena had been keeping her at for over six years. Devastation and fear flooded her.

"I knew it." Lena's quiet voice belied her stoic glare. Somehow, it was worse. "I don't swing that way. Not like you."

Sandpaper rasped over Andy's exposed heart. She understood it was only Lena's armor, but it was still cold and unyielding. It hurt more than anything else had ever hurt. More than Lena telling her to get used to their broken friendship. She'd seen the real Lena again, only to have her yanked away. Grief overtook Andy, losing her again so quickly. She'd hoped for a second they could start again.

Voices echoed close by.

"You kissed me," Andy countered. Her heart hurt like a fresh bruise.

"I hate you, Andy Phillips. With everything in me."

Strangely, there was very little emotion exchanged in the volume or tone, but Andy felt like she was drowning, held under water by the weight of their collected history.

How had she let this happen?

Chapter Eight

Not yet noon, Lena sat by the pool, while the heat of the day already pressed in. The breeze from the ocean should have kept things cool for at least another hour or so, but the winds overnight had blown away the marine layer, or what the locals like to call the June gloom, a normal condition caused by an inversion, which usually kept things cooler in the morning. Without it, direct sunlight heated things up a bit earlier than usual. The locals complaining about temperatures near the eighties needed to spend a summer in Phoenix, where typical June highs were above a hundred.

"I wish I could lounge around the pool all day." The acerbic tone of her mother invaded her peace.

Lena looked up at her mother, who cradled Lourdes. "Good morning to you, too, Mother."

"Is this what you do in Arizona all summer?"

Lena schooled her expression. "It's too hot to lounge in the summer there. But I have a job."

"You mentioned you had a week off. It's been longer than that."

"It's been five days. Are you saying you're sick of me?"

"Did you hear those words emerge from my lips, Selena? How you can lie here in the sun is beyond me. It's terrible for your skin. It ages you faster than you imagine."

Said the woman who looked fifteen years older than her fifty-five years. Some of it was her spackled-on makeup, but mostly, it was being a hateful bitch. There'd been a time when she wouldn't have allowed herself to even think something like that. Was her mother hateful? Yes. A bitch? Also, yes. So, when it came to her mother, she deserved it and then some.

"I've decided to take a leave of absence." She didn't have to tell her she'd tossed a grenade and left.

"What does that mean?"

"I need a rest." She waited for her mother to berate her.

"I imagine the social media thing doesn't help."

"It does. It feeds my soul." Although she hadn't created new content since she'd been back home.

"Too bad it doesn't feed your bank account."

"Don't worry, Mother. I'm fine financially."

She wasn't rich, but she'd be comfortable until she found another job. Her agent was already working on it. She'd hit the speed dial while walking out the door of Insight Phoenix, her chunky-heeled Madisons crunching satisfyingly in the parking lot gravel.

The trouble was jobs in the top markets didn't open up often. It could take some time. Why'd she decided to stay with her mother was a mystery. It had to be some kind of subconscious masochistic thing urging her to confront the mountains of childhood trauma she tried to keep buried. The half-dozen therapists she'd hired and fired over the last several years would have a field day with this.

Lena got up. "I have a lunch thing," she said on her way to the house. By lunch thing, she meant she'd go by the shop to see if her father wanted to go.

Like the mystery of why she'd decided to stay at her parents' house, she had no clue why she decided to ask her father to lunch. Other than dinner the first night, he'd been an apparition since she'd arrived. His dedication as absentee father was the one thing she could count on. No one talked about how he preferred staying in his office apartment at the shop, rather than go home. It had been this way her entire life. With an emotionally abusive mother and a neglectful father, why did she come home at all? One of her fired therapists said it was a form of self-sabotage to validate her feelings of insignificance. She expected her father wouldn't accept the invitation, and when he didn't, she could feel sorry for herself. Plus, she could escape her mother and possibly trigger her bitter jealousy. The trifecta of dysfunction. Her therapist would be proud.

Her mother followed her into the house. "I need you to pick up a few things at the grocery store. I promised my famous artichoke dip for book club this week."

"Sure." What happened to grocery delivery? She'd spent more time at the grocery store in the last five days than she had the three years she'd lived in Phoenix. "I'll grab the list on my way out." She'd suggested she text it once, only to trigger a twenty-minute lecture on the evils of technology. A list would be on the counter for her.

Half an hour later, the door chime sounded at her dad's store. She'd barely taken her sunglasses off, when she was enveloped in a ferocious swaying hug, accompanied by clicks and hums.

"Hey, Joanie." She returned the hug with her own ferocity, wondering how she'd gone so long without one. Eyes welling, she held on longer.

Her dad's first employee, Joanie had been hired to greet customers and make appointments. Now, she was a one-woman show and part owner of the business, responsible for everything on the home installations, from job bids to payroll, while her dad focused on the commercial side.

"Your dad said you were in town. How long?" It didn't feel like being judged when Joanie asked.

"It's open-ended."

"Not a medical thing? There's too much of that going around."

"It's just a vision thing."

"Oh no. Vision?"

"Yeah, I can't see going into work anytime soon. Ba da boom!" Lena mimed hitting a drum.

"You are your father's daughter." Joanie giggled.

She wanted to say she wouldn't know, but Joanie knew how it was. She knew everything.

"Speaking of my father, is he in?"

"He's probably at Glenn's. He's filling in while Glenn recovers."

"Glenn?" The only Glenn Lena knew was Glenn Phillips. Joanie couldn't mean him.

Joanie nodded. "Glenn, of Phillips Pools and Landscapes."

"Right," Lena said as if she'd just forgotten. He hadn't mentioned it at dinner. Talk had been superficial that night, as usual.

"Your dad's burning candles at both ends these days." Joanie looked worried. "Make sure he eats, okay? And if you're in town for a while, come back. I'd love to catch up."

Lena soaked up another hug before heading to Glenn's store. She thought about blowing off her lunch idea. But she was curious. One degree of separation and all that. Self-sabotage seemed to be her theme today.

She was about to get out of her car at Glenn's, when her breath caught. A stunning woman in sandals, black leggings, and a form-fitting athletic tank, walked out of the store. It couldn't be.

Andy Phillips was ten feet away and Lena couldn't breathe.

It felt like someone slammed a fist into her chest.

Andy Phillips. The last person she should want to see. They'd left so much hanging.

She watched until Andy disappeared around the building. Twenty seconds, and Lena's world was upside down. Even more beautiful than she remembered, Andy apparently still had devastating power over her. Andy had always been the match to her gasoline.

Holding the steering wheel, she banged her head against the headrest. She'd frozen. What else could she have done? Andy probably still hated her. A couple of kisses couldn't have changed that.

After composing herself, she cleared her head with a drive down the Strand with the top down, watching the Pacific Ocean sparkle. Feeling refreshed and more like herself, she pulled into the grocery store parking lot half an hour later. She hadn't managed to put Andy out of her mind, but her heart had settled into a steadier rhythm. Andy fucking Phillips. She needed to be more careful to avoid unintentional run-ins.

The cooler air inside the store provided blessed relief from the heat radiating from the asphalt of the parking lot. She overheard a couple blaming the heat on the Santa Ana winds, but it was a low-pressure system over Southern California, which would dissipate by tomorrow, bringing lower temperatures. She didn't need the National Weather Service to know that.

"Drats!" A quiet voice said from the direction of the empty shopping carts. An elderly woman with her hands full wrestled with a stuck cart.

"Can I help?" Lena asked.

"I think they design them to do this on purpose, just like the catawampus wheels." She stepped back, giving Lena room to defeat the obstinate cart.

"I always underestimate the number of items I'll end up getting, too." Lena freed the cart, and the woman dropped the groceries into it with a grateful smile.

"And I always seem to pick the cart that doesn't want to let go. I imagine the reluctant ones as a kindergartner not wanting to be left on the first day of school. My son says I'm a kook with my imagination, but my granddaughter tells me anthropomorphizing inanimate objects shows a high level of empathy. My son may be right, but I like my granddaughter's perspective, so I go with that."

Lena smiled. "I like how your granddaughter thinks."

"She's my heart."

"You're lucky to have each other." It made Lena sad thinking how she'd never had that kind of relationship with a grandparent, or anyone else. For a brief period in grade school, she'd had Andy, who'd built blanket forts during sleepovers, where they snuggled together as they slept. Innocent. She longed for those days, but shut it down immediately. She had no right to those dreams. Seeing Andy again brought up old memories.

After the woman trundled away, Lena grabbed a handbasket for her own shopping. Still smiling over the exchange, she browsed the shelves, thinking she needed more interactions like that in her days. The very short exchanges with Joanie and the woman just then had been the highlights of her week. Pathetic.

Tossing cheese into her basket, she felt untethered and in need of distractions. She thought about her social media presence. Her subscribers deserved better. She should focus on them.

After adding frozen spinach to the basket, she paused in front of the canned artichoke hearts. The top of her mother's list was specific: *NO STORE BRANDS!* Bougie much, Mother? She grabbed the name brand, but her eyes were on the store brand. She snickered. What if she got both and hid the name brand? She could watch her mother have a coronary before she whipped out the name brand. Even in her fantasies, her mother didn't laugh. Lena knew not to poke at venomous snakes. She switched her mother with a cobra. Much better.

Smirking, she rounded the endcap offering artisan breads, nearly colliding with another cart. Her "sorry" was interrupted by a delighted gasp.

"Fancy meeting you here, lollygagging near the breads," the woman she'd helped with her cart said. A bonus interaction.

"What can I say? I'm a sucker for a rustic sourdough."

The woman leaned forward, conspiratorially. "The cinnamon raisin bread gets me every time."

Lena laughed until a voice from the past sounded around the corner, raising the hair on her arms.

"I have about half an hour before I need to get home to Billie. Do you want to stop at Dad's before I take you home?"

Lena's past appeared behind the older woman and froze. She was in a hot air ballon caught in a down draft. Wide eyes greeted hers. She'd have recognized the deep brown irises featuring lighter brown starbursts anywhere.

"Did someone call freeze tag?" The older woman's similar brown eyes flicked between them.

Unable to breathe, Lena broke the law of no dead air. Seconds ticked by. Another cart exited the row.

"Enjoy your shopping," Lena managed. She couldn't feel her body. It wasn't until she closed her car door that she noticed she still clutched the basket of items she hadn't purchased. There was no way she could go back in to pay.

If the mere glimpse of Andy leaving her dad's store had hit her hard, the sighting in the store was a collision of two blackholes. She sat in her car, dazed. Everything she'd tried to forget was released in a violent eruption, annihilating her in just one look.

"Stop it!" she said, slapping the steering wheel, ignoring that she probably looked crazy. At least she'd put the top up. Her stupid mind couldn't erase the face she'd never been able to forget.

"Fuck," she intoned, dropping her forehead against the steering wheel. "Fuck, fuck, fuck."

❖

Andy missed her exit. Even with navigation, it was the second time during the short drive to the hospital. She blew out a ragged breath and circled around again. Two missed exits, running a red light, rolling over the curb at a corner, and starting the drive with the emergency brake engaged for the first block qualified her as a menace on the road. She'd been the width of a shopping cart away from Lena Holmes and the whole world had slipped away. Replaced with cold tile beneath her feet, the scent of chlorine in her sinuses, and the vibrating tension of confusion, expectation, and the fear of shattering into carbon particles being the only thing between her and the only person who'd had sole possession of her heart.

And still did.

If they hadn't had a cart between them, she would have unnecessarily waved a hand through her to see if she was real.

Lena Holmes was real, all right.

It was almost too much to take in. Why hadn't she prepared for this eventuality? Oceanside was their shared hometown, after all. They both had family here. Was it too much to ask the universe to save her from reliving the worst years of her life?

Lena fucking Holmes.

How did this girl—this woman—still affect her like this?

Her thoughts continued to spin wildly, but she finally arrived at the hospital. Not necessarily in one piece emotionally, she parked her car. After hitting the parking stone, of course. Because why wouldn't she? Jesus. Reverberations of the past propelled her forward. How she made it through the hospital entrance, into the elevator, and finally to her dad's room, she couldn't explain. But entering the room always brought her back to brutal reality. The first sight of him every visit, encased in casts, and the side of his face swollen and bruised, never stopped assaulting her. Today she was grateful for it. It silenced the shock of seeing Lena.

Every time she'd arrived, he'd been sleeping. This time was no different. Taking a seat in the uncomfortable armchair next to his bed, her freakout resurged, albeit at a lower level of turmoil. Even asleep, her dad managed to ground her.

In the safety of her dad's presence, she let her thoughts wander. Honestly, she probably couldn't stop them anyway. She'd always expected anger or rejection to be the primary response if she ever saw her ex-best friend again. Either that, or that she'd be consumed with memories of their last interactions when Lena's kisses had lit a flame that had since become a sort of hell's fire. Both of those could have easily been her response. But they hadn't. Instead, she'd been reminded of the bond they'd once had, because out of nowhere it had seized her the moment their eyes met, and it was still there, tying her to Lena. Out of the three, it was absolutely the most painful.

"What's got your face all scrunched up like that?"

She looked up to see her dad watching her. He looked blissed out on pain medication. She popped up, gave him a careful hug and kiss, and plopped back down into the armchair, bruising her tail bone on the softest part of the dangerous furniture. She wondered if it was a revenue stream for the hospital.

"Just something I saw today. It's not important."

"You look like you saw bigfoot."

Interesting choice of words. "You were probably just seeing the pain I'm still in from the night I tried to sleep on this beauty." She slapped the arm of the recliner. "I'm thinking of getting one for the house. Maybe downgrade you from the comfortable chair you already have."

Her dad laughed, but it was more like a giggle. And that made her laugh.

"What did you get up to today?" he asked.

"I visited Gloria to see how she's holding up in your absence."

"I'd wager she's doing fine."

"You'd be correct. She showed me around and offered to show me the books and project schedule. I told her I wouldn't know an accounting ledger from a fifth-grade math book. But the schedule looks busy."

Her dad limply flapped the hand attached to his good arm. "She runs the store better than I do. She's made me redundant, taking care of all the bidding and scheduling, and she's been doing the books for years. With Sander and William on sales, there's nothing left for me to do anymore except play online solitaire and look handsome. Gloria runs the show, and Robert will fill in if need be. You're off the hook."

"Robert Holmes?" No wonder he'd called her mother. Gloria must have asked him to. Her mind slid back to seeing his daughter at the grocery store.

"The one and only Robert Holmes of North County Saltwater Pools. He knows the business, so it's a cake walk to him. Not that Gloria lets him do anything."

"Oh yeah?" she said. "She definitely seemed like she had a handle on everything today."

"She reminds me of your mom. Independent and confident. Just like someone else I know." He regarded her through squinted eyes. It was nice to see him in a good enough mood to tease her. It took her mind off of Lena.

"Speaking of Mom, she demanded daily status reports."

"Your mom is good people."

Their divorce hadn't severed their connection, which Andy loved.

"She's okay, I guess," Andy deadpanned. "Do you know when you get out of here?"

He looked almost giddy. "Tomorrow."

They talked logistics but didn't get far before her dad started to fade.

Andy stood. "You get some sleep, Dad. I'll come back around dinner."

He didn't open his eyes but waved her off with his flapping hand. "Tomorrow, 'kay?" She barely understood him but got the drift. Good thing, too. She had a lot to do to get ready.

A few hours later, Andy was proud of what she'd accomplished. She didn't bring it up to her dad because she knew he'd say no, but they needed wheelchair access to the house. It had been too late to hire a company, so she'd called her dad's office manager, Gloria. Within an hour, she'd sent one of their crews over with all the materials needed to construct one, and they had it up in less than two hours. Her dad would hate what it did for the curb appeal, but he couldn't do much if it was already built.

Billie, becoming quite the supervisor, managed the project from the porch swing. Andy had just finished cleaning up the worksite, when footsteps up the driveway made her turn.

"Hey, Andy," Robert Holmes said.

She met him at the edge of the lawn. Despite her reaction every time his name had been mentioned since she came back, she'd always liked him. He'd spent a lot of time at their house over the years. His hair had started to gray and the lines around his eyes were deeper, but he was still stupidly good-looking with a killer smile. Just like his daughter.

"I was just thinking how you and Lena used to pal around. Random how memories pop into your mind." As he spoke, the warm smile dimmed in his blue-green eyes. Exact replicas of Lena's, who hadn't been smiling this morning. She'd looked spooked. Had it only been hours since she'd literally stood two feet away from her? She wondered what he knew of their falling out.

"Yeah. It's been a few years," she said noncommittally.

He seemed to shake free of his thoughts. "Is there anything I can help with to get ready for Glenn's return? Don't let him know I offered to help, though. He about ordered me not to fuss." He gestured toward the ramp. "Brilliant idea. I wasn't looking forward to lifting him up the steps."

"I think he'll focus on his prized roses the ramp is now hiding," she said. "But the transport company will get him settled."

Robert chuckled. "He does love his roses." He strode closer to the ramp, patting the handrail. "Need me to move furniture?" He stuffed his hands into his pockets. "I mean, if it isn't stepping on toes. All anti-fussing aside, I know he'd do the same for me."

He looked so earnest, she couldn't say no. The rental company had already set up all the stuff, but she invited him inside to see if there was anything he could do.

When they reached the porch, Billie jumped from the swing, performed a lazy stretch, and followed them into the house.

"Who's this?" Robert knelt to pet her. "Does she like to be held?"

"That's Billie. She loves anything that keeps her from using her four perfectly capable legs."

Robert picked her up and Billie proceeded to bathe his face with enthusiastic kisses. "She's adorable."

"Aren't you allergic to dogs?" Andy remembered Lena couldn't get a dog because he was severely allergic.

"I just don't have one because I work such long hours."

Andy wondered why Lena's mom had lied, but it wasn't her business.

"Me too. I take Billie to doggie daycare, so she doesn't feel so alone."

"He's going to hate this," Robert said. He scratched under Billie's chin while scanning the living room. Most of the furniture, except for her dad's recliner, had been moved against the walls to make room for the hospital bed.

"He absolutely will."

"Wanna swap out this smaller TV for the bigger one in his room?" Robert asked. "He's going to spend all his time out here. He'll want the bigger screen."

"That's a great idea," Andy said. It was weird that he knew about the television in her dad's room, though. Maybe he'd helped carry it in.

"He'd probably rather use his own bedding than the hospital stuff they brought, too," Robert said after they'd moved the TV. When he went to the linen closet to get it, a nice feeling fell over her knowing her dad had such a great friend. Maybe she didn't have to worry so much about him being lonely.

Chapter Nine

2013—The Last Summer Before College

The ready whistle sounded while Andy rotated her torso one way and then the other before checking that her goggles were seated properly and her swimsuit wasn't inching up. Crouching, the tips of her fingers pulled against the edge of the platform, she waited for the horn to start her first race. Two hundred yards. Eight laps. Seven turns. She was in lane seven. Seven was her lucky number, and seven was her lucky lane.

She synced her breathing to the silent count in her mind. The horn blared. Everything faded from her perception. Muscle memory took over. She hardly noticed when she entered the water, when her kicks started, how long the glide, or when the tips of her fingers broke the surface. She focused on her arms, pulling her forward, scooping, rotating, scooping, rotating. Most of the other swimmers didn't exist. Her focus was on the smooth and even movements of her body and counting how many times she hit the wall and flip-turned to go back. She didn't stop until her finger touched the side of the pool eight times. Looking at the board, she saw her name on top. She'd won.

Lena was two lanes over. She'd felt her throughout the race like she always did. Not distracting, just there. It was stronger since Lena had kissed her. Before then, Andy had ignored it, focused completely on her race. She couldn't ignore her now. Lena's presence was like a solid thing, hovering near, a focal point. She hated it and craved it at the same time.

She would have thought the new awareness would drag her down or steal her focus, but it didn't. Just the opposite. It almost felt like it made her stronger, propelling her forward. It didn't make sense, but her times had improved. So, there was that.

She hadn't spoken to Lena since the graduation ceremony, with Lena keeping her distance, and she'd done her best to ignore Lena. But Lena's proximity hit differently now. Things had shifted between them. She tried to rationalize it. They had kissed and she couldn't stop thinking about it. But nothing had changed relative to why they hated each other. It was just this new heightened awareness.

She got out of the water, pulling the back of her swimsuit down out of habit, making room for the next heat. Her glance swept to Lena, whose eyes were already on her. She expected her to make a crack about something. Maybe call her obsessed or a perv or something. Nothing. Not even a scowl.

They just grabbed towels and watched the other races. They repeated this a few times as the meet progressed, as she and Lena swam in the same mid-length races. It was weird not anticipating Lena's next aggression or volleying micro-aggressions at one another. No one seemed to notice this odd-for-them behavior. At least no one mentioned it. But more than once, Andy had the strange sensation that the counterbalance of longing was missing now. She almost wished Lena would insult her to reset whatever it was. Weirdness would feel better than the missing interaction she'd come to count on.

At the end of the meet, Lena muttered what had sounded like a begrudging, "Someone ate their Wheaties this morning. Your times were amazing."

It took Andy a few seconds to get over the shock. By then, Lena was already entering the locker room. Coach waved Andy over to talk about her races. She barely registered their conversation.

Shivering in her wet towel and swimsuit, she finally extracted herself and made her way to the locker room, which was empty and eerily quiet. The warm shower was a blessing.

Afterward, she stood at her locker, wrapped in a towel. The unnatural quiet was still unnerving. She'd rarely been there alone. Feeling like a first grader afraid of their own shadow, she fought the urge to hurry as she pulled on her underwear. Unable to resist, and still feeling creeped out, she had to look around to make sure she was alone. Shaking her head at herself, she pulled on her T-shirt. The thin material of it stuck to her damp skin, momentarily trapping her head. Realizing her arms were restricted and she was blind to her surroundings, the sense of vulnerability returned. Sensing someone watching her, she slowed her movements and untwisted the fabric. She knew who it was. She always did. Her fear disappeared to be replaced with something else. Finally, she freed her head and pulled the shirt down.

❖

Fantasies were one thing, but Lena never thought she'd kiss Andy Phillips. Andy hated her. But she had, and now she was mad and embarrassed at herself. Which was worse? Kissing her? Or blaming it on her? It was a little of both, she supposed, but more than anything, it was because she'd liked it. More than liked it. She couldn't think about anything else, and it was driving her insane. She relived it over and over. Her entire body sizzled with the memory and longing. She couldn't stop staring at her during swim meets, imagining doing it again. Andy had to notice her staring. Every time Andy looked over, she'd caught it. Lena had been embarrassed but hadn't been able to stop. It took almost half the meet before Lena figured out that if Andy caught her staring a lot, that Andy was looking just as much as Lena was. The idea both terrified and excited her.

Lena tried to distract herself after she'd kissed Andy. She had a lot of things to do before she left for college, which was coming up fast. But even that hadn't kept her mind off how soft Andy's lips had been and how gentle she'd been. But more than anything, she couldn't stop thinking about how Andy had been just as into it as she had. Andy had liked it, too. And that's what she had to distract herself from. Knowing it made every difference.

So, she'd gone through all of her clothes and spent hours reorganizing her bedroom so it wouldn't be a kid's room when she came home for visits. Not that she planned to visit often, but her parents probably expected it. She daydreamed about college and the freedom she'd finally have. She couldn't wait to make a new start, far from the mother who hated her and the father who wished she didn't exist. More than anything, she'd be relieved her mother couldn't embarrass her in front of Andy, who had perfect parents and a family who loved her. Lena and Andy would be long gone, and free from the threat of her mother telling Andy how awful she was or calling Andy a pervert. There was no telling what her mother would do. All she knew was that without her or Andy around, there was little chance her worst nightmare would come true.

It sucked that it required them leaving for different schools and separate lives. It killed her to know that there was a big chance they'd never see each other again. It had been hard enough knowing Andy would leave still hating her. She'd already wondered how she would manage without Andy in her life, but now that they'd kissed, she didn't know how she could survive without getting to do it again.

Did Andy think about the kiss as much as she did? About how fucking amazing it was? Did she know how soft her lips were? Or how good it felt being so close to her again? Did she tingle all over remembering how their bodies still fit together after all this time and she still smelled like she did when they'd snuggled in the blanket forts they made? Did Andy know she made her feel seen for the first time since they'd stopped being friends? Because she knew Andy had seen her. Had seen what she thought, and how she felt. Andy had seen all the way inside her, had seen her real self, and for the first time ever, Lena had felt safe.

They'd leave for college soon, both of them having worked hard to graduate early. Lena had done it to get away from her parents and the people who called her a friend but didn't know the first thing about her. But most of all, she couldn't stay if Andy wasn't here. She remembered how Andy had loved her once when no one else had. And that she hadn't always been a burden and invisible. Even if it had turned to hate, Andy still saw her. She'd known her once, and had cared about her, and that gave her a light in an often-dark world. Knowing Andy was around had been the only thing that got her through sometimes. As painful as it had been all these years keeping Andy at a distance, and even with all the shit they'd been through, it would be harder to live here without at least getting to see her.

When the meet was over, she slipped away during the celebration of their win, needing to be long gone by the time the teams left the rec center. She almost made it, too, drawing what felt like her first full breath in hours when she stepped out of the rec center. But Crystal was sitting at one of the picnic tables, probably waiting for her current boyfriend. She went through them so quickly, Lena wasn't sure she knew his name. What she did know was she couldn't walk past her without some sort of consequence, so she walked over.

"Hey, Crystal," she said, hoping she didn't sound as anxious as she felt.

While they chatted, the teams streamed out, and Lena tried to hide her distraction as she watched for Andy. Finally, Crystal's boyfriend showed up, and they left, leaving Lena on her own and she hadn't seen Andy. Hoping she'd passed without her noticing, Lena started toward the parking lot, but when she saw hers and Andy's were the only cars left, it was as if she didn't have control of her body.

She stopped just inside the entrance to the silent locker room, expecting it to be empty, but hoping it wasn't. Why was she doing this to herself? But what she saw was Andy next to her usual locker, struggling with her T-shirt. Lena's blood pounded to see that other than that, she wore nothing else but her underwear. Lena's body flushed at the sight of Andy's entire torso on display, including her breasts, and she should have left, but she couldn't. Sensations she'd never felt had her feet glued to the tiled floor. When Andy finally pulled the T-shirt down, her eyes went directly to Lena, as if she'd already known she was there. Lena didn't care if Andy knew she'd watched.

Looking softer, and so, so pretty, Andy's expression was undecipherable. She'd always been pretty. But in this moment, Lena felt the impact of it to her core. Even fifteen feet apart, Lena got lost in her brown eyes, open wide, watching her. A warm tingle spread through her. All she could do was stand there, staring back. She should be embarrassed. She should give Andy privacy. But she couldn't bring herself to leave. Her voice was inaccessible.

Again, her body seemed to control itself. She took a few steps forward and stopped, biting her lower lip. A buzz lived low in her stomach. She couldn't decide if it was fear or excitement. The unfamiliar feeling grew stronger. She stepped closer, stopping on the other side of the bench between them. Her gaze never faltered, and Andy's stare remained steady. Something electric was between them. Her heart raced. She could barely breathe. Andy's eyes remained glued to hers. Lena gripped her own arm with the opposite hand, fighting the urge to reach out. She braced for Andy's expression to close off, but it didn't. She seemed to be waiting to see what she would do.

She took a deep breath, rounded the bench, stopping within a few inches of Andy, whose breath was hot against her face. Please don't be wrong, she thought on repeat, slowly closing the distance. When their lips finally met, Lena expected the powerful rush she'd experienced before, not the delicate tingle spreading from the softness against her lips. The tightness in her shoulders melted when Andy cupped her jaw. Slow-moving electricity flowed down her back. Last time had been learning and sensory overload. This was giving and receiving. Undemanding. Soft. Warm. Everything in her body was aware of Andy's lips, how they moved, how they tasted. How much Andy wanted this, too. She already knew she'd never forget the way she felt now.

In the months following their first kiss, Lena sometimes wondered if she'd dreamt it. But she knew this mouth. She'd known these lips. She had replayed that kiss until it was burned into her memory. This kiss, though. It was the collision of blue stars. The becoming of a supernova. They were floating outside their bodies, removed from everything except each other. Her only focus was Andy and the lips pressed against her own. Lena opened her mouth, seeking more. Needing more. When Andy's tongue met hers, she spiraled into light, awash in sensations created for this alone. Sensory language only their bodies could understand coursed through her, expanding beneath her skin. When Andy ended the kiss, it took Lena a second to understand, and when she opened her eyes, Andy had pulled back. She looked dazed, staring deep into her, still cupping her jaw, and the heat of that hand seemed to scorch Lena's skin. And then, Andy's hands were at her waist pulling them together. Lena didn't have a way to describe the reaction she had to the connection of their bodies. All she could do was take it in. She slid her hands around Andy's waist, grasping the back of her T-shirt, as much to keep from floating away as it was to keep her hands from the discoveries she knew they could make. The ones she'd longed for but was also terrified of what they would mean.

Instead, she let her lips explore, tasting and teasing. She surrendered, holding nothing back, her pleasure rising to heights she couldn't have possibly imagined. When she pressed Andy against the lockers every sensation in her body intensified. How could she have known taking control would thrill her like this? Pressing into Andy, she tried to express how affected she was by her, but Andy was already telling her she knew by the way she gripped her waist like she was afraid to let go. Lena didn't want her to. She wanted more.

Her body demanded she satisfy the need for air, and she reluctantly released Andy's lips. With the pause came the slightest semblance of control, and Lena realized it wasn't just lack of air causing her lightheadedness. She was beginning to feel overwhelmed. Eyes still closed, she brought her hands to Andy's incredibly beautiful face. She didn't need to see it to know. It was what she saw every time she closed her eyes. But this time she could touch it. She stroked the underside of her jaw. Resting her forehead against Andy's, they caught their breath. Her lips missed Andy's and she gently kissed her, pulling back to gaze into her eyes, where she witnessed a galaxy of emotions, some of them heart-wrenching, others pulsing with energy, still others without names. She relaxed the pressure against Andy's body, loosening her tight hold but not releasing her. Their touches were gentle and light.

As minutes ticked by, they didn't speak. Lena wondered what Andy was thinking, how she felt. She imagined their hearts beating in sync, absorbing what was happening. Warmth filled Lena's body as Andy rested her head on Lena's shoulder, her face against her neck, in an unexpected act of trust and tenderness. Unaccountably, Lena wanted to cry. She shivered when Andy brushed her lips across her skin. In a way, it was more intimate than anything else they'd done. Without ever having experienced affection, Lena had never imagined anything could feel like this. She mirrored Andy's pose, her face against Andy's warm neck taking in the warmth of Andy, who smelled of pool water and something floral, probably her shampoo. She wanted to stay like this forever.

Several minutes passed, and neither of them moved. Their breaths had settled into one rhythm. The initial sense of the unfamiliar had eased, while the amazement remained. Lena had stopped trying to memorize everything about the encounter and was simply living in it.

The slap of Danny's sandals neared and stopped. Their bodies tensed, but they didn't move. In that moment, Lena didn't care if anyone saw them. She just wanted to hold and be held by Andy. The overhead lights clicked off, and the footsteps moved away. The late afternoon sunlight filtered in through the high windows, the light through the thick tempered glass dimly illuminating the silent room. They lifted their heads slowly in unison, their eyes fixed on each other. It felt like awaking from a dream, and the chill seemed to blow away the dream-like fugue they'd slipped into. Lena slowly stepped back. Her legs hit the bench, and she stilled, abruptly brought back to reality. Andy watched her, and a mix of feelings churned inside Lena. She'd have to examine them later. Right now, the only one she could focus on was despair.

She touched her own lips, unsure of what to do. Andy held her gaze. Lena thought she should say something, but how do you find words for what they'd done after what they had been to each other for as long as they had? She backed around the bench before turning, leaving the locker room without looking back.

Chapter Ten

Nothing called up memories quicker than a scent, and aside from the ocean air mixed with seasonal foliage smells, chlorine in an indoor pool was probably one of the most evocative to Andy. Still an avid swimmer, she'd been in plenty of pools, but the Oceanside rec center came with a unique combination of smells that enveloped her as soon as she stepped into the building. It was poignancy at its finest, the reminder of her roots, the bestower of mostly fond memories, and a few shitty ones, too.

"Hey, stranger!" a familiar voice called to her as she selected her old locker key from one of the many hooks mounted on the wall beside the service counter. Some things never changed, like the rows of locker keys, her dad's landline, and the slap-slap of Danny LaPonte walking in flip-flops. He'd managed the rec center since before she'd taken her first swimming lesson and hadn't changed a bit: sun-weathered, in his leathery skin, with pale lines radiating from the corners of his eyes. His long white hair, and outfit of vintage OP beach shorts worn with a homemade tie-dyed T-shirt, identified him as an OG surfer. Throw in a puka shell necklace when he had someone to impress and…Shaka, my dude.

"Danny!" she said as she went in for a hug. "I thought you'd be retired by now." She hadn't been to the rec center since she'd left for college. Seeing him just dialed up the intensity of nostalgia she'd been wrapped in since her return.

"Just call me a barnacle. They're gonna hafta scrape me off to get me outta here." He chuckled. "What brings you to O'Side, dude? You missin' your old dad? I heard about the gnarly tumble he took. Bad news. Bad news. Sounds like he'll be rockin' and rollin' soon enough, though. But, fuck, man. Havin' to chill in a body cast is no bueno."

"He's for sure not into the forced chilling. But it's not a full body cast. Just his legs and one of his arms. He's out of the neck brace and can temporarily take off the torso brace when he wants a break."

"Fuck, man," he repeated, shaking his head slowly. "Sweet it's not a body cast. I had to wear one once when I tried shooting the pier and hit one of the pilings full on. The cast was itchy, man, and I'd traded my TV for weed, like a week before, so I just listened to the radio most of the time and talked to my bros when they came around. Don't ask me how I used the bathroom. I've blocked those memories." He rubbed his eyes as if reminding himself not to go there.

"I'm staying with him until he's mobile. His friends drop by." And by friends, she meant one friend. Robert, who was there now. He was the only person her dad wanted to see, aside from her. "He chased me out this morning and I decided to get a few laps in."

"Don't let me cramp your style, dude. Go swim, little tadpole!" He flapped his arms toward the pool. Tadpole was what they'd called the kids in her swim lessons.

Grinning at the happy memory, she headed for the locker room. The place might as well have been sealed for the past twelve years. Everything was the same, down to the green subway tile on the walls and white tiled floor. Even the gray lockers were the same, albeit sporting several more coats of the same gray paint. Only the old corkboard for notices and pool schedules had changed, replaced by one with locking plexiglass doors. Although Danny kept the place as clean as it could get, the decline over the last twelve years was evident. Her dad would say "You can't polish a turd" about slapping a coat of paint on a building, but that's not what it was. It was more like the spirit of the once thriving place hadn't been fed. It made her a little sad, even as the lack of renovations allowed her to take a step back in time.

She went directly to her old locker at the end of the first row, and just like that, she went back in time to right before she left for college. This nostalgia wasn't about the décor, though. It was entirely about Lena, and not fifth grade Lena. It was the grown-up Lena and the kiss that had set a bar so high, no other woman had ever had a chance. Andy shocked herself about explicitly calling that out. She knew it was why she was broken, but sometime in her freshman year of college, she'd deliberately started closing off the thought when her mind started to go into the why of it. Because, if she did, the next part was about the loss of Lena, and that pain was more than she could handle. After an entire semester of grieving her, she'd forced herself to move on. She'd managed to regain most of herself over time, but the part that would have opened her enough to a relationship had been closed off. And part of her didn't want to change it. This was her now. From the exhilaration of the kiss that had defined her life, to the way she held a part of herself back when she met someone new, this was who she'd become. And she wouldn't let the ghost that had haunted her all these years disturb the peace she'd found.

So why had she come back to the very place she'd lost the missing piece of her?

❖

The day was already off to a shitty start. Lena was hiding in her room, feeling like the grade school girl who'd rather go hungry than face her mother. She didn't have to leave her room to know her mother was in another one of her moods, stomping all around the house before the sun had even thought to peek over the distant Sierras. She was probably cleaning something that didn't need it. If her mother had been a storm cloud, Lena would have advised sheltering in place. And when she hadn't been able to go back to sleep, she'd done just that, staying in her room, checking email only to find two more thanks-but-no-thanks in response to positions her agent had explored for her over the last two weeks. Positions in her field were slim to none for anyone who wanted a large market and decent salary, and the only open primetime slots were aggressively protected by non-primetime talent waiting for their own shot. She loved broadcast work. Love, love, loved it. She had a plan B in teaching or research. She'd just rather it be in the field she loved.

"Selena!"

When she'd been a kid, her mother would have scolded her for shouting in the house. But the rules were different for Helena Holmes, whose barbed personality had sharpened over time. She put her laptop down to find her mother in the kitchen making yet another fucking grocery list.

"What's up?" she asked, stifling a sigh as she entered the room.

Her mother jumped as if she hadn't heard Lena approach.

"You creep around the house like a spirit, Selena. Make some noise when you enter a room or something."

"I'll get a bell to put around my neck." Lena's tone was teasing but her mother took her literally.

"That's ridiculous. Just clear your throat or something."

Lena stifled another sigh. "You called?"

"I need a few things from the grocery store."

She never asked. She assumed. And it was every damn day. She shopped there enough that the employees greeted her by name. Between that and essentially turning herself in after shoplifting the groceries when she fled the scene of her head-on collision with her past, she was a freaking celebrity at the store. Her ethics wouldn't allow her to just forget the heist. She'd been compelled to call the store to confess, insisting on paying for the ill-gotten goods, and while the store manager had been surprised at her honesty and told her not to worry about it, she'd insisted. So, although she resented the hell out of her mother for sending her there every day, the sense of belonging when the chorus of hellos greeted her was a daily pick-me-up and an excuse to get out of the house. Fucking pathetic.

She gathered her keys and reusable bags. The loneliness of shopping alone was better than listening to her mother stomp around all day. To shake things up, Lena tried an alternate route while she failed to ignore her anticipation of possibly seeing Andy there again. She'd tried to tell herself it was really dread, but the disappointment each time she didn't see Andy couldn't be explained away. The question was, what would she do if she did see her? That was a question without an answer. After stealing frozen spinach and cheese, she was capable of anything.

Her inability to not think about Andy as demonstrated by her internal ramble, was probably why the alternate route took her by the rec center. It had been a second home to her at one time, and somewhere she and Andy had spent a lot of time together as friends and enemies. It looked the same after all this time. Some of the landscaping was more mature, but the one-story brick building with glass brick inlays was as she remembered it, from the spindly palm trees thrusting their fronds into the sky, to the pristine flower beds. The small lot where she used to park her car for swim practice had been repaved, and she wondered if the picnic table was the same one she and Andy had carved their names into. A monsoon of memories hit her hard at that memory, and she found herself pulling to the curb. She didn't stop with the intent of going in. She just wanted to look at it.

Who was she kidding? She knew why she was here. It was a goddam mystery why she hadn't visited it before. Some of the best and worst things she'd ever experienced were here. She didn't have to go in to remember them. The memories were tattooed on her heart and soul.

She was at the glass doors without considering if it was a good idea. Cool air instantly made her skin prickle with goose bumps. She scanned the lobby. An image of Danny's tan face, long hair, and unnaturally white teeth took her back in time as she listened for the rhythmic slap of his flip-flops on the carpeted floor.

The silence was odd. She remembered it teeming with activity. But midmorning on a weekday when school hadn't closed for the summer was probably a slow time. The clanging of metal weights indicated at least one person was here. She noticed they'd replaced the wall behind the front desk with floor to ceiling glass. The upgrade had been a good call. It opened the space. That's not what she'd come to see, though.

The faint smell of the indoor pool crept into the lobby. She wished she could bottle it up to take home with her. Despite the beautiful pool at their house, it was saltwater and not the same. She'd spent countless hours in the rec center pool. At one time, she couldn't get the scent of chlorine out of her hair. The STEM school she'd attended focused on intellectual pursuits, so they'd partnered with the rec center to give students access to physical activities. She'd leaned toward aquatic sports because Andy had, and after they weren't friends, she stuck with swimming because Andy had. Swim team had been her best sport. She hadn't been great, but Andy had.

She waited at the counter for a few minutes to see if someone would show up. When no one did, she decided to check things out.

The layout looked the same. Two wide entrance ways opened to a tiled wall, blocking visibility into the locker rooms from the lobby. An identical wall and set of entrance ways directly opposite opened into the pool area. A flood of emotion carried her toward the locker room. How often had she walked through this entrance? Ignoring the silence and occasional clatter of metal, she could almost hear the voices and slam of locker doors echoing through the high-ceilinged room. Nostalgia wasn't why she'd come here. Twelve years of feeling as if she'd left a piece of herself behind in Oceanside had. Being here clicked something into place, like the missing piece had been inside her all along.

She was reminded of the fateful moment when she'd arrived at the border between her childhood and her future when she noticed the locker at the end was partially open. A swim cap and a pair of goggles lay on the bench before it. When the water in the showers turned off, she realized time had progressed without her. She almost laughed. She probably would have if being here didn't remind her of things she'd tried to suppress for years. Things that still haunted her. The most agonizing had been the last time she'd been here, on this step, just before she'd sealed her fate by kissing Andy for a second time. She hadn't been able to forget how the first one had revealed the potential of who they could be, and the second had forged something between them that wouldn't break. A fate she'd been tortured by ever since.

But what was all this about fate? She didn't believe in it. There wasn't a powerful entity who determined every action they took to get them to a predetermined goal. What was the point in that? The thought broke the spell.

She sighed. Getting lost in the past was a surefire way to waste the future. She snorted. She should get a T-shirt made. She headed to the restroom adjacent to the locker room. The restrooms at the store weren't her favorite place to visit.

The trip down memory lane hadn't destroyed her. Maybe it had actually been good for her, she thought as she washed her hands. She was a different person. She'd seen Andy a couple of times, and she'd survived. The person she'd been stuck on for years was only human. She would find a way to revive her heart and move on. Andy was just an unfairly beautiful human, whose every movement still entranced her. Of course, she would have feelings. She wasn't that emotionally stunted.

Sometimes debilitating shame overcame her, when she remembered it had been twelve years since she'd seen Andy. She should be over it. Over her. But feelings lived on a timeline all their own, didn't they? No matter how hard she tried to lock them away. It was only natural that reminders about the single most pivotal point in her past would dredge up all these memories and emotions. It didn't mean anything. Sure, she'd ghosted more than one therapist who'd insisted she was allowing her past to define her future. She could see the validity in that statement. But it wasn't anything she didn't already know. She'd been shitty to Andy when they'd been kids, and she didn't deserve absolution just because she'd been a kid. Even back then she'd known it was wrong. If she hadn't done things her mother's way, with harsh words and being mean, things would have probably been different.

But she couldn't change the past. She accepted her actions had caused this pain that hadn't grown easier, even after twenty years of a broken childhood friendship. What she couldn't accept was how she'd caused Andy so much pain.

It was their connection. She was sure of it. They'd always had a deeper than usual bond. It had kept them linked, even when it had been stretched so thin, it should have broken. But it never had. It might have been easier for both of them if it had. She'd expected time and distance after they'd gone off to college to make the bond fade away. Time and distance destroy relationships, right? But it hadn't. And now she knew she'd live with the guilt of hurting Andy for a long, long time. It wasn't just about grieving the loss of a childhood friendship, or a stupid crush she'd tried to bury. They'd both grown up. They'd both built lives away from their hometown. Her own wasn't as fulfilling as she'd dreamed, but she liked the person she'd become. Mostly. But even with lives neither of them knew about, when Lena was quiet, she could still feel the connection. Knowing Andy was in town explained why it felt stronger. All of this had flashed through her mind in the time it had taken to wash her hands.

She shook her arms and blew out a breath like she'd done before a heat at a swim meet when she was a kid. She felt better. It was good she'd come here. She felt a little more grounded now after visiting the scene of her last interaction with Andy. She hadn't crumbled. Progress. One last look in the mirror and she blew out another breath. Time to move on.

"Holy fuck." It flew out of her mouth before she could stop it. Andy whipped her head toward her. She wanted to look away, but she couldn't. Andy Phillips stood near the open locker she'd always used on the end of the row, wearing nothing but a T-shirt and panties. Lena reeled at the flashback to all those years ago.

Thankfully, the T-shirt was pulled all the way down this time, not showing off her flat stomach, or the soft curves of her breasts. Just thinking about it short-circuited Lena's everything.

Andy smiled uncertainly. Even if her eyes were guarded, it was an improvement from the incredulous look in the grocery store.

"Um, hi?" Andy said after a few awkward seconds of way too silent silence. A pause where Lena noticed how long Andy's hair was, the wet strands hanging over her shoulders, leaving damp spots on her T-shirt. Andy's skin was still pink from the shower. She looked fresh and a lot like she'd looked in high school. She'd barely aged. "You okay?" Andy tipped her head.

"Right. Yeah. Hi." Lena felt herself blush. Not knowing what to do with her hands, she pushed a strand of hair behind her ear and shoved them into her pockets. "I just had to pee." Pee? What was wrong with her?

Andy pulled on a pair of shorts she'd been holding. More glitching out happened for Lena. Andy looked sexier putting on clothing than most women looked taking it off. And Lena was staring. She swiveled her head up, to the side, focused anywhere other than Andy. Laughter brought her gaze back. Despite her inability to human properly, the sound did things to her. It had back then, too. Stop it.

"Back to the scene of the crime, huh?" Andy sounded collected. Lena felt anything but.

"Huh?" Andy didn't ease in, did she?

"You know. The last time we were here."

How did someone look so hot in just a T-shirt and shorts?

"I—I'm not. I mean." Lena couldn't think.

"I know. Weird, right?"

"There was no one at the desk so I, um." Words. Where were her words? Because Lena may be the on-air professional, but Andy had always been the poised one.

Andy tipped her head again. "I get it. Being in here. And it's us, so." Andy's brow furrowed. "Do you want to grab coffee? Or tea? Or something?" Okay, so maybe Andy wasn't completely poised. Still, she completed her sentences. But was she really asking her to get coffee?

"Sure," she heard herself say.

"I know a place." Andy collected her gear, putting it into a bag she pulled out of the locker, and slung it over her shoulder. Andy's graceful, confident movements had always captivated her. And she was staring again.

"Sounds great." Lena's voice was pitched higher than usual. Her stomach was full of butterflies? Bats? Pterodactyls? Andy was now less than two feet away. Again, with the questioning look.

"Are you okay?"

Lena realized her hand was on her stomach. She dropped it. "Nervous, I guess." Nerves usually made her honest.

Andy nodded slowly. "Me too."

Outside the building, the sunshine felt good on her skin after the efficient air-conditioning. "I'm over there." She pointed to her car, the only one parked near the rec center.

"My car's at my dad's house. Wanna meet in twenty at Seaside?"

"I can drive," Lena said. But could she? Could she avoid hitting other cars in this weird awkward trance? That would be mortifying.

Andy seemed uncertain for a moment before she headed toward Lena's car. "Nice. Can we put the top down?"

Chapter Eleven

Andy had almost no recollection of how she ended up in Lena's car. How had her legs even worked? Riding in a car with Lena Holmes was not on her schedule for the day. Or even her life. Yet they were going to coffee. No big deal, right? She had a faint recollection of suggesting it, with her own voice, but it couldn't have been her. Also, Lena watching her dress? How had she managed not to get tangled in her shorts and fall on her face? The only explanation was that she'd died from the shock of seeing her, and she was a ghost riding in this car with the top down, sitting like she sat here every day. Far more plausible than seeing Lena while half-dressed, remaining calm, and coherently suggesting coffee to her very attractive ex-best friend and mortal enemy who'd teleported from the past. A mortal enemy she'd kissed and, twelve years later, it was still the best kiss she'd ever experienced.

Lena looked over. Was she thinking the same things? Could Lena tell she was freaking the fuck out? After a rough start, Lena now looked relaxed. Not to mention gorgeous with the wind blowing through beautiful hair the sun seemed to live in. Andy was relieved they couldn't talk much over the noise of the wind. Instead, she concentrated on not making a fool of herself while she watched tourists trying to swim in the crashing surf. Andy held her hand in the current of air rushing by, wondering what she'd do when they got there, and she had to be coherent.

Lena pulled into the dirt parking lot behind the coffee shop and hopped out of her car like she had a pair of perfectly functioning legs. Not to be outdone, Andy made her legs move, too, and somehow managed to make it to the shop without embarrassing herself. At the door, as if they'd choreographed it, they both turned to admire the beach. The breeze and view helped settle her, and she knew she'd forever link the aroma of brewing coffee and the sounds of seagulls to this moment. She couldn't believe Lena Holmes stood less than a foot away from her. She didn't know how to feel.

"This place is great." Lena put a hand on Andy's arm "Are you okay?"

"Just a little thrown," she said, opting for the truth.

A barefoot guy in swim trunks, squeezed around them, turning back after seeing the sign that read, "No shirt. No shoes. No service," and headed to the service window a few feet away where a sign read, "No shirt. No shoes. No problem." So very San Diego Andy thought, amused each time she saw the sign. This time the hand on her arm eclipsed her amusement.

Lena seemed to realize she was touching her and quickly pulled her hand away. She let out a long breath. "Glad it's not just me."

Andy led them to the counter, where they stood behind a sunburned family of four. Andy looked at Lena and they both shook their heads. Only a week or so back home, and she was judging tourists like a local. So pretentious. She didn't want to delight in their shared reaction, but she did.

"I'm not sure what to get." Lena studied the chalk menu behind the counter.

"What do you like?"

"I'm normally a basic drip girl."

Lena was hardly basic, and definitely no girl, Andy thought. She'd grown into a full-fledged woman. Who'd totally checked her out at the rec center but seemed to have trouble meeting her eyes since. Still, a steady buzz played in her stomach.

"Andy?"

"Sorry?" She never knew she would like the sound of her name on Lena's lips again. It had been a very different story until about fifteen minutes ago.

"What do you recommend? Iced or drip? Or something in between?"

Coffee was Andy's language, so she leaned into it. "It's all good. I usually go for the Ecuadorean. It's rich, but not too rich, with hints of something flowery." Andy stopped before diving in too far. Not everyone appreciated coffee as much as she did.

Lena shook her head. "A coffee snob? Who knew?" She sounded amused. Andy took it as a compliment. "Ecuadorean it is."

Coffee in hand, they went out to the deck where Andy found an open table. The background sounds of the beach helped her relax.

"A girl could be tempted to move here for this coffee alone. And the view? Perfect." Lena sipped her drink and Andy struggled not to stare.

"Where do you live now?" Too personal? She had no idea what Lena would consider too personal. She half expected her to break into a sneer and berate her for interrogating her.

"Phoenix. Going on three years."

"What do you do there?"

"I was the chief meteorologist and weather anchor for a news station. It's the biggest station in Arizona for broadcast, and the digital channel has a solid reach from the gulf, all of Arizona and Nevada, most of the panhandle, and New Mexico." She paused. "Not that you asked for market information."

"It's impressive, though. Isn't digital streamed globally?"

Lena nodded. "We have subscribers all over. But our main density is in those regions. Local news and weather are like that."

"Meteorologist, huh?"

Lena nodded. "It was always my thing."

"I sort of expected you to go into something environmental."

"Meteorology is part of the environment," Lena said over the top of her cup. Her eyes had a twinkle in them Andy had never seen, and she wondered if Lena was teasing her.

"I think you know I meant climate change."

"I figured," Lena said. Andy couldn't look away from the twinkle. She remembered how Lena's blue-green eyes changed color depending on her surroundings. Right now, they were the color of a wave falling into a barrel with the sun shining through it. The twinkle just enhanced it. Lena looked down at her cup. "I changed my focus in college. I like pattern analysis. I do a lot of it to forecast weather by studying past events, present conditions, and other data. Not all of us are forecasters. Just like any science discipline, we pick our niche. I'm sure you have your own in marine science."

Andy didn't miss that Lena knew she'd gone into marine biology. It wasn't a leap, considering her interest in it as a kid. "Initially, it was deep ocean research. It's fascinating, but reefs are more accessible." Like coffee, she could go on and on about her research, but she was measuring everything she said and did. She couldn't believe they were here together. It felt surreal. "I really got into the ecosystems of reefs back in high school."

"I remember. You took first at the science fair with a project about them."

Lena looked at her, not quite from the corners of her eyes, but close. Andy immediately knew why. What an idiot. She bought time with a sip of coffee.

The goddamned science fair where Lena's project should have won. Andy cringed. Lena's project had been exponentially better, and after the challenge to the judge's ruling, she'd been given co-first place after the fact. Not nearly good enough. The damage had been done. She still remembered Lena's expression.

Andy slouched, wanting to crawl under the table. "I didn't deserve it."

Lena waved a hand. "Why does it matter? I was too immature to thank you back then. So, thank you."

"For what?" But Andy thought she knew.

Lena tilted her head to the side again. "For sticking up for me."

Andy sat up. "How did you know?"

Lena smiled and the twinkle was back. Her smile did things to Andy, but that twinkle did even more. "I saw you talking to the judges. But the boss judge told me when they gave me co-first." She leaned forward, her elbows on the table. "That makes me respect you even more."

"Even more than what?" Andy wanted to kick herself for asking. She was like a little kid asking for validation. In a sense, she was.

"Lots of things," Lena said dismissively. Andy wanted details, but if Lena didn't want to elaborate, she wasn't going to beg for it. Especially after getting closure on an event that had haunted her for years.

"What kind of judge does that? He made an error. Your project was brilliant."

"What kind of person stands up for someone they hate?" Lena's smile was gone, her gaze intense. "It was…" Lena puffed out a breath, very obviously fighting emotion. "It was unexpected."

"It was the right thing to do." Regardless of what they'd become by then, at one time they'd been best friends. And best friends stuck up for each other. "So, what about now? What made you leave Insight Phoenix?"

Lena looked surprised. "What makes you think I left?"

"You said 'was the meteorologist' a few minutes ago."

"Nothing gets past you, does it? I needed a change."

"What kind of change?"

Lena shrugged, but it looked forced. "You could say the derecho was bearing down on me."

"Gusty wind?" It made sense she'd use a weather metaphor. It sounded ominous.

"It's more than gusty."

Andy nodded. "And that means move on?"

"Preferably before there's any damage."

"Are you still talking about your former job?"

"I am. But it's not always about work."

"I'm intrigued." Andy leaned forward.

Lena rested her chin on the back of her overlapped hands. "You're the intriguing one. I always knew you were more complex than you let on."

Holy abrupt subject change. Totally understandable, but what the actual hell? Everything about sitting here with Lena was unreal.

"Same," she said. "The intriguing part. I always knew you were complex." An almost imperceptible flash of something crossed Lena's face but was gone before Andy could identify it.

"Obviously," Lena said.

"Obviously?" Had she missed something?

"Obviously, I'm intriguing." First the twinkle and now…wait! Was she flirting? Andy instantly disintegrated and reassembled right then and there. At least she felt like it. "I have so many questions." She barely heard, because, WTF?

"Like what?" Andy asked. The calm voice that came from her mouth couldn't be hers.

Lena shifted in her seat. "I don't know…I might not like the answers."

Andy laughed until she figured out Lena was serious, which reset her system. She'd have to deal with the whiplash later, but she sensed Lena was showing her insecurity. Her lack of poise at the rec center had been disarming, but this was peak fragility. "I'm not a scary person. I'm not out to hurt you. I never was."

"Would it surprise you if I already knew those things?" Lena asked. Andy didn't have a response. "You're surprised. I can tell."

"I am." Andy smiled uncertainly. The moment had shifted so quickly.

Lena continued to smile but Andy could already tell the difference between her news anchor version and a genuine one. This was the former. She was pretty sure there were a lot of other versions in there. "Okay, here's a question. Ready?"

"Lay it on me," Andy said. Lena was almost too still. The pulse racing under her jaw was the tell that Lena was trying hard to appear as if she was relaxed. Maybe it could fool some people, but it didn't fool her. Or maybe she was deluding herself into thinking she had that kind of insight into Lena.

"Do you think we could wipe the slate clean?" Lena swallowed hard. She was most definitely nervous. Andy wondered how hard it had been for her to bring it up. She wasn't sure she could have.

Andy considered the question. "How long have you wanted to ask that?"

Lena looked at her hands. "Honestly?"

Her question was a throwaway idiom, buying time. Lena seemed to be weighing the possible answers, indicating she saw this as a crossroads point in their conversation. Andy's world was tilting, knowing Lena was so invested.

"Only if you feel safe," Andy said.

Lena's gaze met hers and Andy wasn't prepared to see the disbelief followed by gratitude in her eyes. She didn't think it was about this singular question.

"Since about fifth grade."

Andy leaned back heavily into her chair. She hadn't expected it. "That wasn't…" Andy didn't know how to say what she wanted to. "But you hated me. Like really, really hated me."

"I hated me. It was never you." Lena shook her head. "I mean, I came to believe I hated you after a while. But even that was really a projection. I lost track of what was real and what was anything else. I just want us…" Her eyes seemed to search the air for the right words. Her shoulders dropped. "I just want us."

Andy was so off-center, she didn't know how she felt about any of this. "I don't know." She hated to see Lena sag even more at her answer, but she owed her the truth. "I mean, how can we just forget it all? We were awful to each other."

Lena stared at her coffee cup. "You mean, I was awful to you."

"It went both ways," Andy said.

"I don't remember it that way."

"Trust me. It did." Andy watched Lena absorbing their conversation. She had no idea how it would be received, but she rested her hand on Lena's forearm. She almost withdrew it when Lena's glance immediately shifted to it. "I don't think we can wipe anything away, but maybe we can see how it goes."

It was like she was watching a rock wall start to crumble beneath Lena's skin. Her tight muscles relaxed but not all at once, as if they were so used to being on alert, they didn't know how. Lena stood up. "I'll be right back. Ladies room."

❖

Sunlight glinted from the saltwater pool in Lena's parents' backyard as if someone had tossed diamonds into it. She squinted at the refractions, watching the light stretch longer, then shorter, and longer again. It was a trick with light she'd used since before she could remember. Whether it was reflections from water, a streetlight, or a studio light, it had always helped her think. Mostly about difficult things. She used it for that now, but mostly to keep from crying. She couldn't remember the last time she'd cried, and she didn't know why she was on the verge now. She'd been on the verge since seeing Andy. Especially when Andy said they could see how it goes. Never in a million years would she have expected it. Let alone ask it in the first place.

She'd always been the queen of confusing thoughts, though. She blew out a breath, closed her eyes, and dropped her head back to the soft cushion of the lounger. The book she couldn't concentrate on slid off her lap. Grateful that her mother would be gone until later in the evening while she accompanied her own mother to Tuesday after-dinner game night, Lena and Lourdes had eaten a light dinner earlier, and were relaxing by the gas firepit, Lena with a nice glass of wine and Lourdes with her voodoo doll chew toy her mother did not approve of. Lena's mind kept drifting to Andy. She didn't have to examine the events of the day to pinpoint what troubled her. She knew.

Today with Andy had been wholly unexpected, but not really. If she was honest with herself, and she usually wasn't, having run into her at the grocery store should have told her it was a foregone conclusion she'd see her again. What wasn't a foregone conclusion was Andy asking her to go to coffee. Also seeing her half-dressed, but that was a completely different thing for her to process.

Them running into each other should have been as expected as the sun coming up. It was going to happen no matter how hard she wished it wouldn't. Given any length of time in geographical proximity, their crossing of paths, would occur as surely as the waxing and waning of the moon. The longer they were in the same vicinity, the more likely it would be. But Lena hadn't expected Andy to be in Oceanside, and she certainly didn't think she could endure her mother long enough for it to happen if she knew Andy was. But that's not how it worked for them. Until they'd left for college, they'd seen each other far more than their proximity warranted. Sure, they'd gone to the same school, they'd frequented the same rec center, and they'd had a few of the same friends. But outside of those instances of forced proximity, they seemed to find the other no matter where they went. They were like highly reactive elements seeking each other out to gain stability. Alone, they begin to lose themselves.

It had been evident years ago when their paths would cross in uncommon situations. For instance, Lena rarely went to the beach. She didn't surf, and the tourists crowded everything. But almost every time she did, she'd see Andy, no matter what beach she went to. And of course, Andy would be shredding waves like a pro just like any sport she tried. One summer, to avoid time with her mother, as a last-minute decision, she'd volunteered for Habitat for Humanity. Guess who'd also volunteered. Naturally, they'd been assigned to the same project. Lena, not allowed to have a dog, signed up to walk dogs after school at the nearby dog rescue. Two days into it, Andy showed up for the same thing. There'd been so many coincidental meetings, Lena stopped being surprised by them. Of course, Andy had accused her more than once of stalking, but by the time they'd been assigned to the graduation speech, they'd stopped questioning why.

Lena hated that it made sense to her without scientific proof, but there was something between the two of them that sought each other out. It wasn't a conscious thing, and Lena didn't believe in supernatural beings purported to manipulate events. Not like Crystal, who'd suggested it after she witnessed it happen. Lena suspected it was a sort of energy thing. Probably the same thing that let her know when Andy was near without having to see her. She just knew. It had been strong by the time they finished high school, and it seemed even stronger now.

No one could convince her otherwise. This thing between them was real, even if she didn't know how it worked.

Today at the rec center was a perfect example. But rather than fight it, they'd gone to coffee, and she'd felt their energy stronger than ever before. It had felt like a dance, smooth and in sync. Something seemed to be at play just below the surface. Something exciting and scary that reminded her of how she'd felt just before each time they'd kissed. As always, a familiar shiver of desire stepped down her spine at the simple thought. The longing the mere thought stirred up inside her was different than anything or anyone she'd ever experienced. Nothing had even come close. She'd give every sexual encounter she'd had for just one more kiss with Andy.

Chapter Twelve

After a restless night of sleep filled with montages featuring Andy, Lena shuffled into the kitchen, desperate for coffee. Unexpectedly, her dad stood next to the coffee maker, hands braced on the counter. There was an identical mug on the counter, already filled, the sugar dispenser next to it. He didn't do sugar in his coffee, and her mother only used sugar-free sweetener, so she guessed it was for Joanie.

"Hey, Dad." She felt like she was intruding. She'd never been in the kitchen alone with him. He usually spent his time in the yard or dining room. Like a guest.

He seemed startled and turned around. "Hey ya, kiddo. I hoped you'd be up." He took a step toward her. She thought he might hug her and tensed, but he stepped back. "Can I make you a cup of coffee?"

She wanted to ask why he was here, but it was his house. And where was her mother? She usually didn't leave for another hour. Lena hadn't heard her come home last night, either. Maybe she should be worried, but that's not how they worked. Her mother had never asked about her whereabouts, so she wouldn't pry into hers.

"Sure," she said about the coffee.

He smiled like she'd just given him a present, which made it weird. It shouldn't be so hard to be around him.

His glance skipped to the front door. "Your mother's taking Grandma to a procedure today," he said as if reading her mind.

That's probably why he was here. Maybe an opportunity for him to visit his own house. The old "Fuck You, I Do What I Want" boogie. Big sigh. While his over-architected and swank office was the probable answer, she wondered again where he usually slept. Given her mother's obsession about what other people thought, she doubted he had his own place. For the first time, she wondered if he had a girlfriend. Her parents had obviously not lived a married life in some time, if ever. And now it was time for the old "Stuff it Back in the Shit I Don't Want to Think About Lockbox" tango. Seriously.

"How's Grandma doing?" Guilt about not visiting her grandma at Sunrise Memory Care swam to the front of her self-flagellation cortex. She'd often visited Sierra Vista where she'd lived before, but the only person allowed to visit anymore was her mother. She wondered if she should just go and sit in a room with her. Not even talk. Her grandma had, at one time, been the only family member who'd seemed the least bit invested in her. There'd been no snuggles or silly moments, but there had been a chocolate shake or two.

"You mother didn't say what kind of procedure. She has a lot of them. I used to think she'd outlive us all." His eyes grew faraway. "Where's the line determining quality over quantity of life?"

His parents had died when he was much younger. So had her mother's father. Lena had never met them. Lena's grandmother, her only grandparent, was the only parent he'd known for most of his adult life. She wondered how close he was to her and if this was hard for him.

He set a cup of coffee on the counter along with all the accouterments. "I should know how you take it."

Pouring half-and-half into it, she wondered why he should. Also, did he expect to drink their coffee together? This whole interaction wasn't just awkward. It made her sad.

"Do you want to have lunch together? It doesn't have to be today," she said. Aside from the dinner the day she'd arrived, she still hadn't seen him this visit. Why did she even care? And why was she doing his job?

He looked as if he might cry. "I'd like that."

"I mean, a person's gotta eat," she said. Someone had to break the awkward pause.

He rounded the kitchen island and wrapped her in his arms.

She hugged him back. What was happening?

When he stepped back, his eyes were watery. "That was weird, huh?"

She almost said no, but it was weird. "A little," she said. Especially since she couldn't remember being hugged by either parent. By anyone other than Andy. She flashed to the locker room. Not gonna go there, though. Nope.

"Well, I'm gonna…" Retrieving the travel mugs, he looked as if he had something to say. Instead, he gave her a sad smile.

When he was gone, she stood frozen, thinking about what just happened. It was the most they'd said to each other in years. Dazed, she noticed he'd left his wallet on the counter.

She dialed his number. Oddly, Joanie answered his phone and said he'd be there in hour or so.

"Oh, yeah. I forgot," she lied. "Do you usually answer his phone?"

"You called the store line, honey."

"I must have hit the wrong number," she said, embarrassed to admit she'd gotten the number from a billboard a long time ago and had never used it. "What would people think?" ran through her mind. Fucking indoctrination. "I have his wallet. I can drop it when he gets there."

"He's visiting Glenn if you want to try there."

After a few minutes of chatting, she rang off. First, she discovered her dad filled in for Glenn at work, and now they were the drop-in-every-morning kind of friends? The weirdness just got weirder.

Not sure when her mother would be home, she fed Lourdes and decided to take a drive. The destination was already in her mind, but she didn't admit it until she pulled up. And sat. Why was she here? Should she call first? Dropping in was probably rude. Excuses and cowardice. Admitting she was afraid, she just wanted to see her. She didn't need to talk to her. She couldn't talk to her. Preferring to remember her grandma from the last time she'd seen her, she started her car and pulled away.

After that, a dark cloud seemed to follow her, making everything seem gray.

Seaside Café crossed her mind. There was sunshine there. And yesterday had been nice. Mostly. Why was she tingling, though? She shouldn't tingle.

The place was packed when she arrived.

She scanned the crowd as she waited in line. Not hoping to see Andy, she told herself. Going out on the deck with her coffee didn't mean anything, either. Then why was she disappointed not to see her? Their table was the only one available. Now it was "their" table? She needed to get ahold of herself.

Settling in, she automatically picked up her phone. What was she doing? She had a gorgeous view right in front of her. Looking back, her life had always been one distraction after another. If it wasn't her phone, it was something else. Since being back in Oceanside, her mind kept wandering to places she didn't want to explore. She wondered if finding distractions had been suppression all along. Probably a way to keep other people out, too. Admittedly, there was no "wondering" or "probably" about it. Considering how many difficult things from her past she'd consistently had to stuff back down since coming back, she'd say all the distracting she'd been doing was a direct correlation with the amount of free time she had now. Nothing new, really.

Sighing, she did more stuffing as she sipped her coffee and opted for getting lost in the view. Who knew how long she'd been lost before a very welcome awareness fell over her?

"I wondered if you'd be here." Andy stood a couple of feet away.

Did Andy think she came looking for her? Desperate much? "It's nice here?" Why did it come out as a question?

"The vibe snagged you, right?" Andy laughed, shaking her head. "I've never used the word 'vibe' in my life. It felt wrong as soon as it left my mouth."

"It's a good vibe." Lena pushed a strand of hair behind her ear, liking the pink staining Andy's cheeks. "I hope you don't mind, I really like the coffee." And drinking it with you. Stop it.

"I couldn't deny you the pleasure of the vibe." Andy shrugged with a crooked grin.

The world tilted when the fifth grade Andy stood before her. Then she saw she had two cups. She stood with a smile she didn't feel, tossing her empty cup into the nearby garbage bin. "I should probably go. It looks like you're waiting for someone. Good thing I saved a table." She almost said "our." She had no right to be disappointed.

Andy offered her one of the cups. "I saw you on the way in and took a chance you'd want a second cup, but I really needed an excuse." Andy shifted her weight from side to side.

Poof! went Lena's disappointment. She looked from the coffee to Andy before accepting it.

"Did you just say 'poof'?" Andy asked.

Had she? "I wished another cup would magically appear. I'm glad to see you aren't immune to my magic." Did she really say that?

"Your magic has always worked with me." Andy's smile twinkled in her eyes.

"Good to know." What was this? Flurries tickled Lena's stomach. "I'm a coffee zealot. Not even human until I have at least three cups."

"Seven or eight for me." Andy looked proud of it.

"Large or true cup-size?"

"Ginormous if they have it. True cup-size can't compete in this caffeinated world."

"I'd be zinging all day."

Andy smirked playfully. "That's not a bad thing, is it? But it makes you a coffee novice." Was this flirting? Lena could usually tell. With Andy, it seemed preposterous. Impossible, even.

"Does seven or eight make you an addict?" Lena countered.

"I'd argue my vice could be worse." Andy shrugged.

"Valid point," Lena conceded.

"I brought someone. Do you mind if I bring her over?"

Did her hot air ballon just hit wind shear? What had she been thinking? "I was about to leave anyway."

"Just a few more minutes? I really want you to meet her." Andy looked so earnest.

"She might want you all to herself."

Andy rolled her eyes. "She'll probably be more interested in you."

"Uh-huh." Weird thing to say, but who was she to judge?

Andy pointed to the railing at the bottom of the steps. "She's super friendly."

A woman about her mother's age was petting a small dog. So, Andy was into older women. "Sure," she said. A quick hello and she was out of there.

Andy was already heading toward her. "Save the table." She was stuck. She turned around so she didn't have to see them hug or kiss in greeting.

"Billie, I want you to meet Lena."

"I really should—" She turned to see Andy holding the cutest little long-haired wiener dog.

Andy put her mouth close to her ear. "This is Selena Grace Holmes, but she hates Selena, so we call her Lena." She held Billie's paw out and Lena shook it, unaccountably touched that Andy remembered her middle name. "Lena, this is the High Priestess, Billie Phillips."

"Oh goodness. Those short little legs and floppy ears." There was only one way to talk to animals and babies. She giggled when Billie gave her hand a lick. She couldn't name Andy's expression, but it made her warm inside.

Billie wiggled. Without thought, Lena stepped closer to make the trade. The back of Lena's hands brushed against Andy's stomach, while their arms slid over each other. Andy sucked in a breath, and Lena felt a very different kind of wind shear. Careening back in time, chlorine and rec center shampoo evoked a paradox of sensation. She didn't step back. She really should have, but her legs wouldn't move. Neither did Andy. Lena chanced a glance. Andy's expression looked penetrating yet guarded. Billie snuggled into her, and still they stood. Andy visibly shivered and dropped into a seat. Lena did the same. The strange moment was over. Billie shifted only enough to get comfortable in Lena's lap.

"You're committed now. She's there until you move her," Andy said, as if the charged moment hadn't happened.

All Lena could think about was how soft Andy's lips had been. Something powerful moved through her, settling low and hot and she didn't even try to ignore it.

❖

What was she doing? Andy watched Lena play with Billie's ears, somehow knowing it was Billie's favorite thing, next to naps. Andy was probably just as happy as Billie, seeing Lena loving on her.

"Do you always come here when you visit?" Lena asked around a sip of her drink. Andy heard the question as if from a distance. She'd moved her gaze from Billie's unbelievably lucky perch on Lena's lap to Lena's mouth on her cup. She wasn't sure if she'd ever found anyone drinking coffee sexy before. But this wasn't just anyone making her heart race.

"Andy?"

Still entranced, Andy lifted her gaze to Lena's eyes. "Huh?"

Lena tipped her head. "I asked if you spend a lot of time here when you're in town."

"I only discovered Seaside about a week ago. It's been three years since I've visited Oceanside." She grimaced about admitting how long it had been. "I know. I'm terrible. My dad deserves better."

Lena put her hand on Andy's forearm. "It was almost five years for me. Two before that. So, no judgment here." She took her hand away, looking as if she'd touched a live wire.

Andy ran her finger along the edge of the table. "I tell myself I'll visit more, but then I get caught up in a project, and next thing, it's been a year."

"Is that your way of saying you're a workaholic?" Lena looked amused but the topic had come up with various people too many times for Andy to brush it off.

She shrugged. "Talia thinks so. But I love my work."

"You're still friends?" A hint of longing briefly surfaced on Lena's face and just as quickly disappeared.

"She and I just happened to get jobs in Monterey. She's staying at my place while I'm here. She's basically my family. She was there when my mom moved to Denver."

"I always loved how close you were. Wait. Your mom's in Denver? Your parents aren't together anymore?"

Andy sipped her coffee. "They split when I left for college. My mom moved to Monterey for a while, then moved to Denver when her sister had some health issues and stayed."

Lena looked sad. "They seemed so solid."

"Still are," Andy said. "Only in a different way."

Lena's gaze shifted to the beach. Most of the surfers had come in from the water and the tourists were migrating down for the day.

"I've always loved your parents. It must be hard to be away from them." She sounded wistful.

"Mom's partner has family in Monterey, so they visit a couple of times a year."

"Does your dad have a partner? Tell me if I'm getting too personal."

Andy didn't think she'd ever think Lena was being too personal. She liked telling her about her life. "It's okay. You were close with them. I don't think he even dates."

Lena focused on petting Billie, who still slept soundly. "I lost them when I lost you."

Andy wanted to hug her but wasn't sure if Lena would be okay with it. "They ask about you."

Lena cleared her throat. "What do you say?"

"The truth. That I haven't seen you. They know a little about what happened, but my mom really misses you. She was always protective of you. I don't know why she felt she should be, but she was. I suppose my dad gets updates from your dad, like dads do."

Lena still hadn't looked up. "I don't think my parents ever noticed about us. I'm glad your mom and dad are good."

"Mostly. My dad says he's good. I mean, other than his accident. My mom and Lydia are happy."

"Lydia?"

Andy nodded. "Her wife."

Lena's mouth dropped open. "How did I not know?"

"She didn't either, until she met Lydia. She and my dad chose to stay together until I went to college. She and Lydia were friends and waited until the divorce before acting on anything. It was all very respectful. I didn't find out any of this until later, though."

"How was your dad about it?"

"He doesn't talk about his personal feelings a lot, but they're still very close, although they don't see each other as often as they want."

"That's amazing." Lena looked pensive. "Do you think your dad doesn't date because he still loves your mom?"

"I think he's past that. He was at their wedding. Everyone likes Lydia Daniels."

"Lydia Daniels?" Lena asked. Andy waited for her to figure it out. Lena's face switched to disbelief. "Not Ms. Daniels? Our favorite teacher from fourth grade?"

Andy nodded. "It was weird at first. She's just as amazing out of class."

Lena looked wistful. "You must have had all kinds of support when you came out."

"I did. Unlike my dad."

Lena looked confused. "Your dad?"

"My dad's dad was not supportive."

"He was gone before you were born, right? How was he not supportive of you?"

"Of my dad."

Lena sat back. "Wait. What?"

"He's bi."

"Your parents are both queer? Did he figure it out later, too?" Lena's expression changed to chagrined. "Sorry. That's rude. It's none of my business."

"It's totally okay. He knew in high school, and he was open about it. None of this is secret. Besides I trust you."

Lena stared at her. "Why should you?"

"Why should I what?"

"Trust me. I've given you absolutely no reason to."

Lena looked almost angry, changing the mood abruptly. Andy knew she was right, though. She needed to be careful. Especially with Lena essentially warning her not to trust her. She should be running away.

But she didn't want to.

"You never gave me a reason not to. You always kept my secrets. Even when everything changed. At least I never heard otherwise. But if you had, we were just kids. You were dealing with a lot of things."

"So were you."

"I get a feeling you had more on your plate."

Lena dropped her gaze and shook her head. Her eyes glimmered with tears. Surprised, Andy offered one of the napkins she'd picked up at the coffee counter. Lena used it and went back to stroking Billie.

"I wouldn't trust me," Lena whispered.

Andy hadn't for a long time, and maybe she still shouldn't. But it felt different now. And even if it was a bad decision, Andy wanted to take this chance. She'd just have to be careful.

"Adult me believes I can trust adult you," she said. "Unless you're secretly scheming to destroy me over there." She covered Lena's hand with hers, feeling the weight of a defining moment for them. She realized she'd been waiting for something like this since the first minutes in the locker room. "I trust you, Lena."

Lena shook her head, appearing unable to look Andy in the eye. When Lena's gaze dropped to their hands, Andy pulled hers back.

She'd never seen Lena cry. Not even when they were kids.

Lena visibly shook herself and pulled her shoulders back. "I've always been jealous of you and your parents. I can't imagine having that kind of support coming out."

"Were your parents not supportive?" It was a stupid question. Andy knew Lena's mother wouldn't be. But Robert might have been.

Lena held her gaze for a moment. "I never came out to them," she finally said.

"You're not out? Or you're not…?"

Lena seemed confused for a moment and then scoffed. "I've just never told them. My mother…well, I don't think I exist to her when I'm not in the same room, and even then…" Lena shrugged, looking toward the ocean, not seeming to really see it.

Andy ached for Lena. She'd known her mother was cold, but not that cold.

"How long are you here for?" It seemed Lena was the queen of abrupt topic changes.

"It remains to be seen," Andy said. Fortunately, she could work remotely in a limited capacity, and her schedule was flexible. "A few months, at least. He's not mobile with the casts, and all. He won't be able to manage by himself for a while."

"You're the only one who can take care of him?"

"My grandma's too old, although she wants to. There are other services and he'd probably rather do any of those than be a burden on me or anyone else. But he'd hate all of it. We have a few things to figure out."

"What happened?"

"Your dad has probably told you the high-level stuff, but with two broken legs, he's basically immobile, which makes him grumpy. He'd never take anything out on anyone, so he internalizes it. I think that's what gets to him more than anything else. He'd be a lot worse if your dad didn't come by so often. I honestly don't know how he does it all and still has time for your family."

Lena looked stricken, and Andy was touched by her concern.

They talked for a few minutes longer, until Lena looked at her phone and said she was late for an appointment before gently moving Billie to Andy's lap and leaving. They'd been talking for nearly two hours by then.

Andy didn't realize they hadn't exchanged phone numbers until Lena had left.

Chapter Thirteen

On day four of not seeing Lena, Andy's spirits were down but not yet broken. When she arrived home after her morning swim and visit to the café, where she'd chided herself for looking for Lena, Robert's truck was parked in the driveway. It was usually gone by the time she returned. She decided to ask Robert for Lena's number. Friends checked in on friends, right? But did Lena consider her a friend?

Bypassing the ramp as usual, Andy hopped onto the porch. Just past the front window, she froze. Distracted by Lena's distance, it took a second to sink in. What had she just seen? Robert leaning over her father? Her father's fingers stroking his dark hair? Their faces too close not to touch?

Unable to decide if she should leave, confront, or act like it was any other morning, she realized it was none of her business. So, she took her time and made more noise than usual entering the house. She almost laughed to find Robert making a point of adjusting her dad's pillow, while her dad thoroughly examined the controller for the bed. Both's hair was tussled.

Her dad cleared his throat. "How was coffee?"

Robert feigned surprise. "Oh, hey, Andy. The coffee shop. How was it?"

"Busy as usual." How could she look at them without laughing? But also, WTF? Stunned? Flabbergasted? You could knock her over with a feather? None of that described her reaction. Her dad and Robert?

"Not surprising. I hear it's the best." Her dad seemed to relax, probably thinking they'd avoided detection. She'd seen what she'd seen, though. A million questions she wasn't ready to ask stacked up in her mind. Instead, she asked Robert for Lena's number and made small talk, before excusing herself to start her workday. Totally normal.

By the time she fell back onto her childhood bed, it really did seem normal. She still had a lot of questions, but thinking about her dad and Robert over the years, how had she not known?

It really wasn't her business. She knew it wasn't her dad's thing to talk about personal stuff. His love was shown in many other ways. One of them was he never lied. He said it like it was and she'd always trusted him. Had he lied about dating Robert? She wasn't sure, but even if he had, it did nothing to test her trust in him. He had his reasons, and he didn't have to tell her why he'd never said anything. It didn't make her not want to know, though.

Between this and Lena's disappearing act, her thoughts were more than a little crowded. She was a scientist. It was her nature to want to know why, and with two major topics competing for answers, her thoughts were spinning like a maelstrom. The only things she knew for sure were, her dad's business was his business, and she couldn't let Lena in too far, but maybe she already had. She needed to fix that. But what if she didn't want too? She needed a distraction from her brain.

Her gaze landed on her desk. Since seeing Lena again, her old journals had been on her mind. She couldn't help thinking about the last entry any time she thought of them, the one right before she'd left for college. She never wanted to feel that way again, so she avoided even looking at them. The thing was, she felt almost as hopeless now. Like some addicts who'd thought they'd conquered their addiction but had a lapse, she'd slid right back to where she'd been at the nadir of their journey. She hadn't expected it. It had been so long, but feelings from their past seemed to seep from the drawer where her words were hidden away. She'd purged and moved on, never rereading any of them. The urge to revisit them felt strange. Almost like breaking a promise to herself. But it wasn't, was it? They were part of her, and surprisingly, a part of her she missed.

Settling at the desk with the very first one her teacher had given to her in first grade, she began to read the chronicle of her life. Several years of evolving handwriting depicting youthful thoughts spread across the volumes. Nothing between the first enthusiastic entry and the one where she'd bared her shattered heart in a way she hadn't done before hinted at the sudden ending to their friendship. The day before, they'd had the "best sleepover in the world." The next, Lena had simply stopped talking to her. Ten-year-old Andy had no idea why. She'd assumed she'd done something wrong. Adult Andy revisited the embarrassment of begging for answers and the torture of getting none. Wiping away tears while she rubbed at the old ache in her chest, she continued to read.

When she reached the part describing her last moment of tenuous hope, Andy paused to retrieve the carefully folded note Lena had dropped onto her desk after four weeks of ignoring her. She placed it next to the journal before continuing. Fifth grade Andy's hands had shook so hard, she'd barely been able to unfold it. That's when she found there were things worse than silence. *People just grow apart, Andy. Get used to it.*

Those words were still tattooed on her heart. They'd emerged, unbidden, in her thoughts throughout the years. The pain they'd initially inflicted having faded in intensity since, but the weight of them remained. It was interesting how, out of context, those nine random words might not seem as lethal as they'd been to her.

Almost a year after receipt of the devastating note, kids had still been talking about the huge fight Lena and Andy must have had. As far as Andy knew, Lena had never spoken to anyone about it, and Andy certainly hadn't. But Andy had overheard two of her friends talking in the locker room. Cara told Ingrid she'd heard Rene tell Lisa, who'd heard it from Maria, who'd overheard Lena tell Bianca that Andy's dad was trying to drive her dad, his business competitor, out of town, and Lena was just being loyal to her father. Andy would have set them straight, but at least everyone finally stopped talking about it.

People just grew apart.

Andy sat in her childhood room, reading the words of the kid who'd poured every bit of her heart and soul into them, knowing they hadn't grown apart. They still had an unbreakable connection twenty years later. Even ten-year-old Andy had known Lena's motives had been out of her hands, which was somehow harder. If Lena had decided she didn't want to be friends, Andy would have been hurt but would have accepted it and probably moved on. But knowing in her heart that Lena hadn't done it willingly had inflamed Andy's sense of justice and triggered a protective love of her best friend. She still hated it, which leaked onto Lena, but she'd mostly stopped reacting to Lena's jabs and had stopped making her own. They continued to be enemies, and Andy could never move on, but it kept them from doing any real damage to one another.

Knowing all of that made Lena's current distance harder to take now.

❖

Early as always, Lena waited for Claire to arrive at Rose's Diner on the corner of Mission Avenue and the North Coast Highway. She watched traffic inch by and tourists flipping through sidewalk racks of sweatshirts and T-shirts as others sorted through knock-off Mexican blankets that would shrink to half their size in the first wash. Although tourists had always been a part of her hometown, she didn't remember this many of them crawling around. Grateful Rose's somehow maintained a predominantly locals clientele, she sank into the familiarity of her past, something she'd never thought possible, and wondered what Andy was doing.

It was a new and unexpected freedom to think about her without immediately having to fight away regret and guilt for the sins she'd committed in their childhood. She felt lighter, even though she'd been avoiding her the last few days for other reasons she'd been trying to work through.

It appeared the diner remained a favorite meeting place, like it had been since their grandparents had been kids. She remembered sitting in this same spot, watching Andy with her friends at the other end of the rows of booths. She'd been with her own friends, but she'd always wished they were more like Andy's who had real connections, instead of worrying about status and spouting veiled criticisms at one another. She'd once seen her here with her parents. Their closeness and obvious love had made her sick with longing. There'd been a time when Lena had wished with every cell in her body that Andy's parents were hers.

Andy had ignored her when they passed, but her parents had stopped to greet her, like they missed her and legitimately enjoyed seeing her again. They'd been interested in what she'd been up to and what college she had picked. She still remembered every word they'd exchanged. When they'd left, it felt like a knife in her heart. Just like it had when Andy had mentioned they missed her and still asked about her.

The scent of coffee and pancakes mingled with those of fries and burgers. She could live without the nausea-inducing scent of frying bacon though. Still, a wave of nostalgia hit when it reminded her of having chocolate milkshakes with her grandmother here. Her mother's mother had been kinder to her than her own mother, but no one would have accused her of being warm. Mixed emotions joined her memories when she thought how her grandmother wouldn't remember Rose's now. This conjured up the painful trip she'd finally had the courage to make to the memory care home two days ago. Her grandmother, once solid and vibrant, now tiny and frail, sat a table's breadth away, and Lena hadn't been prepared for the sweet old woman smiling and interacting with people, including her, although there was no recognition at all when their eyes met. Lena could only bear to stay half an hour, but she was glad she went.

Her thoughts were all over the place.

"I can't believe you're here," Claire said, pulling her up for a hug, something they'd never done in the past. Now, Lena wished they had, despite the unfamiliarity of it. Surprisingly, she found she'd like the chance to get used to it. "What's it been? Ten years?"

Lena hated small talk. But she'd endure it until they reacquainted themselves. Claire was one of the few acquaintances from high school Lena would call a friend, although she'd faked disaffectedness, secretly intimidated by Claire's innate confidence and ability to look fantastic even in sweats and a rumpled T-shirt. She looked like a mom now. Apparently, because she was. She laughed when she said she looked forward to a reason to change out of her usual uniform of an oversized T-shirt and yoga pants. She currently wore a pair of linen shorts and a sleeveless button-up shirt. She was still pretty with the same kind, unpretentious spirit she'd had in school.

Claire caught pregnant soon after graduation, just after she'd married Josh, her high school boyfriend. He'd worked a few odd jobs for a while after graduation, until joining the police academy, landing a career in law enforcement. Three kids and a mortgage later, they had all the happiness in the world now, according to Claire. Lena believed it, and regretted not going to their wedding, thinking it wouldn't last. Glad, she'd been wrong, Lena happily accepted when Claire suggested lunch after running into each other at the grocery store. What was it about grocery stores and old friends in this town?

"Twelve years," Lena said with a sigh.

"God. That long? We're getting old."

Lena didn't think thirty was anywhere near old. Maybe having kids made people feel old. Claire had been positively giddy when she told her that her mom had taken the kids so they could have lunch in peace.

"Time sure flies," Lena said against her disdain for small talk.

"Have you seen anyone else since you've been back?" Claire distractedly studied the menu.

"I ran into Andy Phillips." Lena looked at her own menu without seeing it, waiting for Claire's response.

As expected, Claire gaped, dropping her menu. "Get out! How'd that go?" Drama had a long shelf life.

"Fine. We had coffee." She didn't add it was twice. Claire already looked like she was queuing up questions.

"Coffee? Together?" Claire sounded as shocked as Lena predicted. "You look fine, but did she come out alive?"

Lena laughed, while the old guilt and confusion snapped back, dispersing the change in perspective she'd had just moments ago. She didn't want to return to thoughts about how she'd treated Andy. She wanted to focus on how things started to turn the second she'd watched Andy exit her dad's shop, and how the thump she'd felt signaled that her heart had started beating again. Sappy nonsense that it was. "We were civil. Guess we've grown up."

Claire cut a swath in the air up and down in front of Lena's head and torso. "You certainly have. You haven't aged a day and look how glamorous you are. And a celebrity. I can't imagine Andy could compete with that."

"Have you seen her lately?" Lena asked, attempting to sound casual.

"Not since about the same time I last saw you."

"She's famous in her own right. At least in science circles." Lena didn't mention the rabbit hole she'd dived into after she'd found the first article Andy had written. She also didn't mention how gorgeous Andy was in the photos she'd found online, which hadn't captured a fraction of it in real life. Based on Claire's disbelieving response to coffee, she didn't want to discuss it with her, especially when she was just trying to figure it out.

"You know, everyone wondered why you and Andy stopped being friends." Claire studied her and Lena pulled on her mask of disaffection, reverting back to when they were kids. Fuck. If she couldn't be herself around Claire, she had no hope with others. Andy came to mind with a flare of hope, and she instantly dismissed it. There was no way she could inflict her shit on Andy. Not after everything. It wouldn't be fair.

"Everyone?" She already knew, but she scoffed like she hadn't cared. But she had. So fucking much.

Claire nodded. "You two kept the hate alive so long we figured it had to have been something terrible. If you hadn't been infants when it started, the obvious suspicion would have been a romantic falling out. But I never believed that lame-ass story about your dads being business rivals, either."

"It wasn't. It was just kid stuff. After a while I didn't even remember what it was." She shrugged.

"Well, what did you talk about over coffee?"

"The normal surface stuff." Lena waved a dismissive hand she hoped Claire believed.

"You know, you mostly ignored each other, but sometimes Andy watched you. Not in a skeevy, or even an angry way. More like interested. I wasn't the only one who noticed. Do you think, maybe she had a crush on you? The allure of the forbidden, and all that?" Unexpectedly, Claire looked abashed, resting her hand on Lena's. "I hope this isn't reviving old pain. I figured if you had coffee, it's water under the bridge. It's not gossip if it's over a decade later, right?"

This was the first she'd heard about the noticing rumor. She stared at her menu, the words a blur in her inwardly focused gaze. Where was that server? Fuck that. She needed to set the record straight. The opposite of straight, actually. She lowered her menu.

"It was the other way around, the crush. But she never knew. So, that had nothing to do with it." And it hadn't. Not in fifth grade, anyway. Not until she'd started fantasizing about attack-kissing Andy in seventh grade, years before she finally did. Twice. After Lena had come to terms with her sexuality sometime in seventh grade. She'd grappled with it for years, all alone, with no one to talk to. God. Those kisses. Something neither of them had brought up. Back to the scene of the crime, Andy had said. It was as close as they'd come. But Andy didn't know she'd been in love with her back then.

She didn't have a chance to see Claire's response, because a woman dressed in Rose's traditional pink uniform and white apron appeared at their table.

"Hi ya, sweeties. Know what you want? Or do you need more time with the menu?" She wore a lot of makeup, which Lena wasn't really into, but she was pretty. Her nametag said, "Rose, too." Cute.

Before Lena could answer, Claire handed her menu back, looking a little shell-shocked. "I'll have the house margarita, please, no salt, and your number five, no cheese, no bun, no mayo, fruit instead of fries. Your nails are adorable." Her voice sounded stunned, but true to the Claire Lena remembered, she managed to emit cheer.

Rose, too's already bright smile radiated. "Thanks, hon. I do them myself."

"Well done." Claire beamed back.

Lena couldn't look at her, but she felt Claire staring. She hadn't read the menu, so she settled on her go-to. "I'll stick with coffee and try the veggie omelet, if you have one. And sourdough toast, please. And what the heck? Let's try the berry waffle with extra whipped cream," she added when she noticed the pin on Rose, too's apron, urging her to give the waffle a try. "Only if you recommend it, though."

Rose, too gave her a wink. "My top recommends are the strawberry shake or the berry waffle. You won't regret it, darlin.'" With a sassy turn and a twitch of her hip, she headed toward the kitchen.

Ugh. Strawberry shakes. Lena swallowed back a visceral reaction from her childhood. She met Claire's stare when she turned back. Here it comes. She leaned back, gearing up.

"How do you stay so fit, eating like that?"

Not what she expected. "Good genes, I guess." She waited for the follow-up.

"You were in love with her, huh?"

Lena nodded, noting the way Claire had intuited her real feelings. She studied the silverware wrapped in a napkin. She'd never been ashamed of being gay, but being in love with Andy had been a secret she'd thought she'd take to her grave. It was a relief to have told someone. The back of her eyes stung.

Claire dropped her chin onto her propped-up fist. "Does she know?"

Lena shook her head. "God, no."

"It makes so much sense," Claire said with a tone of dawning amazement. "There was so much tension. Sometimes it felt like we were in a Disney direct to streaming movie. It's a wonder some of us didn't break into spontaneous song. Some people hate those movies. I adore them." Claire looked all dreamy, and Lena couldn't help but laugh. But her mind had traveled back in time to when she'd kissed Andy, and a shiver ran down her spine. If Claire noticed, she didn't say.

As she and Claire enjoyed their lunch and caught up, Lena's thoughts about the rift between her and Andy ran in the background. She knew the tension between them had been obvious to others back then. Maintaining the façade had been a constant sleight of hand and exhausting. Unfortunately, it also required keeping everyone at a distance to protect her secret. Taunting Andy had helped distract from the guilt and feelings. Until she'd kissed her, dismantling all the protection she'd built. Thank God, it had been right before they left for college.

Chapter Fourteen

"Selena, I need you to take my books down to the library. The front desk will have a new stack."

Reluctantly pausing her task, Lena turned to find her mother standing in the doorway of her bedroom. She swore she'd shut the door before sitting down.

"I can run them by right after this is submitted." She turned back to her laptop, helping Lourdes climb into her lap. The sweet girl seemed to know when Lena needed a little affection, and since her mother was gone so often, Lourdes probably needed some of her own. They'd become attached and Lena dreaded having to leave her, whenever that might be. Hopefully, soon.

"If Preston goes on break before you get there, the person filling in for him might not let you use my library card." Her mother sounded put out. She always did when Lena didn't jump at her requests.

"I'll wait for him to get back if he's not there. I need to get this finished." She returned to the urgent email her agent had sent.

"You have all—"

"Mother. Give me a few minutes." She was going to catch hell for her tone, but she had to finish.

"Selena Hol—" Her mother's voice was as hard as granite.

Lena turned with what she hoped was a non-confrontational expression while she seethed internally. "I have about ten minutes to respond to my agent before he meets with the hiring manager for a position I really want. I need to focus. I'll go in a few minutes if you leave your card on the kitchen counter."

When her mother didn't say anything for a moment, Lena was dumbfounded. Had she really defused a tirade? She was hesitant to hope that maybe, just maybe, they'd finally achieved some sort of accord. The idea was so momentous, she felt it physically. It was hard to concentrate on what she was doing.

"You shouldn't put things off until the last minute." Her mother perched on the edge of her bed. "I'll just wait here."

Still not as caustic as usual, it was irritating how her mother disregarded her needs, privacy, boundaries, and just about everything else. Anxious about the deadline, she didn't engage. Instead, she took a deep breath and tried to remember what she'd been doing.

Just three minutes past her agent's request, she hit send and closed her laptop, saying a little prayer to whatever entity was listening. The Denver job was perfect. She had to get out of here. The market was seventeenth largest, and the job offered an equal mix of on-air presence and research. In addition, Denver had a dynamic weather pattern, making it a welcome challenge. Andy's mom lived there, too. She didn't want to think about why that made a difference, but it did.

She risked a minute to settle her blood pressure before facing her mother, who peered performatively at her thin gold watch before standing up. The cold flat stare her mother leveled at her scared her. She hadn't been scared of her in years. When she was within a foot of the chair and looming over her, she pointed a manicured finger at her, and Lena felt smaller than she'd felt in at least two decades. Lourdes shivered in her lap. Lena, frozen in place, couldn't move to soothe her. Her mother had never struck her. Would that change today?

"Interesting that the deadline was set at five minutes past the hour. You have always been a liar." Her mother's reasonable volume was chilling. Had the delay Lena had so naively thought might be some sort of turning point, given her mother time to get into a more lethal battle posture? Or had her mother developed an advanced level of malice? "No one will hire you with that kind of disrespect for other people's time, Selena. You've always been a worthless weight around my neck. I keep asking myself why I allow it." Her mother went on, but Lena didn't hear it.

When her mother slapped her card on the desk, exiting the room, Lena barely noticed. As soon as her mother's finger was in her face, a cold blanket of disassociation had fallen over her. She sat there for a long time before she could move. Lourdes standing in her lap licking her face was probably what roused her. Slowly, her body thawed, allowing her to slump into her seat. She drew the first deep breath she'd taken since her mother stood up.

Just one interview, she prayed as she sat there. One fucking interview from one of the dozens of positions her agent had vetted.

The more time she spent here, the closer she came to committing heinous crimes, which wasn't hyperbole. Her old job was still cycling through weather anchors, according to Rory, who'd turned down the evening slot out of principle, which made her want to cry. What was with all the crying lately? Phoenix was also dropping viewers and subscribers like a cold front coming over the Phoenix Mountains. She wasn't proud of enjoying the comments and DMs from the viewers who missed her, but she needed all the good feels she could get right now. It would kill her soul to take a step backward, but Fuckwad Lance was a cakewalk compared to Helena Holmes.

The direct route to the library took her through neighborhoods she'd roamed like an alley cat in her childhood. She'd expected nostalgia, but time changed most things, and many of the original bungalows had been replaced by homes of drastically different styles, or four times the size. Some streets looked vaguely familiar, others she didn't recognize at all. All of them made her miss Andy, though. She felt it so much stronger being in Andy's old neighborhood.

About a block away from the library, she arrived at a particular intersection she knew well. Andy's house was on the next block.

The desire to stop was almost undeniable. The only thing that stopped her was how rude it would be to come unannounced, especially with Andy's dad recovering from whatever injury had required a cast. She didn't have Andy's phone number, though. She barely slowed down as she passed it. The ramp was new, but the rest looked exactly the same. Her heart physically hurt as she continued on. At the next stop sign, she made right turns until she turned back onto Andy's block. This time she slowed but still didn't stop. Would Andy know she'd avoided her since she'd left so suddenly? At the intersection, she turned again, circling around one more time. She drove so slowly, the car stopped of its own accord, and she idled in the street, staring at the house she knew as well as her own. She felt an almost physical pull. If she hadn't recognized the intersection, she might have driven right past.

Oh, shut up. When had she started lying to herself again? The pull she felt was familiar. She'd never been able to deny it.

She parked the car at the curb.

Memories washed over her, as had a million others in the last few days. God. The love in this house. Swimming and eating honey and peanut butter sandwiches on the picnic table under the orange tree. Short walks to the rec center for swim practice. Lying on their stomachs in Andy's bedroom, drawing pictures of horses and giraffes. On the front porch in their swimsuits, red mustaches from fruit punch staining their upper lips, each of them taking turns kicking their feet against the porch post they'd worn the paint off to keep the swing moving.

Lena was caught in long-ago moments when someone sitting on the same porch swing stood up. Her stomach flipped.

Andy hopped from the porch into the sunlight. Halfway across the grass, she stopped. Lena felt the hesitation before Andy waved.

Embarrassed for being caught creeping, but ashamed even more for staying away, Lena exhaled a shaky breath, nearly getting out of the car before turning it off. Standing on legs tired from running away, she'd say she was conflicted about seeing Andy again, but she wasn't. She was conflicted about what it might mean.

❖

Andy knew the red Mercedes with tinted windows and the GLAAD sticker on the rear bumper making a third trip down her street. She had recently ridden in it. But even if she hadn't, she'd have known. The owner hadn't been to her house in over twenty years, but the almost vibrating expectancy she was almost always aware of, had increased throughout the morning, propelling her outside minutes before the car made the first pass down her street. She watched it drive past more slowly a minute later, and on the third pass, it moved so slowly, Andy got dizzy from holding her breath. When it stopped, she hardly remembered how she ended up on the lawn.

Lena looked uncertain when she stepped onto the sidewalk. Andy's skin tingled taking in the glints of sunlight in her long auburn hair blowing in the ocean breeze. When Lena pushed her sunglasses onto the top of her head, Andy took what felt like her first full breath in days.

"Hey." With a shy smile brightening her almost timid expression, Lena slid her hands into the back pockets of her shorts. The move pulled the front of her button-up sleeveless shirt tight across her chest. Andy pretended not to notice that, or the deep neckline.

"Hey back," Andy said. Neither of them moved.

"I was in the neighborhood. I thought I'd swing by."

"Three times?"

Lena walked closer, stopping about five feet away. She scanned the front of the house. Andy had the feeling she was avoiding looking at her. It made sense. This wasn't neutral ground like the coffee shop. They were standing in a yard they'd spent many an afternoon playing in together. A lot had happened since then.

Lena stepped closer. Close enough for Andy to smell the familiar floral scent of her, reminding Andy of a walk in the neighborhood, just before dark in early summer.

Lena scrunched up her nose, something Andy found adorable. "Creepy, huh?"

"Beat-up white vans with drivers offering candy or puppies are creepy."

"I prefer subtler ways to stalk my victims. Three passes to lure them onto the grass, then I snatch them up." Lena lifted her shoulders, hands still in her back pockets. Had Andy ever admired bare shoulders the way she was now?

"What do you do with them when you have them?"

Lena's cheeks reddened. Andy could count on one hand how many times she'd seen her blush. "I don't know. You're the first person I've lured."

"I guess we'll both find out, then."

"It's hot today," Lena said, pulling at the low neck of her blouse.

Andy laughed at the obvious change of subject. She wasn't sure if the heat sweeping through her was more from embarrassment or from standing in direct sunlight. "Wanna get out of the sun?"

"I'm on my way to the library for my mother."

"You're a few blocks off route."

Lena ignored Andy's observation.

"It took three passes for me to get the courage to stop." She nodded at the ramp. "That's new."

Lena pushed a strand of hair behind her ear. The gesture was reminiscent of young Lena. The quaking in Andy's stomach from earlier became bolder. All this action in her stomach was new but not a mystery. Lena, by far, was the most attractive person she'd ever known. But really. It was simply Lena. And Lena didn't hate her anymore. Leaving Andy defenseless and terrified. But mostly excited.

"It's temporary, but my dad won't be walking for a while."

Lena looked sheepish. "I didn't realize it was so bad."

Watching Lena squint, Andy moved toward the house. Lena followed. "He'll bounce back. I'm sure your dad's told you some of it."

Andy told her the details. Lena's brows drew together as Andy spoke.

"Sounds awful for both of you."

"We're getting into a routine. He has aides for an hour in the morning and early evening. They bathe him, check wounds, and deal with most of the other stuff."

"Can I drop food off or something? What would be most helpful? Cooking? Cleaning? Run errands? Keeping one or both of you company?"

A lump formed in Andy's throat. "A cleaning service already does most of the cleaning and laundry and I take care of errands. I love my dad, but we need a little time apart each day. He hates to be fussed over, and I get a bit of cabin fever."

"You were always on the move. Getting into trouble, looking for new things to try. I could barely keep up with you."

Andy gave her a mock glare. "You were complicit."

"If you say so." Lena rolled her eyes and again, she looked like the younger version of herself. But then she didn't, and her beautiful grownup eyes grew distant. But a small smile indicated the memories were pleasant. "We certainly had adventures." She rested a hand on Andy's arm for a second. Patted it, and took it away, like she did it all the time. The touch caused sensations that didn't remain in her arm, but it was the casual touch that didn't cause Lena to jump away that made the oxygen in her lungs seem thin. "So, it's food or company." Lena grinned at her.

They'd walked up the winding ramp and were standing in the shade. Andy laughed. "Our freezer's packed. Our neighbors have a schedule they don't take lightly. Three squares a day, no deviations. Some must think we have a family of ten living here."

"That's heartwarming." Lena put a hand on her chest, but then she smirked. "You're taking the long route to telling me you want company. How shall I split my shift?"

Andy was about to deliver a snappy comeback but stopped. They'd had some flirty exchanges both times they'd had coffee, but Lena had started it each time. She wasn't sure Lena would respond well if Andy started it.

"Your dad and the aides are the only people he's comfortable with. So, you're off the hook there, too."

"Guess it's just you and me, then"

She couldn't read Lena's feelings about it. She assumed she was good, or she would have taken one of the outs Andy had given her. Also, Lena had just emerged from hiding after four days. She wasn't sure she could trust her about disappearing again. She needed to be careful about getting too used to her company.

"I like spending time with you, but you don't have to entertain me. I'm sure you have things to do while you're here." The admission about liking Lena's company had slipped out unintentionally, but she meant it.

Lena opened her mouth as if to say something but closed it like she'd changed her mind. After a moment of seeming to study Andy's face, she looked away and then back. "I do, too," she said quietly.

"You sound suspicious," Andy said.

"Suspicious? Of what?"

"I don't know. Suspicious usually means someone feels things might not be what they seem."

Lena looked uncertain. Following a pause, she squared off with Andy, as if trying to be brave or convey something important. "I worry that you'll disappear on me."

Andy almost said it was more likely to be her, but if that's what Lena felt, it would be mean to be dismissive, especially with their past. Then she thought she understood. Lena was probably projecting. "Like a sort of payback? For back then? Or the last few days?"

"Both, I guess. I wasn't thinking payback, but I guess that might be a reason you'd do it."

"I'm the least scary person you might ever meet." Andy meant it, but she wondered if Lena was talking about herself. "Do you want to go inside where it's cooler? I made lemonade."

Chapter Fifteen

Andy led them directly into the kitchen, while her dad snored loudly in the other room. Despite being late morning, the inside of the house was dim, and the TV was off for a change. She winced at the potpourri of mancave and hospital room, wishing she had a candle or something. Lena didn't seem to mind as she crouched to pet Billie, who'd toddled from the living room into the kitchen to sit on her foot.

"She's claimed you. By virtue of your obviously comfortable foot, you're hers now."

Lena looked up, eyes sparkling. "I'm a willing captive."

The comment shot a spark into Andy's lower body. "So, we could stay in the kitchen and whisper, go out back where the flies are swarming, or to my room where it's cool, fly-free, and we can make all the noise we want." She heard how it sounded as soon as it left her lips. "I mean not whisper. Just talk."

"It's fine." Lena's face was too still. She was uncomfortable. Andy had had years to learn.

"Let's get that lemonade."

"Got any popcorn?" Lena asked.

Andy grimaced. "I'll stock up." She was touched Lena remembered her mom used to give them popcorn and lemonade for snacks.

Minutes later, she closed the bedroom door. With her back to the room, she squeezed her eyes shut, bracing for the memories entombed within these walls. When she turned, Lena was examining a poster.

"Where's Billie?" Lena asked.

"Likely in the recliner next to my dad's bed. She's appointed herself his guardian." She wished Billie was there as a distraction.

Pointing to a poster of a periodic table, Lena laughed. "You're such a nerd, Andy Phillips. I don't know why I thought your room would look the same. The poster of indigenous plants of coastal Southern California and the desk are the only things I recognize. You were going to be a horticulturist."

"Seahorses are more interesting." She kicked off her flip-flops and perched on the end of the bed.

Lena looked over her shoulder, scrunching up her nose. Andy thought it was adorable. "Ugh. The dried seahorse display."

"That my grandpa gave me. Remember the funeral you insisted on?"

Lena nodded. "We performed it in the flower bed by the porch." She gave Andy a half smile. "Afterward, your mom made us chocolate chip cookies. I loved how your house always smelled like fresh-baked cookies."

"Chocolate chip was just for you. Always with walnuts."

Lena gave her a dubious eyebrow raise. "She made them all the time. Not just for me."

Andy shook her head. "Only when you came over. You told her they were your favorite."

Lena rolled her lips inward. "Mine never baked." She turned to study the poster again. "This is definitely the room of a young scientist."

Andy caught a glimpse of Lena's expression as she turned back to the poster after abruptly changing the subject. A memory surfaced of Lena thanking her mom for cookies as if she'd given her a puppy. The tone Lena had used when she said her mom didn't bake was the complete opposite.

Andy never liked Lena's mom. She hated her now for the look of dejection on Lena's face.

"Do you still have space stuff in yours? And posters of bands. You were so into music. I'll bet you have posters of clouds and tornadoes now." Andy pulled her legs into a crisscross. Who would have thought they'd be in the same room, let alone this one?

Lena looked sad. "A few in my home office. My mother turned my old room into a craft room two weeks after I left for college."

"Your mother crafts?" It seemed incongruous from what Andy knew of her.

"Nope." Lena was still again. And strike two for Lena's mom.

They navigated a maze of paths cut through tall-sided pathways lined by sensitive or off-limits topics. They both seemed to tread lightly. Andy reached back to retrieve her glass from the bedside table where she'd placed it. To do so, she stretched across her bed. She caught Lena staring and biting her lip when she sat up. It wasn't an unfamiliar look. Andy had seen it twice before, and it sent heat pulsing through her.

"You're nervous," Lena said quietly.

Andy was, but she thought she'd hid it well. "Why do you say that?"

"The ice in your glass sounds like a windchime in a derecho." She laughed, almost self-consciously.

"Do you feel like you're in danger?" Andy had meant it as a joke, but Lena looked serious.

"Am I?"

What kind of danger was Lena afraid of? She could only guess. "Never with me," she said, holding her gaze. "Wind seems to scare you. It's the second time you've mentioned a derecho."

She shrugged. "I'm safe if I avoid it."

Were they still talking about the weather?

"Behind something solid?" Andy asked.

Lena paused. "I've never had anything like that."

So, not the weather. This Lena wasn't the stoic kid or Teflon teen she'd known. Nor was she the confident on-air personality Andy had watched hours of videos of in the last few days. This was the vulnerable girl she'd seen in the locker room the last time they'd kissed. She seemed to be searching for something. Maybe their old connection? Andy wished she had the courage to tell her the link had never broken. At least for her. She was reaching back to her right now.

"Never?" she asked.

"Not in a very long time." Lena's eyes never left hers. "I miss it."

A shiver vibrated through Andy.

"I miss it, too." Andy swallowed hard, hoping she wasn't revealing too much. "This is weird, right?"

Lena released a breathy laugh as she lowered herself into the desk chair. "Hanging out with you? Or being in your room?"

"Both."

Lena huffed. "Understatement of the year."

She pushed her fingers through her long dark hair. Andy watched, mesmerized by everything Lena did. Being like this with her, gradually opening up to each other, was the terrifying elation of flinging herself from the high dive, but realizing she forgot the dive she was supposed to do. For the first time in twenty years, it felt like they could find their way to being friends again.

Lena's gaze dropped to the floor. She'd gone completely still, which had always been her reaction to highly emotional situations. Her mouth became a thin line. Andy's chest tightened, seeing the quiver of her chin just before tears escaped her eyes. Lena's pain seeped into Andy. Before the coffee shop, Andy had never seen Lena cry. This was the second time now. Lena began to unravel right in front of her, and she didn't know what Lena needed anymore.

Lena closed her eyes, placing visibly shaking fingers on her forehead. One finger repeatedly smoothed her eyebrow, seemingly holding on to her last thread. When a quiet sob issued from behind her tightly closed lips, Andy finally moved. She slipped to the edge of the bed, leaning forward.

"Hey," she said softly. Lena dropped her face into her hands, unable or unwilling to respond. Andy sensed her collapsing inward. Her barely perceptible sobs tore at her. Everything in her wanted to pull Lena into her arms. But the Lena Andy had known had never accepted comfort, even when she'd accidentally hurt herself when they'd been playing. She'd just dusted herself off and kept going. One time she'd ridden her bike into a parked truck, gashing her forehead. She'd picked up her bike, ready to ride away, but there'd been so much blood. Andy had to pull her home by the straps of her overall shorts, where Lena's mother just told her to put a Band-Aid on it.

"See? No big deal." Lena had said on the way to the bathroom to get the Band-Aids, as if she'd expected as much. It was only when it wouldn't stop bleeding that Lena's mother took her to urgent care. But she told Lena she had to clean up the mess in the bathroom first. Andy sat Lena on the edge of the bathtub with a towel to her head while Andy cleaned it up.

Lena came back from urgent care with thirteen stitches, and she hadn't cried once.

Seeing Lena cry now was heart-wrenching. Her silent sobs and ragged breaths hurt so much to watch. Fuck it. She went to her, carefully gathering Lena's hair away from her face to rub between her shoulder blades, making little noises she remembered her mom making when she was a kid. Lena stiffened at first, but gave into it, not quite fully relaxing, but seeming to find comfort.

Aside from handing Billie to her, Andy hadn't been this close to Lena since fifth grade, the kisses excluded. It was like dancing in an electric storm. There was nothing sexual about it, but the energy they exchanged was profound. Andy stroked Lena's back, trying to absorb her pain.

❖

Being this close to Andy was safety. It was letting go and knowing she wouldn't just float away. Nearly a lifetime of emotions played through her. Many she hadn't stored away as securely as she'd thought. Both good and bad, and even the good ones hurt when she remembered she'd lost them. And God, did she hurt.

"Hey, you," Andy whispered.

She knelt before her, tucked a wad of tissues into her hand, and closed Lena's fingers around them. She didn't take her hand away after, though, which made Lena want to cry even more. So, she used her hair as a curtain to hide her face while she wiped away tears and snot. She probably looked like shit. Blotchy with puffy red eyes. At least she hadn't bothered with makeup this morning.

"Well, this is embarrassing," she said, followed by a shaky sigh.

Tenting her hand over her eyes, she leaned forward, resting her elbow on her knee, unable to find more words. She absolutely hated Andy seeing her like this. Her mother's words rang in her ears. "Stop it right this minute, Selena. It makes you look ugly and weak. No one wants to see or hear it." Lena had seen Andy cry, and while it had ripped her open every time, knowing she was usually the cause of it, she'd never thought Andy was weak, and she'd never been ugly.

"I'll get water," Andy said.

Lena finally looked up. Andy's gaze pierced her, seeming to read her soul. How did Andy do that? Lena, unguarded and vulnerable, knew Andy could hurt her so easily right now. But then again, Andy could have destroyed her at any time. She'd never had protection from her.

Lena reached out, grabbing Andy's wrist with shaking fingers. It was so warm, and Lena felt Andy's pulse racing under her fingertips. Her warm brown eyes were dark, continuing to look right into her, and Lena would have given anything to know what she saw. How could she breathe when Andy looked at her like this?

She stood. "I'm sorry."

Andy's brow creased. "Crying is nothing to be sorry for."

"No. I'm sorry," she repeated, her eyes still searching Andy's. "So fucking sorry." Her voice broke.

Andy opened her mouth, but Lena stopped her.

"You never deserved what I did. Sorry isn't enough, but I'll say it a million times. I'm sorry. I'm sorry. I'm sorry." Lena's voice fell to a hoarse whisper. With every declaration, she squeezed Andy's wrist tighter. Andy's eyes glittered with tears as she brushed back the hair on the side of Lena's face with her other hand, finally resting it against Lena's cheek. She'd never felt anything so gentle. She pressed into it. Andy's touch seemed to close a circuit, allowing the chaotic energy that flowed between them to even out.

"I've never needed an apology," Andy said quietly.

In that moment, the sensation of something clicking into place quieted the almost constant sense of dread Lena had lived with for having hurt the one person in her life who mattered to her. She took a breath, exhaling shakily, releasing the regret of missed opportunities and what-might-have-beens. Knowing she'd still have to work through years of guilt and pain, those five words had just given her hope that she and Andy might find a place in each other's lives again. God, she'd missed her. It felt like she'd been given a second chance, and she would do anything to be a person who deserved it.

Lena closed the space between them, the warmth radiating from Andy telling her this wasn't a dream. They were really here. Like when she'd kissed Andy all those years ago, and she'd had to convince herself they'd really kissed, because there was no way Andy would have let her. But they had. And here she was again. And Lena wanted to kiss her again so badly, she thrummed with it. Something had shifted. Their once fractured connection was strong enough to hold her, and she was going to kiss Andy now. Everything that had happened since she'd decided to quit her job had led her to this moment.

A warm breath caressed Lena's lips before she pressed hers against Andy's, and Andy's quiet sigh slipped into her mouth. Inexplicably gentle, the reunion of their lips sent a tide of sparks traveling just underneath her skin. Less than a second in, the kiss had already dismantled her.

In a haze, Lena reacquainted herself with the taste and feel of Andy's lips. How they moved against hers. How warm and pliant they were. How they were Andy's lips and they could be anything and Lena would love them, but they were perfect and she sank into Andy, losing herself. Lena couldn't fight this any longer. Especially when Andy slid her hand to the back of her neck, gently pulling her closer. Lena dissolved into stardust.

With the swell of Andy's breasts and the plains of her stomach against her, the warmth that passed between them short-circuited her brain. Lena encircled Andy's waist with both arms. The action seemed to ignite something in them. Andy's approving moan and soft surrender when Lena pressed her hands flat against her lower back and Andy arched into her sent a tremor rolling down Lena's spine. Digging her fingers into Andy, she was barely able to breathe imagining her fingers on Andy's bare skin. Knowing what more was, Lena had been dreaming about doing it with Andy her entire adult life. Whether they ended up there, or not, simply kissing Andy again was enough to burn her down to embers.

Their previous kisses had been a crackling fire. Not quite innocent, but nothing like this, where their bodies molded together, their hands roamed, and the confidence in the kiss fed an inferno she was more than ready to be consumed by. Desire surged through her, turning their languid exploration into an urgent need that every one of her senses was involved in.

Before Lena knew what was happening, Andy slowed the kiss before breaking it. Lena wasn't even close to finished, and her entire body cried to go back in. It took a moment for Lena to find her voice.

"You're good at that." Her voice came out breathy with tingles still dancing on her lips. "I don't wanna stop."

"I could say the same for you." Andy smiled at her and Lena would do anything to keep that smile on Andy's face. "I don't, either. That's why I'm checking in."

"I think we do it well together. A-plus for form and execution."

"We're three for three," Andy said.

It was the first time she'd mentioned the kisses from twelve years ago. Had she been thinking about them all these years, too? A shiver ran through Lena at the thought. She seemed to shiver a lot lately.

Andy leaned back, but not far. She ran a hand up and down Lena's arm, causing goose bumps to rise in its wake.

"Do you need to take a breather? You were upset and we jumped right in there."

Andy's expression was so earnest, it made Lena's heart ache.

"You're the kindest person I've ever known, Andy Phillips."

"I just want to make sure you're okay before anything goes too far."

That sounded like Andy wanted more. Nerves and excitement fueled a desperate need, but she couldn't bring herself to say it aloud. This was Andy and no words would ever be enough to say yes in a way that expressed how she'd give Andy everything she had to give, plus all the things she didn't have but would give if she had them. Her body decided for her. She slid her hands up Andy's sides, over her breasts, and fisted the front of Andy's T-shirt, pulling her close. Their hips and breasts crashed together, and she stared into Andy's eyes, showing her the intensity of her need before crushing their mouths together. She bit Andy's lower lip, sucked it in, and ran her tongue over it. Releasing it, she searched for Andy's tongue, teasing it as she thought about teasing Andy until she shattered. How she knew the electric pulse accompanying Andy's release would flow into her, letting her experience Andy's pleasure at the same time. Years of craving was conveyed in her kiss. It wasn't about sex. It was about trust. It was about repairing old hurts. It was about becoming whole again.

They still had a lot to talk about, and she didn't know if she'd survive if this turned out badly, but Lena knew one thing. Her heart had only started to beat again when she'd seen Andy walk out of her dad's store, and that alone was worth any risk.

Reducing the intensity of the kiss, she let her hands roam across Andy's back, teasing along the hem of her cropped T-shirt, before finally inching her hands beneath it, satisfying her craving to experience the warmth and softness of Andy's skin. It was exactly as she'd always thought it would be. Lena whimpered, and Andy's moan vibrated into Lena's mouth.

It was Andy who shivered this time, arching into Lena when she ran her hands up Andy's spine. Gaining confidence, and desperate to explore Andy more intimately, Lena dipped her fingertips under the waistband of Andy's shorts, slowly drawing her fingers along toward the front, and back again. If there was any residual doubt about what she wanted, Lena pushed her hands lower inside Andy's shorts, cupping Andy's ass through her underwear. Shifting her thigh between Andy's legs, pressing herself against her.

"Fuck." Andy moaned as she kissed Lena again with a heat and demand Lena couldn't get enough of.

Andy's lips caught her bottom lip, sucking it in, releasing it to do the same to her upper lip, while she ground against Lena's thigh. When Andy bit Lena's lower lip, a roar of sensation washed through Lena, and she pulled one hand out of Andy's shorts to tangle her fingers in Andy's long dark hair, fisting it, eliciting a low moan. Lena whimpered. When had she ever whimpered? Never, that's when.

Their tongues met again, and surging pleasure mounted low in Lena's body, like magma beneath tectonic plates, building pressure that could only be released by an earthquake. With Andy rocking against her thigh, a shivering wave of incandescence ran up Lena's spine. Not enough to make her come, it still spiked her need. And when Andy threw her head back, exposing the column of her neck, Lena trailed a path of open-mouthed kisses, along it, her teeth skimming the smooth skin. She paused at the muscle joining her neck to her shoulder and gently bit it. The tremor she felt move through Andy intoxicated her.

"Lena. Fuck." The words were a loud whisper, tickling the stereocilia in Lena's ears.

In the rare moments she'd allowed herself to fantasize about what it would have been like if they'd taken their last kiss further, Lena had always imagined a gentle exploration, where awe and tenderness would set the pace. She'd never expected the kind of urgency she felt now.

Lena was lost.

Pressure coiled deep inside her. Her demanding physical response spiraling beyond anything she'd imagined. She'd never risen as quickly before, never this high, never this intensely. It was overwhelming.

And they'd only kissed.

Chapter Sixteen

Andy couldn't tell up from down when Lena pulled her head back by her hair and kissed her neck. Andy almost screamed with the pleasure of it. No one had ever made her let go like this. Because no one had been Lena.

Lena's touch shot bolts of electricity to every nerve in Andy's body, increasing her arousal to levels unknown to her until now. She trembled with it. Why were they still standing when a bed was only feet away?

They were doing this.

If making out had her ready to explode, she couldn't imagine how sex with her would be. She wanted this. She needed to see and touch and taste every inch of her. She imagined having Lena below her, above her, beside her. She didn't care. She just had to have her. She'd wanted it for so long, Lena's hands on her, her fingers inside her.

It was surreal. They were in her room where they'd played Legos, and all she could think about was Lena inside her. The girl who'd devastated her twice. Now, in the same room where they'd played together as kids, she was kissing her again, clearly on the way to more. Heart pounding in her ears, body thrumming with anticipation, Andy knew she'd lost all control. And she didn't care. It felt wild and free. Because, before this she'd been living half a life, and one minute of this was worth more than all the minutes she'd spent without the woman who'd always owned her heart in her arms, driving her crazy with her hungry lips.

Hungry lips that had just been pulled away.

Lena's eyes were filled with concern. She cradled Andy's face.

"Hey. Where'd you go just now?" she asked.

"What?" Andy asked with a smile, leaning in again.

"You seem preoccupied." Lena smiled back, her warm hands still cradling Andy's face.

"I am. I'm preoccupied with how much I want you." Andy kissed Lena's palm, surprised by her own candid admission.

"Oh yeah?" A slow smile crept across Lena's mouth.

Andy felt drunk with it. "Yeah."

Lena searched Andy's eyes. Her smile was gone. "After everything we've been through? I guess it's my turn to check in. Are you okay to take this further? I mean, you should have written me off for good years ago, but you didn't."

Her words pinched Andy's heart. "I'm more than okay, Lena. It's more than sex. It's us. That's why I'd never write you off."

"I was awful to you."

"It went two ways. As much as I hated you sometimes, I'd catch a glimpse of my best friend." Andy wasn't sure she could effectively explain how she thought Lena was as much of a casualty in their war as she was.

Lena dropped her forehead on Andy's shoulder. "Being here feels like coming home. I want what we had before everything went to shit."

"You want milk and cookies? Play a little Legos?" Andy teased her, her lips pressed against the side of her head. Lena caught one of Andy's hands and pressed it against her lips. The sensation was both tender and erotic. Andy had never experienced either feeling, yet they both coursed through her now, along with others Andy was afraid to name. "I think we need to make some new memories in here. Don't you?"

Lena gave a short laugh, muffled against Andy's shoulder. "What do you have in mind?"

"For starters, I was about two minutes from coming against your very sexy leg. We could finish that. I've also been thinking about going down on you." Andy closed her eyes, imagining Lena lying on her bed, ready for her. She smiled and shrugged. "Or we can play Legos."

Lena lifted her head. "Maybe after we burn off some of this energy."

"Do you have anything in mind?"

Lena pulled Andy's face toward her, merging their lips in a searing kiss. When she broke it, she left her lips against Andy's. "I want to keep doing this."

The entirety of Andy's body grew incredibly warm, and she too, spoke against their lips, breathing each other's air. "What is it we're doing?"

"I know what I hope we're doing," Lena said with a teasing grin.

And then she kissed Andy slowly, deeply, and with purpose. Andy grew dizzy with desire, and when Lena pulled back, her eyes still closed, Andy's stomach dropped into a freefall taking in how beautiful she was.

"You still haven't told me what you hope we're doing." Andy's voice was a whisper.

"What do you want?" Lena asked.

"I'm scared, but I want to see where this could lead. I want this. I want you. I want us in every way. That's what I want. Now tell me what you want."

Lena wrapped her arms around Andy's waist, resting her head on Andy's shoulder. Andy pulled her closer, needing the nearness. When Lena looked up, her soft eyes glittered with tears.

"Where do I hope this is going? Right now, I hope we're on our way to getting naked," she said, shaking her hair back with a sexy smile. "I want to show you how I feel and know you in ways I haven't before. I want to touch you everywhere." Her eyes blazed into Andy's. "I hope I make you come."

"I promise that won't be a problem." Andy's fingers trembled as she slid them along the smooth curve of Lena's jaw. Lena's throat moved when she swallowed and Andy kissed her neck, humming as she tasted the warm skin, trailing her lips down to Lena's collarbone, dipping her tongue into the hollow at the base of her throat. When Lena whimpered, Andy found Lena's eyes, seeing desire in them. She slid her hand to the back of Lena's neck and pulled Lena's mouth to hers. Kissing her deeply, hoping to show Lena how much she affected her. "I can't wait to feel you against me," she said against Lena's lips, taking in their softness, knowing she could kiss Lena forever. But she wanted other things, too. "I've dreamed about touching you, and you touching me. I want to be inside you, Lena."

"I'm going to make you come first," Lena said. Her voice was low. Her breath tickled Andy's lips.

Andy tangled her fingers in Lena's hair, pulling her closer, kissing her deeply, moaning into her mouth. Her core pulsed at Lena's words and trembled as Lena's fingers traced under Andy's waistband again, stopping at the button, sending a bolt of anticipation through Andy. Lena broke the kiss and locked eyes with Andy as she unbuttoned Andy's shorts, eased the zipper down, and leaned in, keeping her lips millimeters away.

"It won't take long for you to make me come." Lena visibly shivered. "I'm almost there and you haven't even touched me yet." The last sent sparks shooting through Andy in every direction.

Andy had never been on the verge like this. The kisses in high school had been chaste compared to this. Lena slid her hand into Andy's shorts, causing Andy to hiss. When Lena pushed into her underwear, a rolling pulse caused Andy to moan. Her clit begged for attention when Lena stopped just before reaching Andy's desperate need. At the first touch, Andy sucked in a shaking breath.

"You're so wet for me, Andy." Lena sounded awed.

❖

Lena fused their mouths together in a blistering kiss. She gently stroked Andy, amazed at being allowed to know her this way. It was as if they'd done this before. Their bodies falling into a familiar rhythm, somehow knowing how to touch one another. Almost everything they did together was like this. Always in sync, even when it was new. Lena shouldn't be surprised how this was, too. She'd wondered how Andy kissed, how she touched, and wanted to be touched. And now she knew. She also knew how Andy moved and sounded, and what aroused her. And hopefully, soon, she'd know what made Andy come.

Andy moaned and broke the kiss. Her eye contact spoke volumes with Lena's fingers stroking her. Lena adjusted her hand for better access, and when Andy stepped back, she nearly cried. What happened? But Andy removed her shorts and underwear, and was back, giving all of herself to Lena, whose fingers slid through Andy's wet heat, every few strokes slipping over her hard clit, which made Andy twitch. Andy kissed her like her life depended on it, her hips rocking against her. Lena moaned as their lips and tongues synchronized with their motions, both becoming more insistent with Andy's quickening breath.

"Do you want to lie down?" Lena asked against Andy's lips. Circling Andy's clit with her thumb while she slowly entered her with two fingers. Andy hissed, her hips rocking slower as if savoring Lena's slow, deep push into her. Lena stilled her fingers when Andy's walls pulsed around them and an answering pulse coursed in her own center. Fuck. She felt so good. Andy wasn't shy about expressing what felt good and it was hotter than anything she'd experienced, making her breathless at the wonder of it. She'd fantasized so much about this, but her fantasies weren't even close to the reality.

Andy grasped Lena's shoulders, staring intently into her eyes. "I'm going to…" Andy closed her eyes, rolling her lips between her teeth. When she opened them again, she caught Lena's gaze and held it. "I'm going to come," Andy rasped. The last word was drawn out as the first tremors shook her. Lena couldn't look away, transfixed by the uninhibited way Andy gave in to her pleasure. She held her with one arm, loving the way Andy's body rocked against her. "God, Lena, you…oh…"

Her name whispered from Andy's lips caused goose bumps to rise all over Lena's body. Rolling waves of anticipatory pleasure issued from deep within her core. Andy came with a gasp, holding it in, as her body went rigid, shaking with pleasure, while Lena watched, transfixed for having been a part of it. She remained inside her, savoring the way Andy's walls rippled in fading pulses around her fingers. Finally, Andy grew still and pliant in her arms, relaxing her head on Lena's shoulder, her ragged breathing smoothing out, as the pulses around Lena's fingers slowed. Andy's heartbeat was the last to calm, thudding against Lena as Andy's arms slowly lowered to her sides, snaking around Lena's waist. Lena gently extracted her fingers, running them lightly through Andy's wetness in a few slow passes before she simply cupped her, enjoying the heat.

"You are so fucking beautiful, Andy. Do you know that?" Lena whispered next to Andy's ear. Andy shivered. Lena withdrew her hand so she could wrap both arms around her, trembling at the sensation of the kisses Andy pressed to her neck. So soft.

"I deflect compliments with humor." Andy's kisses gained more ardor. "Can I show my appreciation with interpretive sex?" Andy lifted her head, her eyes were soft, belying the joking tone of her voice. "I mean, for the compliment and the earth-shattering orgasm?"

"If you must." Lena breathed out in feigned exasperation while she ached, thinking about how fucking hot it was to watch Andy come undone. Nothing had prepared her for it. Her body thrummed. She craved to have Andy's hands on her. To release the charge of energy building with every second in Andy's arms.

"I do must." Andy kissed her, talking against her lips, breathing her same air. They seemed to do this a lot and Lena found it erotic as hell. "Not to kill the mood, and I'm an orgasm too late, but my dad's on the other side of the wall. He's a little hard of hearing, but the television is off, so we probably should be quiet."

Lena wasn't sure she was capable of quiet, but she'd say yes to anything Andy asked. "I'll give it my best."

Andy stepped back, peeling off her T-shirt and sports bra in one motion. She pointed at her, waving her finger up and down. "And all of that needs to come off."

"All of it?" Lena had trouble thinking at the sight of Andy's toned body. It was, by far, the most beautiful body Lena had ever seen. She forgot what she was supposed to do. She took a step toward Andy, drawing her hands down Andy's arms, her eyes following the path of them. She wanted the soft skin against her lips, Andy's beautiful breasts in her hands, her nipples hardening against her tongue. She was about to put her hands to work, when Andy stepped back, dropping onto the edge of the bed, taking all of that gorgeous body with her. Lena prepared to climb on top of her, but Andy indicated her clothing again.

"I'm waiting."

Lena's eyes rose to meet Andy's and Andy's expression, along with her teasing low voice, sent tingles through Lena's body. She felt drunk with it. When had she been so affected by a woman like this? Andy leaned forward and trailed a finger up Lena's thigh, stopping at the hem of her shorts. The tip of her finger teased under it. Lena's center pulsed.

"I need to see you, Lena. Please." She must have paused to admire for a little too long. Andy's eyes pleaded, and Lena couldn't refuse. Not that she would have.

She slowly unfastened the button and zipper of her shorts, pushing the opening apart for Andy to see her lacy pink underwear. Andy dropped back onto her elbows, her teasing manner from a moment ago replaced with desire. "I'm still rocked after watching you. How your eyes reacted when I touched you." Her breath rushed out. "How you looked when you came." Lena unbuttoned her sleeveless shirt.

Andy scooted up the bed, settling against the pillows, watching her, one arm flung behind her head, absently running her fingers over her own stomach. Lena crawled onto the bed. Lena felt the electric charge humming in the half inch between them when she lay next to her. Replacing Andy's fingers, she strummed up and down Andy's abdomen, loving the ripple of muscles beneath the skin. Andy shut her eyes, humming her pleasure. Still frames from years ago lived in Lena's mind when she'd secretly admired Andy's back and shoulder muscles at swimming and diving practices. The way Andy had somehow managed to rotate and bend into poses in the split seconds before hitting the water during a dive. Watching her at the beach, especially when she came out of the water, holding her board under one arm, unzipping the top of her wetsuit with the other. She'd been gorgeous, her body a constant source of fantasies over the years. And now she was touching it.

Andy didn't let her play for long. She pulled Lena onto her, humming as Lena lay atop her. A long drawn out yes issued from Lena when their breasts met for the first time, resulting in a pleasure Lena could live in forever. It had always been a race to orgasm with the few women she'd been with. Most of the time she'd left satisfied, but she'd never felt this. This want of connection. The desire to learn how another body moved under her touch. The feel of skin against skin. When it was Andy's skin against hers, there was nothing like it.

Sliding to the side, Lena's body still half on top, her leg over Andy's, her center pressed against the firm column of Andy's thigh. It wouldn't take more than a few passes against that muscled limb for her to explode. But she didn't want it to be her first orgasm with Andy. Reluctantly, she broke contact. Lena kissed Andy deeply and her arousal grew higher. "Full disclosure. I'm about three strokes from coming. It'll either be so fast I won't have time to scream, or my sounds of pleasure will shatter the windows. It can go either way."

Andy rolled her over, pushing Lena to her back, and within the curtain of her dark hair, she hovered above her. Her smile was soft like her eyes, and Lena couldn't look away. Not that she tried. Sex had never felt like this. Like it mattered. The unfamiliar intimacy stunned her, but maybe it shouldn't have. This was Andy. And the pure wonder of it shook her.

Andy lowered herself, and when their skin touched again, excitement flared within her at the softness of it. The smoothness of it. The warmth. The fucking pleasure of it made her catch her breath. But the most exquisite thing was Andy looking at her as if she was the only thing she saw. Andy tenderly pushed Lena's hair behind her ear and traced the shape of it. She did the same to the slope of her brow, the contour of her cheek, and the lines of her lips. Finally, Andy kissed her, exactly like she'd touched her face. Reverently. Making Lena aware of every touch. With feather-like kisses, Andy slowly kissed her way to Lena's ear, making all the hair on her body stand up. The soft kisses and warm breaths caused her to tremble. Andy might not have to even touch her to send her over the edge. But she needed Andy's touch. She pressed her hips into her as an invitation to participate in what was going on between her legs.

"I'm going to make you come, Lena Holmes," Andy whispered next to her ear, just before she bit it, dragging her teeth over the lobe before letting it go. "But I'm going to do it slowly. I'll savor every inch of you and make you ask for release."

When those words reached the parietal lobe deep within her brain, Lena was closer than she'd ever been to an orgasm without being touched. Impatient, she claimed Andy's mouth, the tension in her body spiraling up in an almost painful torture. She felt like a supernova ready to explode. Reluctantly, she pulled herself from the kiss

"I'm asking you now, Andy. Please fuck me as hard as you can right this minute, or you'll make me cry."

She didn't recognize her own voice.

Chapter Seventeen

Only eighteen hours had elapsed since Lena had left Andy's bed, and now she was in her room, second-guessing every decision she'd ever made in her life, and fighting her desperate desire to go back to Andy's house. An internal voice reminded her it probably wasn't a good idea, and this was the time to leave. She reminded the voice she'd done it once and it had broken her. She wasn't sure she'd survive leaving her again. She'd never disobeyed the voice, and the fact that she didn't have the slightest desire to leave was a big deal.

Because wow. That's what she had to say about sex with Andy. Just wow.

After leaving for college, when things got difficult, she bailed. She hardly questioned it. To her, the decision was as simple as analyzing a zonal flow diagram when predicting cyclone behavior. Theoretically, using pattern analysis, she'd make an educated decision based on a dependable forecasting diagram. Of course, as everyone knows, theory and reality are two very different entities. Weather doesn't stick to the paths you chose. If independent events, relational effects, or conditional and subjective probabilities aren't factored in, the ability to predict the path and strength of a cyclone is compromised. Thus, making a confident decision to evacuate becomes difficult, and the shit hitting the proverbial fan is what you get. That's what made her a good meteorologist, and a habitual runner-awayer. She just needed to remember people make bad choices. Good intentions devolve. And, yadda, yadda, yadda. Thus, instead of extreme weather events and climate change, she took her dependable diagram and factored in emotions and stupid bosses or declarations of love from women who'd claimed they were good with a one-night stand, to forecast the direction of the storm and make the right decision. Thus, she analyzed the situations fast and with as little emotion as possible, to make the best decision based on the forecast model. Boom. She knew her next move.

Yesterday, after the most incredible experience of her life, which normally would have created the conditions for the perfect storm, she didn't want to run. Not this time. Running from Andy had been the catalyst for her habit of running away when difficult situations came up in her life. But what if she hadn't run? What if she'd chosen another path instead of running? Like, what if she'd faced the situation? Would her life be different? Probably. Every new decision opened a new set of possibilities. Maybe Andy would have ended up hating her for other reasons, and they'd have gone their separate ways anyway. Maybe they'd have stayed best friends, and she wouldn't have kissed her because it would have been too weird. Or maybe they would have stayed best friends and still kissed, fallen in love, and life would have been…well, she didn't like thinking those thoughts. That particular example hurt too much. The point was, what if she'd done anything else but run? Would she still wonder what could have been? Would she have regretted the decision immediately? Would she have still been too weak to take it back? Would she have still lied about the reason, doubling down on a bad decision? All of that aside, she wished she'd chosen Andy instead of fear. At least she wouldn't have thought of herself as a coward for the rest of her life.

So, here she was, wondering why, after a lifetime of running, she didn't want to run now, knowing the perfect storm was on the way. Was it just for the sex? What a stupid question.

With Andy, nothing between them would ever be "just" anything. She had no words for what it meant. An army of emotions, yes. But words? She could describe how her body was still thrumming. She could admit that eighteen hours later, the play-by-play was on repeat in her head, leaving her in a state of constant arousal. It had definitely been more than just sex.

Sex with Andy had changed everything. It flipped everything she thought she knew about herself on its head.

And here she was, back to yesterday afternoon, wondering if it would destroy her.

It didn't matter. She was all in. No reservations. She chose them this time.

A vibration in her back pocket made her jump. She kept her cell silenced so her mom wouldn't get nosey when she received a call. It didn't keep her mother from getting pissed because Lena never answered her calls, though. Like yesterday when she'd called twelve fucking times, leaving a message each time, asking Lena when she'd be home with her library books. Lena wanted to scream she'd be back after she finished having the best fucking sex of her life. Instead, she'd said she'd run into an old friend and time had gotten away from them. As it was, her mother was going to give her shit no matter what the circumstances were. Her mother was lucky Lena had even remembered to get to the library before it closed. God, it had been hard to leave Andy's bed. She shivered with the echoes of Andy's touches playing over her skin.

She slid the phone from her pocket.

She didn't recognize the number of the caller. She was about to send it to voice mail when it stopped. Seconds later, a text notification from the same number popped up.

Hey. I was just thinking about you. What are you up to?

Lena's stomach did a cartwheel. *Do I know you?*

You knew me in the biblical sense just yesterday, Andy texted.

You need to be more specific, Lena teased her.

I was the one who gave you two orgasms.

I believe it was three, but who's counting? Lena shivered, remembering.

My mind wasn't on math. Your dad gave me your number. Hope you don't mind?

Along with the cartwheels, butterflies took off to make dramatic swoops in her stomach. Had she ever felt butterflies from a text? Had she ever felt butterflies, period?

It depends. What was it you were thinking about me? Lena held her breath.

So many things.

Lena wanted to know. *Be specific. Hold back zero details.*

How about I show you?

I think that can be arranged. Who was she? All theoretical thoughts about running from this woman were gone. Also, could butterflies stampede? Because the ones in Lena's stomach were definitely stampeding. Was there something more stomach quaking than a stampede?

What are you doing right now?

Eager. I like that. Lena tried to sound cool, but she was anything but.

I just know what you want, is all.

Intense body memories caused Lena's hands to shake. Andy really did know what she liked. She'd demonstrated it very well yesterday.

What would that be?

Maddeningly, Andy's answer didn't come until almost three minutes later, and Lena impatiently waited.

An Ecuadorian drip with room for cream. Not what she expected, but why did that even sound sexual?

And here I was thinking you wanted...

Lena intentionally sent the text without finishing it. Andy again made her wait, but this time it was only a minute.

Are you going to finish?

Oh. I finished. Lena sent back.

You're killing me. And you have a dirty mind.

I do. And it's all your fault, Lena wanted to add.

And now I'm thinking I want to come inside.

I feel like that's a sexual reference, but I don't get it. Lena teased her.

I'm outside. I was going to take you to coffee if you're up for it. But now I have something completely different in mind.

Lena lifted a slat of the blinds and looked out. Andy's car was parked across the street. A bolt of heat rose through her. Even as it caused the old panic to flare. If she had a normal family, she could invite Andy in. But not when her mother could be home at any time.

Coffee sounds good. All of it does. Be out in a minute. She said, hoping Andy would stay in her car.

❖

Andy glanced across the console at Lena, who looked soft and lost in thought. Was she thinking about sex yesterday? Because Andy couldn't stop thinking about it. Her body kept remembering, too.

"We're here," she said as they pulled into the lot behind the café. "What are you thinking about over there?"

"Oh, you know. Einstein's theory of general relativity. How long the gestation period of otters is. When and if I should kiss you. Just the things most people think about on a seven-minute drive to the coffee shop."

Andy swiveled to face her. "You think most people wonder about when to kiss me?"

"They do if they have eyes."

"You have eyes. Beautiful luminous eyes." Andy fell into them, happy she could do that now. "Did you figure it out?"

Those beautiful eyes expressed so much. Lena leaned toward her, her arm against Andy's on the console. Lena's eyes drifted to her lips and Andy's stomach bottomed out.

"I know the answer to 'if,' but I'm sorry to say not the 'when,'" Lena said.

Fuck. Did Lena know how much power she had over her? "If your answer to 'if' is 'yes,' you're correct. What's getting in your way about 'when'?"

Lena bit her lower lip. A spiral of desire wound through Andy's stomach.

"What if I said I didn't know?"

"That's what they call answering a question with a question. I demand a re-answer." Andy said.

The corner of Lena's mouth rose, making Andy's stomach drop.

"You want a statement? I don't know."

"I believe the rule book specifically states that once one offers a question as an answer, one is not permitted to change the question-answer to a statement. There's a penalty, I'm afraid."

"I must have skipped that section," Lena said.

"Lucky I know the rules, then."

"What's the penalty?"

Andy leaned toward her. "A kiss."

When their lips met, the heat from the day before flowed over Andy like molten lava. She knew yesterday hadn't been a one-time thing for either of them, but she wasn't sure if Lena was ready for more so soon or needed time to regroup. Andy didn't need time, though. She wanted more. So much more. God. Just remembering the way Lena tasted, and fucking hell, the way Lena arched when she came. She worked to resist crawling over the console. She slid her hand into the hair at the back of Lena's neck. She'd always known her hair would be soft, and when Lena paused their kiss and leaned into Andy's hand with a soft moan, it tested Andy's control, and she brought their lips together with more fervor, loving the press of Lena's lips against hers. Feeling the electric surge dive straight between her legs. Despite the heat rising with every second they kissed, a shiver raced through her, spiking Andy's arousal to heights she'd never known.

Feeling Lena's tongue teasing her lips was almost as erotic as Lena's fingers sliding into her, and Andy released a low sound of surrender when Lena expertly traced the inside edge of her lips, before gently biting her lower lip and releasing it. She repeated the same sensual action to Andy's upper lip, adding more heat to the arousal echoing through Andy. Lena had slowed the kiss, setting off thermal plumes deep within Andy, who'd felt pressure expanding in her core since the moment she'd awoken with the scent of Lena in her bed and on her body. She desperately wanted Lena's hands on her again. She wanted Lena's fingers on her clit, her desire so sharp, she almost felt her. It drove her so crazy, she wanted to beg Lena to touch her. But she didn't need to. Lena had her hand between Andy's legs, pressing against her, rubbing the fabric of Andy's shorts. Heat flared under Lena's touch, assuaging the ache while driving Andy's arousal rapidly to the crest. She shifted in her seat, holding Lena's hand against her so she could slip her hand under the short skirt Lena wore. Despite pushing the fabric of Lena's underwear aside, she couldn't quite reach what she wanted. Lena solved the problem by breaking the kiss to slide down in her seat, spreading her legs. She arched, pushing her breasts up, and a memory of watching Lena come yesterday produced a rolling throb thundering through Andy. She was so close.

"I want to watch you come when I do. I'm so close." Andy breathed out.

Lena opened her eyes, finding Andy's, capturing her. Lena's hand picked up speed between Andy's legs, and they both cried out as they flew over the edge. When Lena's brows raised, Andy almost felt the energy of Lena's pleasure flaring into her. Her orgasm hit her like the impact of a cannonball aimed directly at her chest.

Breathless and throbbing, Andy dropped her head against the headrest to regain some composure. The waning pulses of the orgasm she'd just had were a reminder of how quickly Lena could turn her into a quivering mess. And based on Lena's response, she'd enjoyed Andy's reciprocation. Andy sure hadn't seen Lena fucking her through her clothing in her car on her to-do list today. With eyes closed, she grinned like a fool.

"Hey." Lena broke the silence. When Andy peeked from the corner of her eyes, Lena was wearing the cutest satisfied smile. "Serious question. Is it considered public lewdness to do what we just did since we kept our clothes on?"

Andy chuckled. "I don't know. It might depend on the local laws. We'd probably have to ask someone to be sure."

"Like the officer who belongs to that motorcycle?"

Andy sat up. A white motorcycle was parked two spots away.

"Was it here when we arrived?" she asked, not sure if alarm was in order.

"I don't know. I've been a little preoccupied."

Just like that, Andy didn't care about cops or being seen. Fucking hell, Lena was beautiful. Andy took the opportunity to look at her. Really look at her. Undeniably gorgeous, with stupidly amazing features, an unfairly beautiful body, and a way about her that could make Andy do anything she asked. She was also intelligent, kind, and talented. To Andy, she was perfect. Despite their differences, and regardless of everything that had transpired, Andy had aways seen the essential kindness of her. It had been the primary reason their childhood conflict had been so agonizing. Not only was she pushed away from someone so special, but she also hadn't been able to move on because Andy knew Lena wasn't the awful person she pretended to be.

In this moment, this beautiful and unexpected moment, seeing Lena so soft from what they'd just done, she was grateful she hadn't moved on. Not even after Lena and her friends had stolen her clothes while she showered, leaving only her wet bathing suit and a towel to walk home in. Or when Lena had tripped her in the cafeteria, resulting in a concussion and seven stitches. Lena had held her head in her lap, crying and calling for help. But when Andy came back to school a couple of days later, Lena had been her normal shitty self and Andy wondered if she'd had a concussion delusion. But she'd never told anyone who tripped her.

There'd been countless painful interactions between them, most of them less significant and not so mean, but Andy hadn't been innocent. She'd inflicted her own types of miseries during their war. Granted, hers had been gnats at a picnic compared to Lena's hornets, and anticipating Lena's next move had been far more exhausting than anything else, but Andy had gotten in her own jabs. Yet, through it all, she'd remembered Lena, her old best friend. Especially when she'd seen Lena struggle at times, as if regretting what they'd become. At those moments, and even now, Andy believed something else was behind Lena's behavior. Either way, it had always seemed like Lena suffered more than she'd ever let on.

"Andy?"

"Huh?" She wondered how long she'd been lost in the past. A quick glance at the clock on the dash said it had only been a minute or so.

Lena caressed her cheek. "You're staring at me, looking a hundred miles away."

Of course, she'd been staring. Lena was the most stare-worthy person she knew. She just hoped Lena hadn't picked up on her thoughts. Some things were starting to make a lot more sense, but she still didn't like thinking about them.

"It's hard not to stare at you. You're stunning. And I was thinking about your hand on my p—"

"Stop!" Lena laughed behind the hands she held over her face. "I've never done anything remotely like it. Not even in high school. Did you?"

Andy shook her head. "I didn't date in high school. No hiding in cars for me."

"We aren't hiding. At most, it's a crime of opportunity." Lena stared this time, her hand slipping behind Andy's neck, her fingers tangling in Andy's hair. "I know you didn't date in high school. I sort of kept tabs. Everyone thought you were dating Mitch Garcia."

Andy shook her head. "He's in Rhode Island now with his wife and two kids."

Lena bit the inside of her cheek. "Can I tell you something?"

"Is this about you trying to get with him in high school?"

"I did not."

"Claire's party? Out by the pool? Ring any bells?" Andy honestly didn't care. For about five minutes, maybe, because it probably meant she was up to something, but when nothing happened, she'd let it go.

Lena's gaze slipped away. "I pretended to flirt with him when Bronson wouldn't leave me alone. I know Mitch thought it might have been real, and I felt bad for doing it. But…" Lena paused.

"But what?"

Lena bit the inside of her cheek again. The gesture was hot, and Andy's body reacted. "You and Mitch were in the hall and I'd been using the bathroom. He was so sweet and loyal to you." Lena seemed wistful for a second or two. "You told him you were gay."

Lena had known. "And you still kissed me."

"Yeah." Lena blew out a breath with a guilty smile. Andy was confident not many people had seen that smile. "There's no way I would have kissed you in the auditorium if I hadn't known." Andy watched a shiver pass through her. "I still had a hard time working up the courage."

"Did you know you were gay, too?" God, Lena biting the inside of her cheek made Andy want to do things.

"Feelings for someone clued me in," Lena said cryptically.

"Feelings, huh? What kind? For who?" Andy could barely breathe.

"Difficult ones for someone who was off-limits." Lena's expression was adorably uncertain after what they'd just done.

"Who was 'someone'?" Suspicion churned in her stomach and not in a bad way.

"I think you know." Lena's expression was serious now.

A shiver ran through Andy this time. She'd been ashamed of having conflicting emotions for Lena back then, and now she knew Lena had them too. "Did you ever tell anyone?"

"About the kisses? Or about overhearing you and Mitch?"

"Both."

Lena shook her head. "Neither. I almost told Crystal. I needed someone to talk to. But I lost my nerve. Crystal would have flipped out. I never got very close to anyone after you. I didn't have a confidante. As far as the kisses, they were too important to me. I knew what I felt, and we were leaving for college. I wanted things."

"You wanted what?" Andy had to know.

"I wanted something I couldn't have."

"How do you know that?"

Lena's eyes were full of something that looked like remorse. "Andy, I was a mess. I still am. But back then, even if you could have found a way to forgive me, I would have been hard to be around." Lena gave her a sad smile. "Those kisses gave me a lot of nice daydreams, though. Night dreams, too."

Andy reached up and cradled Lena's face in her hand. "I wish I could have been there for you."

Lena put her hand over Andy's, leaning into her touch. "I wish a lot of things. And you were there. Just not in person."

That last part both crushed and elated her. "My mom says you can't change the past. All you can do is move forward with new information. It's helped me through a lot of tough times."

"Your mom is amazing." Lena's wistful tone elicited a tenderness in her that made Andy want to wrap her in her arms.

She was learning so much and a lot of emotions were rising in her. Tenderness for sure, but also desire, which kept blowing her mind every time she remembered she could act on it now.

Lena narrowed her eyes. "I know that look."

"Then you know I'm thinking lewd and unlawful thoughts."

"Do you still want coffee?" Lena asked with a suggestive smile.

That's all it took for Andy. She started the car. "Your place or mine?"

"Yours."

As kids, they'd hardly ever hung out at Lena's house, and when they did, they stayed in her room. Andy hadn't thought much of it back then but was beginning to figure out why.

"Do you think you can be quieter this time?" She glanced over with a grin.

Lena returned her grin. "It depends. Are you going to make me come so hard I can't remember my own name again?"

Heat washed through Andy. She'd never forget the experience of discovering Lena's body for the first time. The highlights kept her occupied as she drove. It was a wonder she didn't crash the car.

"Should we go in through the back?" Lena asked when they arrived. They stood next to Andy's car. Lena's dad's truck was in the driveway. Lena had mentioned she hadn't come out to him.

"My dad's for sure awake. He might appreciate us going in through the back. But don't think I'm hiding you."

Lena tilted her head, resting her hand on Andy's arm. The heat from before flowed between them. "Back door it is."

"It reminds me of the times you used to sneak over." Andy noticed Lena's shoulders drop along with her smile. Andy wondered what she'd said.

Lena sighed. "I just wanted to be with you." The vulnerable beauty in Lena's eyes captured Andy. "My parents argued. Well, my mom yelled, and my dad sat there until he'd get tired of it and leave. Then my mom would take it out on me." She said it as if describing a bad restaurant experience.

"Did your mom hurt you?" She couldn't bear to know.

Lena froze, and then with visible effort, she breathed out. "Not physically."

Andy's heart ached. "I had no idea."

"I didn't want you to. I was afraid you wouldn't want to be my friend if you knew."

"God, Lena. Why did you think that?"

Lena looked down. "I worried you'd believe what she said. It was bad enough I started to believe it. Before I drove you away, I was mostly worried she'd go off in front of you. Or worse, that she'd go off on you. I'd only invite you over when I knew my dad wouldn't be there. She stayed in her room and left me alone those days. When you were there, she didn't have to deal with me."

Andy pulled her close, humming like her mom used to do. She loved how Lena melted into it. She needed it as much as Lena. "I wish I could've done this then."

Lena issued a weak laugh. "Your scrawny arms would have been heaven to me."

She breathed in the smell of her. "My scrawny arms, huh?"

"They aren't scrawny now."

"I wish I could have been there for you," Andy said.

Lena lifted her head. Andy was surprised to see tears in her eyes. "Me too." Despite the tears, Lena's gaze drifted down to Andy's mouth. "You are now, though."

Chapter Eighteen

How'd your date go with Lena yesterday?"

Andy nearly dropped the beer she'd just opened. Thankfully, she was in the kitchen, and her dad didn't see.

Hoping she didn't look as rattled as she felt, she placed his beer on the hospital table near his good arm, along with a plate of homemade shortbread cookies from Mrs. Rafferty. Her dad had been watching a documentary on Netflix which had just ended, and he was flipping through the menu to find the next one. The smile he gave her in thanks was probably sincere, but his normal good nature wasn't reflected in it. Cabin fever was really bad when a cold beer wasn't helping.

"You doing okay, Dad?"

His days consisted of visits from Robert, when her dad seemed to shine the brightest, and the two hours with his aides, which wore him out. Netflix and naps filled the time in between. In the monotony, he'd become depressed and grumpy. She tried to stay upbeat around him. Which wasn't difficult lately because of Lena.

"As well as can be expected," he said. His typical answer lately.

She pretended not to have heard the date question as she took a seat in the recliner next to his bed. She watched him browse. At least he stayed away from true crime. She didn't want either of them worrying about serial killers among them, not when her dad was a sitting duck. It's always the most unassuming ones. The thought of four-foot-nine, house-dress-wearing, cookie-making, Mrs. Rafferty being a serial killer amused Andy. But there was no getting around the fact that her lawn had always been just a little too perfect and the cookies she brought by were just a little too good.

"Now you answer mine."

"Answer what?" She wasn't convincing even to herself.

"Your date with Lena." To his credit, he didn't sound exasperated.

"It wasn't a date. We went to coffee." Had he heard them? He hadn't said anything, but that didn't mean much.

He stopped lifting his beer and did one of those huff-laughs of his. "I asked how your day was."

"Oh. It was good," she said. Of course, he'd been there when she'd asked Robert for Lena's number.

"Thinking about making a move?"

She studied her dad. What had gotten into him? He never asked personal questions. Not because he didn't care. He just didn't initiate it. He was always there to listen, though. They were beyond making moves, but she wasn't ready to talk about things yet. He took a swig of his beer while watching her out of the corners of his eyes. He was invested. Weird.

"I'm not sure what making a move means," she said, dodging the question for now.

He rolled his eyes. She'd never seen him do that before. This was Twilight Zone territory.

"Are you asking me if I'm interested in her?"

He rolled his eyes again. Apparently, he was an eye roller now. This time it was accompanied by a sigh. "I'm asking for Robert. You asked for her phone number and Helena said she saw Lena getting into a car yesterday before she left to visit her mother. She described your car."

"You're asking this for Lena's dad, who heard from Lena's mom she'd seen us together in a car? Based on that, he wants to know if I'm planning on making a move on Lena? To report back to Lena's mom? Just because I picked Lena up to go to coffee?"

Her dad shrugged. Andy wondered how something like going to coffee could be construed as clandestine. Even if it had been, given what they'd done in the car, and then had sex all afternoon. They were adults. No one was cheating on anyone. At least she and Lena weren't. Stop. It wasn't anyone's business.

"You can tell him I'm not planning on making a move." A technicality, given the moves had already been made.

Her dad seemed satisfied with the answer, but she hated minimizing this thing, as if it was inconsequential. It wasn't. Not that it had to be anything more than it was, but they'd been together twice now. Three times, including the parking lot. And based on their good night kiss, she knew they'd do it again.

Her dad flipped through Netflix options while her mind drifted. Electric charges raced along her skin as she thought about yesterday, which was uncharted territory, but far from inconsequential. Their history meant they were being careful, not that she was one to throw caution to the wind. She had serious trust issues to work through. Sometimes she was certain she could trust Lena with her life, that everything that happened when they were kids was just that. Kid stuff. Things were so different now, and it had only been a week.

On one hand, it was unbelievable how easy it was to forget about everything and move into the place with each other that they'd both wanted but never thought possible. On the other hand, the ease in which it had happened really was unbelievable. And how could Andy trust it wouldn't destroy her? Lena had royally fucked her up, even if they'd only been kids. Plus, for a big part of the week, Lena had disappeared without a word and hadn't provided an explanation for it. She'd just left her hanging. It had been torture, and she'd felt like she was back in fifth grade all over again. Yet, as soon as Lena showed up again, Andy was right back to acting like everything was wonderful.

She couldn't help wondering if she was being reckless with her heart. It was scary how Lena could make her feel this way when she'd walled herself off from being hurt by anyone else since the day Lena had dropped that folded up note on her desk. At the same time, she couldn't deny the way she felt.

Yesterday had been incredible. After they'd gone into the house through the back, they'd fallen into bed immediately, inpatient for more of what they'd started in the car. Eventually, they'd fallen asleep after a few rounds of intense sex. When she'd woken, Lena had been snuggled tightly against her, like they'd been sleeping together forever. She'd wanted to wake her for more. Instead, she took the time to admire the slopes and plains of Lena's face and body as she slept. She looked younger, a slight smile playing on her lips. Andy let her eyes roam over her neck, her shoulders, her arms, knowing exactly what was under the sheets beyond. The pressure of arousal pulsed between her legs. Something else settled around her heart. It's where Lena lived, and always had.

Feeling peace she'd never known, she'd wrapped Lena in her arms, falling back to sleep, waking again when the alarm in her phone sounded quietly next to the bed. She silenced it as carefully as she could without waking Lena. It was dinnertime, but she didn't want to get up. She wanted to get lost in Lena until they fell asleep, and wake to do it all over again.

"I should be creeped out with all the staring you do," Lena said with a sleepy voice. "But I think I like it. Especially when your eyes are all soft like that."

"Like what?"

"Like after you come." Lena snuggled against her, tucking her head against her chest. Andy melted. She stroked her fingertips along Lena's side and Lena arched into her. Andy absolutely loved being the cause of Lena's pleasure. She also loved how the sheet had slipped down, revealing Lena's truly beautiful breasts. Andy drew circles around a perfect nipple, envisioning taking it into her mouth. Lena arched again, voicing her enjoyment. Just like that, they were lost again.

She decided on sandwiches for dinner.

❖

Flashes of light intermittently flared as the late afternoon sunlight struck the rippling surface of the pool Lena gazed across from her favorite lounger. Beneath the sunlight decorated surface, the automatic cleaner made erratic patterns across the floor of the pool, reminding her of Andy's fingers making random paths along her body. These kinds of thoughts had been drifting through her mind all day.

Lena had spent most her day in a miasma, playing back memories of the last two days of truly phenomenal sex, daydreaming about seeing Andy again, and how fucking happy she was to have her in her life again. It felt like she'd regrown a missing limb. Even if she didn't know where it would go after they went back to their other lives, it was an unexpected and overwhelming bliss she'd already learned to crave. If Andy hadn't needed to take her dad to appointments, Lena would probably already be with her.

Her pleasant daze was interrupted when one of the filter hoses snaking around the pool breeched the surface, startling her with a spray of water. Giggling, she set her unread book to the side and took her sunglasses off to dry them. So, she was a giggler now, huh?

After her father had finished cleaning the pool he'd left to go "check on some things," which she knew was code for visiting Glenn. She wondered if he was keeping up Glenn's pool for him while he was laid up. What a ridiculous question. What would people think if he didn't?

What would people think?

She refused to spoil her giddy mood with that old recording.

It had been a good day. Thoughts of Andy had butterflies dancing in her stomach, and her dad must have known her mom wouldn't be there, because he'd come over during the day for a change. She hadn't felt one way or the other when he first arrived, and they hadn't said much. but the visit was much easier than the morning he'd made her coffee, and she hadn't felt like a stranger in his presence. That had been nice.

She picked up her water-splashed book and headed to the house, pushing her sunglasses to the top of her head before sliding open the glass door. Squeezing her eyes closed to help them adjust to the dim interior after the bright sun, the air-conditioning cooled her sun-warmed skin.

"Another day by the pool, I see." Her mother's voice wasn't loud, but it made her jump.

"I didn't see you." She still couldn't, but she tried to keep the annoyance out of her voice. Being startled by anyone else would have made her laugh.

"I'm not surprised. Your head has been in the clouds. I'm surprised you haven't walked in front of a car yet." From some people, the comment might have been teasing. Her mother delivered it as an indictment.

"Just decompressing from all the work stress." Why justify her good mood? Letting her mind wander wasn't a crime.

"Speaking of cars, I saw you get into one yesterday."

Her eyes had finally adjusted, so she could study her mother's expression to gauge the situation.

"I believe it was that girl you used to play with as a child."

"Oh, yeah." A zing of horror shot through her. Where had she them? At the coffee shop? They'd stayed in the car, so it was unlikely. But she'd recognized Andy, which made her nervous. She'd learned long ago not to say anything more than necessary. Her mom was an expert at turning anything into a weapon, and she wasn't about to give her a blade.

"Why would you possibly want to spend time with her?" her mother asked.

Her mother did that thing where she pretended to be casual, but she was waiting. It was always a trap. The pause grew uncomfortable, but Lena wasn't stupid. The other day had been horrible, even if her memory was doing that thing where it categorized the event but removed all the painful details. Any sense of equanimity she'd began to feel around her mother had vanished.

"Well, don't let me interrupt whatever you're doing. Will you be home for dinner?"

Lena and Andy hadn't made any specific plans. Andy would call or text. But her mother's question sounded more like a threat. Especially because they didn't eat meals together.

"I have plans with a friend."

"Is that 'friend' the person from yesterday?"

Her mother's eyes had taken on a predatory gleam. Lena hadn't seen that look since her early years in college. Her stomach churned.

"Do you have plans?" She tried to divert the topic.

"Why would you care now?" When her mother's voice sounded as if there should be a hand flapping accompaniment, nothing good ever came of it.

Why had she thought anything had changed? Just because she was thirty fucking years old? Her mother had been working up to this. The other day hadn't been a singular throwback to the bad old days. Her mother had been establishing the dynamic. Making sure Lena knew her place. The demands to run errands. The lack of boundaries. The absence of routine. The unending criticism. Lena had walked right into an exact replica of the world she thought she'd escaped. Why had she thought she had some sort of immunity for being an adult now? Also, knowing her family for what it was—an emotionally abusive mother and a neglectful father—should have given her some control over her actions and responses. What a joke. What a goddamn fucking joke. Acidic bubbles of defeat eroded what she'd thought of as her nearly healed spirit.

She prepared for the tirade, reminding herself she was a functional adult. Her mother's words weren't gospel. They were abusive and meant to hurt. She was not the person her mother said she was. She wasn't the person her mother said she was. She wasn't the person…

"…who your father can't stand. As soon as you showed up, he's been completely unavailable. The pool's neglected. He hasn't…"

Shame washed over her at the mention of her father, followed immediately by anger. He can't stand being around me. Those were her mother's words. He was supposed to take care of her, not the other way around. It was her mother who…

"…ruined the family and my life. I might have been able to make a new life for myself, but I've been forced to take care of you as if I was a single mother. I wish you'd never been…"

Maybe she's right. She hadn't really tried to be a good daughter. But why would she? Her parents never acted like…

"…perverts. The whole family. I used to feel sorry for their little girl, but she's just like her father. The apple doesn't fall far from the tree. That man should be arrested the way he influences your father. Paula's just as bad. I should have gone to their house after I caught that girl all over you, basically sleeping on top of you. I always wondered why you two built those blanket tents."

Was that why her mother hated Andy? She'd seen them cuddling? They'd been kids. It was the only affection Lena ever received.

I was selfish. I don't deserve that kind of love. It's best to walk away. And the apple and the tree? Was this about Andy's dad? She'd said he was bisexual and had always been open about it. And Glenn and her dad were friends. But influence? Things made a little more sense. Her mother hated Andy by association. If she'd known some of this, she might have guessed her mother would have made a fool of herself if she tried to confront the Phillipses. They would have…

"…tried to turn you into one of them. I know you preferred it over there. I'm sure you wished Paula was your mother. Honestly, I should have told her to keep you. I wouldn't have had to deal with…"

That would have been nice. She would have been so happy. *Am I just like my mother, wishing my life was different?* It was too late to think about what…

"…people thought? I looked like a laughingstock letting you associate with them and their brat. They wouldn't have wanted you around if they knew who you really were. I'm glad you broke off that friendship, before I had to tell them how useless you are. You can't keep a job, let alone find a man who'll put up with you. You ruined our family. I could tell your friend now. I probably should. As much of a disappointment as you are, I can't have you running around town..."

Her mother's threats to confront Andy shouldn't have scared her anymore. Andy would know it wasn't true. But what if Andy thought she was like her mother? The apple doesn't fall far from the tree. Lena had been terrible to Andy. Her head was a mess.

I'm a good person. I'm a good person. I'm a good person.

She had no idea how long she'd been repeating it before she realized the tirade had stopped and her mother was gone. Just like when she'd been a kid. Last time had been a full shut down. This time was more like when she'd gotten a little older. She wasn't sure which was better. Both left her drained and feeling hopeless.

Lourdes lay curled up on the carpet near her feet watching her. Over the last few days, her mother had been less attentive of the little beast, and Lena wondered if her affection had been less authentic and more about making Lena feel inferior to her dog. It would have been just the kind of fucked up thing her mother would do.

Lena leaned forward, holding out her arms, and Lourdes jumped into them. It was hard to question if she was a good person if a dog loved her.

Chapter Nineteen

Lena wished the derecho would come.

The words of her mother tumbled in her head, and she fought off the habit of letting them wrap her in a gloom of believing she didn't deserve the things she craved. Love. Acceptance. Happiness. Yet, all the old recordings she'd tried to destroy over the last few years kept playing.

She needed the derecho to come and blow her on to the next place, to distract her from the reminders of who she used to be, to give her a brand-new start free from the fucked up past she couldn't seem to shake. She waited for the sound of the wind.

There was one problem. She didn't want to leave this time. Besides, running had done nothing to fix her. It only caught up and she'd run again. Lena was tired of running. She wanted to be with Andy.

Sitting on the bed, her back against the pillows, and Lourdes in her lap, she ran her fingers through the little dog's hair, watching her preen, with the corners of her mouth curved up, and her little pink tongue lolling out in a smile. All Lourdes wanted was a warm lap and her hair played with.

Her mother's words from earlier still tumbled in her mind. As a child, she used to blank them out as soon as her mother was done. When she and Andy had been friends, she'd sometimes gone over to her house because Andy always made her feel better. After she'd ended their friendship, she'd had nowhere to go.

She was just so exhausted and tired from holding it all in.

Lourdes stood on her back paws and gave Lena a kiss on her chin before darting under the little blanket Lena had bought for her and coming back out with her tennis ball. Smaller than a golf ball, it fit perfectly in her tiny mouth. She dropped the ball next to Lena, looking up at her expectantly. Lena's eyes welled up at how sweet she was. She tossed the ball and Lourdes raced after it, bringing it back to drop into Lena's hand.

"I have a surprise." Lena pulled a bag of treats from a drawer and Lourdes immediately went through all the tricks Lena had taught her.

When she opened the new bag, Lena gagged at the smell of bacon.

She was eight years old, and her mother had stormed from the room after another one of her tirades. Lena couldn't remember what had set it off, but she'd been getting ready to prepare her own birthday dinner, so that's what she continued to do. The bacon sizzled on the stovetop for her sandwich, crinkle fries were in the oven, and she'd just blended up a homemade strawberry shake. Her favorites.

After turning off the burner under the bacon, she jumped down from the chair she'd been standing on to get the spray can of whipped cream. She squirted some into her mouth and was getting ready for another, when the smoke alarm went off. Instead of turning the burner off, she'd turned it all the way up.

She'd already turned off the stove and opened a window, silencing the alarm, when her mother rushed into the kitchen. Fresh from the earlier tirade, her mother launched into her. By the time her mother finished, her shake had melted, her fries had grown cold, and she needed to start over, but her mother grabbed the packages out of her hands and told her she could eat the food she'd prepared and watched her pick the burned slices out of the charred grease. Knowing her mother would check, she'd eaten the meal and cleaned up her mess.

Taking out the garbage, she started to cry. She hadn't cried in longer than she remembered. Without thinking about it, she found herself walking to Andy's house. She'd never walked there in the dark, but she kept herself from getting scared by a new trick of watching the light from the streetlamps lengthen and shorten by squinting through her tears. She wasn't going to let her fear of the dark keep her from seeing Andy. When she got there, Andy had been excited to see her because she had a birthday gift.

Over twenty-two years later, the only thing Lena wanted to do was see Andy.

Hey. Lena sent the text before she could overthink it.

Hey back. Andy's response was almost instantaneous.

Can I call you?

Sure. Everything OK?

Not really.

She never admitted to not being anything other than fine to anyone, even herself. Who wanted to be around that? But Andy had seen it a few times recently and she'd stuck around.

Her phone rang less than a second after she sent the text. She wasn't surprised.

"I was just about to text you. What's going on? Do you need anything?"

Lena sighed into the comfort of Andy's voice. It had been so long since she'd had someone to lean on, and it had been Andy back then, too. Even if Andy hadn't known it. How had she ever shut Andy out?

"I hear you breathing. Do you need to just do that for a while? I've got time."

She wanted to cry. Andy understood. Andy, who'd probably never felt this kind of hopelessness and lack of power. Andy still got it. Andy, who'd never had no one to turn to. Andy, who…her thoughts screeched to a halt.

Hadn't she, though? Hadn't Andy felt hopeless and powerless, with no one to turn to when Lena pushed her away? Yet, Andy was showing up for her. She wasn't sure how many of these revelations she could take. She was spinning and couldn't stop.

True to her word, Andy let the silence sit between them. Because, yeah, Andy had been here before. That's why she always knew what to do. Lena took in a long, shaky breath.

"I meant it when I said I was good with just hanging out on the phone. But I can come over or pick you up. I can meet you somewhere, too. Whatever you need."

She swallowed through the tightness in her throat. "I'll walk over. Like before. Is it okay?"

"More than okay. Need an escape? Or is it just me you want to see?"

"Both." It came out as a whisper.

"I'll talk you over. Cool?"

"Yeah," she managed.

Besides her phone, she didn't take anything with her or even fix her hair. She thought about bringing Lourdes, but that would end up bad. She just started walking and Andy told Lena about the impressive work of the transport company and how her dad's appointments went.

Depending on how fast she walked, it took about ten minutes, plus or minus. So, it didn't surprise her to see Andy and Billie headed toward her about five minutes later. Andy hadn't said she was meeting her, but Lena knew she would. She couldn't find her voice again, but she smiled. She couldn't help it. Andy was the only person she wanted to see. The only person she wanted at all.

When Andy held out her arms, she walked right into them without missing a step, instantly surrounded in their comfort. How had she lived without this for so long? She wore her lying-around-the-house leggings and old swim team T-shirt she'd stolen from Andy years ago. It had ARS written in faded Sharpie on the tag. The R stood for Renee. She'd worn it to threads, and would never answer the door dressed like this, but she hardly thought about it with Andy, who'd never given her a shred of judgment. Not even at the worst of their feud. She listened to Andy's breathing and counted her heartbeats. She'd never felt so safe.

Lena shifted to look at Andy. It had been mere hours, but she'd missed her.

"Hey," she said, barely above a whisper. She really was undeserving of this unyielding presence in her life. Every minute Andy gave her was a minute she never expected. She wouldn't take another one for granted.

Andy scanned her face, worry etched across her own. She leaned back, sliding her hands down Lena's arms, intertwining their fingers. "You ready?"

Lena looked at her feet. "But what about Billie?" The small dog lay across her feet, snoring. It gave Lena more comfort than she could explain.

Andy shrugged. "I guess we stay here all night." Fortunately, Billie had heard Lena say her name and was already pulling at her leash in Andy's hand.

She led with her nose in the air, Andy and Lena just behind, holding hands. Andy had been the only one she'd ever held hands with, and that had been when they were little. This felt as if it was another way of communicating, one that didn't require words. Which was good, because she needed to organize her thoughts. A person who offers to breathe with you is a person who knows when to let you set the pace.

They walked, soon passing Andy's house, Lena not stopping and Andy not mentioning it. This quiet walk, holding hands, was just the thing Lena needed. Various scents hung in the mostly still evening air, with the last magnolias of late spring still holding on in early summer, giving off their heady perfume. Creeping violets with their powdery smell, the subtle sweet wisteria, and the spicy, smokey aroma of star jasmine added their aromas to the bouquet. The ever-present scent of freshly cut grass, fragrant eucalyptus, and the moist soil releasing the day's heat worked as a base to round out the smell of home. It evoked so many things for Lena, but the main one was Andy. The perfumed landscape of their hometown was imprinted on her. Sometimes, wherever she was, she'd pick up a phantom waft, and she and Andy were nine again, having meaningful conversations about the probability of micro nebulas floating in the air around them. Lena had a custom scent made trying to capture it. It didn't, but it was close.

Andy stopped, and Lena took in a deep breath. They were in front of a house featured in her very best memories. This part of their neighborhood was replete with creative landscaping, quirky art installments, and other shows of personality. Lena pressed into Andy's side, and they studied the house. Even in this neighborhood, it stood out, its quirkiness just a little quirkier and its creativity just a little more creative. The xeriscaped landscaping, with decorative rock beds, featured a surprisingly accurate rendition of *The Great Wave of Kanagawa* by Hokusai in the main bed, painstakingly represented in colored rocks. A tsunami of memories hit Lena as she looked at it. They'd stopped here often during their wanderings. Lena had even written a story about it once. Andy had given her a drawing she'd made of the house for her eighth birthday, something she'd thought about less than an hour ago. They call it synchronicity, these meaningful coincidences. But right now, she called it healing.

Barely visible, a *For Sale* sign lay faded and worn amid dried weeds and the withered corpses of a cactus bed. The faded *No Developers* sign told her why the house had never sold in a neighborhood of scrape and scape lots.

At one time, the rocks had been contained within sharp borders but now bled together. Weeds grew through degraded weed barriers, and tufts of grass lined the edges. Once vibrant but now faded yard ornaments leaned wearily in random displays the owner didn't seem bothered to tend, or maybe worse, was bothered but couldn't. Most of the plants had died, while a few invaders had taken over. It still projected a certain mystique in its neglected state, an unintentional Havisham Garden. It wasn't the same garden it once was, but maybe it was better for this moment. It seemed a perfect metaphor for the disarray of her own life.

❖

Andy watched Lena. For Andy, the wave house was "their house." It captivated Lena, who captivated her. Like the smell of magnolias, the house elicited some of her favorite memories. After Lena had broken things off, she'd often come alone. It had never been the same, but sometimes she'd needed to remind herself the memories of what they'd had would always exist, even if their friendship hadn't. It was especially poignant now, with Lena beside her, holding her hand, her head on her shoulder, looking at a ghost of their childhood friendship.

"I've always loved how much you loved this house," Andy said quietly, the first words spoken between them since they'd started walking.

Lena squeezed her hand, something she'd done occasionally as they'd walked, as if she had to prove Andy was still there.

"It's our house." Lena's voice was reflective.

A soft alley-oop stirred in Andy's stomach. "It's kind of sad to see it this way, huh?"

"Maybe it's just a reminder that everything eventually goes to shit no matter how much we try to prevent it." Her reflective tone had turned flat.

It crushed Andy's heart to hear. "You really think that?"

Lena shrugged, still taking in the yard. "It's been my experience."

Andy squeezed her hand but didn't try to convince her otherwise. If that's how Lena saw things, who was she to try to change her mind? It hurt her heart, though.

They stood in their own thoughts for a while longer.

Andy finally shifted. "Wanna head back? I should make sure my dad finished dinner without falling asleep in his plate."

They'd walked about half a block. "Your dad falls asleep in his food?" Lena asked.

It was Lena's first real sign of animation since Andy met her halfway. She laughed. "It's just a thing we say when someone's tired at mealtime. I did it a few times as a baby and my parents thought it was funny. I'm sure your parents have things they laugh about from your childhood."

Lena went as still as she could while walking. The kind of too still Andy recognized when Lena tried to deal with her emotions. She felt far away. Her precarious emotional state worried Andy. She seemed so lost. She let go of Lena's hand and slipped it around her waist. How was it possible she got to do this? A few steps later, Lena stopped, pausing a few seconds before she moved into Andy, burying her face against her neck. Andy shivered at the feel of Lena's face against her skin.

"How do you do it?" Lena asked.

"Do what?"

"Always know what to do. You should open a business."

"I'd have exactly one customer."

"Who?"

"Just you."

"Just me?" Lena lifted her head. Andy worried she'd told Lena something she shouldn't have.

"I mean, I haven't really been in a position to comfort anyone." She didn't know how to explain it without sounding pathetic.

"How many people have you dated?"

She'd dreaded this question. Did hookups count? She'd had a lot of those. But dated? Never. How could she tell Lena she thought she was broken? Besides, they were here to talk about what had upset Lena. Lena looked at her and Andy felt exposed.

"I don't know what a lot means to you. But if dating means some sort of committed relationship with defined expectations, I haven't had any of those." It was embarrassing to say. "I've never gone out with the same person more than once."

Lena stopped yet again. It appeared she couldn't speak about a lot of things when in motion. She shook her head, mouth open. "There's no way women aren't begging you to go on a second date with them."

Andy didn't want to tell Lena she made it clear from the start that it was only sex. "I don't see the point if I know it won't go anywhere."

"You just don't want a relationship?"

She hadn't even talked to Talia about this. Sometimes she ached with how much she wanted one. "I do. It just hasn't happened."

"Maybe you haven't tried with enough people?"

Andy felt her face go hot. The number of women she'd "tried" with was embarrassing. "Well, um." She would give anything to know what Lena was thinking.

"It's obvious you've had plenty of practice." Was she really teasing?

"I'm not sure what that means," Andy said, not sure she wanted to hear Lena's response.

Lena stopped again. "It was a compliment, Andy. What you do with your body seriously doesn't matter to me unless we decide otherwise. What you do with your heart does, though. I'm not a jealous person, but I can be insecure. I wouldn't want to share you if we, um, well, it's too soon, but we can decide if it comes down to it." Lena started to walk but stopped again. "You've really never seen someone more than once?"

"Yeah." Andy grimaced.

"How do we factor into that?"

Andy felt like she'd just fallen into a puddle that was way deeper than she'd expected, and the water was over her head. The last few days had been some of the best of her life. Being with Lena and getting to know her again, especially in this whole new way, had never been an option before. So, she was in a sharp learning curve. Normally, Andy was a planner, which was the scientist in her. But she was going against her nature. She was giving in to what was happening, not trying to figure out what it all meant or how things would go. She had to. So many things were uncertain, she knew she'd ruin it if she did it any other way. To her, they didn't factor into anything other than what they were doing and seeing where it would go. And somehow, this felt right to her.

But did it feel right to Lena?

Abruptly, Andy wondered if she'd done something wrong. Should she have been talking to Lena about some of this? Because if she had, she'd only have said how happy she was, and how she didn't want to fuck anything up by overthinking it.

It occurred to her that maybe Lena thought she was more invested than Lena was. Or just the opposite, that Lena might be more invested than her. Was Lena panicking? Had something else come up that Andy hadn't even thought of? Was Lena thinking about cutting everything off? Again? And, oh God, that made Andy's chest tight. Was this the derecho Lena had been talking about? Had she triggered Lena's signal to run? She wanted to run before Lena had a chance to. She couldn't take it again.

"Hey." Lena moved closer.

It was like a starting horn at a swim meet. Andy's mind went still and all she could see was Lena's eyes. And they were kind and concerned. Andy was rubbing the middle of her chest. Lena wrapped a hand around her wrist, much like she had the first time they'd been together.

"Where were you?" Lena asked.

"I actually don't know." It wasn't a complete lie.

"Do you want to talk about it?"

Lena's voice was soft. Her eyes were kind. She was still here. Had Andy really been about to run from this? She blew out a breath to reset.

"Sorry. You called me to talk. We've gotten off track."

"Can we talk about what's happening here first?" Lena tilted her head. "You look terrified. What's going on?"

Andy should have hidden it better. "I'm just sorting through things. Things have happened so quickly and…" Andy searched for the words.

"I know," Lena said, her thumb stroking Andy's wrist. It felt so good. But she'd agreed it was too quickly. Maybe Andy hadn't been off base.

"That's why—" Lena began.

"Maybe we should—" Andy said at the same time.

Both raised their hands.

"I need to—" Lena said again.

"I think—" Andy started again.

They paused, the frustration on Lena's face evident. It would have been comical had Andy not felt like she was losing her best friend again. Her anxiety spiked.

"Let me get this out." Lena's voice was firm.

"I've enjoyed every—" Andy tried to interject, anxiety swelling inside her.

Lena put her hand over Andy's mouth. "Goddamn it, Andy. Just shut up for a second and let me say—Ah. Fuck it." She surged forward. Everything around Andy went still at the sensation of Lena's lips, hot on her own, possessing hers with a sudden hungry, needy intensity that Andy returned with everything she had to give. The thing she'd wanted to say had died on her lips, only to be replaced with something so much better. In seconds, they were dialed up to the last notch on the control panel. This was what Lena did to her. The sounds Lena emitted from deep in her throat, drove white-hot currents of lust straight to Andy's center. Her racing thoughts and tangled fears of moments before were distant memories now.

It was only the passing of a car, the sounds of laughter, and shouts of "Get a room!" that brought them back to reality. Andy looked up to make sure the car hadn't stopped, but Lena was having none of it. She pulled her in for another searing kiss. Desire and need were in complete control.

"What was that for?" Andy managed when she could speak.

"I just had to. Your lips were right there and I had to tell you how much I love everything happening between us. It felt like you needed to hear it."

The streetlight directly above illuminated Lena's eyes, highlighting their blue-green depths, flooding Andy with a surging tide of desire and promises of more kisses to come.

From their very first kiss, Lena had been able to ignite her like this. They were uncontrollable and beautiful fire, dangerous and consuming. Andy would rather die than have the inferno of them extinguished.

Lena took her hand. "We need to get somewhere private or I'm going to resort to something more indecent and lewder than what we did in the car yesterday."

Chapter Twenty

They couldn't get to the house fast enough. Lena was almost pulling her along the sidewalk. Even Billie seemed on a mission to get back home, foregoing all the sniffs and explorations she usually insisted on during their walks.

Andy slowed them several feet from the driveway, gesturing toward a truck parked behind her dad's. "Your dad's here. He usually doesn't come by this late, with my dad usually going to sleep before the sun goes down. We could go in through the back."

Lena considered it for a few seconds before she scoffed. "We're not teenagers sneaking in after curfew. The front's fine, if you think your dad's okay with it. I could give a fuck about what my dad thinks."

Andy absorbed Lena's comment. That and the several references Lena had made about her mother over the last few days, made her wonder what was going on. She made a mental note to ask Lena about it when they didn't have other things on their minds. With the way Lena's hand rested on her ass as they walked up the driveway, she was pretty sure Lena was on the same track. The time for layperson's therapy was over for the night. Her sole mission was to get Lena under her as quickly as possible.

At the bottom of the ramp, a quick glance and a nod made Lena smile. They walked to the far side of the porch, boosting first Billie, and then themselves. "Like old times. Huh?" Lena asked. "If I wanted to keep up with you, vaulting fences and taking shortcuts were a necessity."

Andy kissed her and put a finger to her lips, before pushing Lena ahead of her with a smile. Lena moved with over-the-top tiptoeing across the porch, glancing in through the front window as she went. She abruptly stopped mid-step, gaping through the window. Andy's stomach lurched. She had a good idea what had caused Lena's reaction. As she passed, she peeked over to see Robert lying next to her father watching TV. They held hands, while Robert cuddled against her dad's side. Not as scandalous as the kiss she'd witnessed, and they definitely weren't as comfortable as they probably wanted to be, but it made the everyday intimacy seem more personal.

Lena stared at her, eyes wide. "Holy shit."

"I know, right?" Andy whispered back, feeling guilty about the relief she felt at not carrying the secret alone anymore.

Lena's expression switched to questioning. "Why don't you look fazed?"

"I'm very fazed," she said. "But I saw them doing something similar a few days ago."

"Similar?" Lena whispered.

"There may have been some kissing. And my dad's hands were tangled in your dad's hair."

"Stop." Lena raised a hand. "May have? Or did? Were you even going to tell me?"

"I've been wrestling about telling you. I really have. There's been so much going on. And, well, it hasn't been in the forefront of my mind with our stuff."

Lena relaxed. "There has been a lot of stuff."

She took Andy's hand, stroking the back of it with her thumb. Her eyes had gone soft. Songs had been written about the way Andy felt. How had she been about to stop things between them just fifteen minutes ago?

"So much," she whispered.

Lena glanced at the window, but they couldn't see their fathers from where they stood. "They're still just holding hands, right?" Lena covered her eyes. "I can't look."

"Are you upset about seeing them snuggled up or about what it infers?" Andy asked.

"More like confused, I guess. But both." She sighed. "I don't know why this is such a big deal, honestly. It's not like I even know my father." Lena pushed her hands through her hair which had only been loosely put up and now cascaded over her shoulders. Andy itched to run her fingers through its softness, but she settled on tucking a strand behind her ear. Incidental touches like this were becoming a favorite thing. She wanted to know more about Lena not knowing her dad, but she'd have to come back to it later.

"We should go in. Who knows what they might get up to while we just stand here?"

Lena swatted her arm. "Stop it."

Andy smiled. "Sorry."

Lena grabbed her arm. "What if they're, you know?"

Andy gestured toward the window. "Take a peek, then."

Lena's eyes widened. "And who's gonna pay for my therapy? Hard pass."

Andy stifled a laugh. She guessed Lena was pushing through the shock.

"I suppose we could go back to Seaside."

Lena looked confused. "Aren't they closed this late?"

Andy arched a brow. "I wasn't talking about getting coffee."

Lena swatted her again. "I can't with you."

"Oh? I think you have. A few times."

Lena's eyes took on the look that caused Andy's heart to flutter and her center to ache. "Let's get this over with. I have plans for you."

Andy was ready to barge in, dad drama be damned. "Rock, paper, scissors? Loser checks to make sure they're not kissing, or something else," she said, and Lena held out her fist. "Two out of three."

"Unless I lose. Then it's three out of five." Lena quickly pumped her fist and came out with paper before Andy had a chance to even start. She wrapped her hand around Andy's fist, which wasn't technically a rock yet. "One for me."

"Dirty cheat. You owe me a cookie." It was their penalty when playing board games. The cheater, if caught, gave the other a cookie, which always accompanied board games at Andy's house.

Lena gave her a mischievous look. "I don't have a cookie." Lena grabbed Andy's face and kissed her soundly. Andy returned the kiss with as good as she got, and then some. The game was instantly forgotten when they moved into each other's personal space.

"I love kissing you," Lena said against her mouth and Andy felt it in the back of her knees. Had it been less than an hour since she'd almost called things off? What had she been thinking?

"I love it, too," she said at the same time a crack of light from inside the house shone directly on them. Robert stood in the doorway. Lena took less than a step away from Andy.

"We thought we heard something." He turned his head. "It's just Lena and Andy."

"What are you girls doing on the porch in the dark? Come in here."

❖

Lena threw herself backward onto Andy's bed, remembering almost too late that she wasn't ten years old. She tucked at the last second, before sprawling onto her back, narrowly missing the wall with the crown of her head. "That wasn't weird making small talk with our dads just minutes after seeing them all cuddled up."

"First, that last-minute tuck and roll you just did was impressive," Andy said, looking genuinely awed. "Second, yes. The awkwardness factor was beyond weird." Andy stood by the bed swirling her finger in the air. "Can you do that flinging onto the bed thing again? It was really hot."

"I'm having a minor crisis here." A bolt of heat flared between Lena's legs at the compliment. What was it about Andy Phillips that turned her desire from all the time simmering, to full on boiling even when her world was in a free fall? She held open her arms. "Come here."

Andy immediately dropped onto the bed, curling up with her, tangling their legs together and sliding her hand under the bottom of her T-shirt, letting it rest on her stomach. The casual touch ignited something in Lena that held all the ingredients for something she didn't want to name yet. Not naming it didn't stop her from feeling it, though. How many times had she lain side-by-side on this bed as kids just wanting to be close to Andy? It had always made all the terrible things fade to the background. As if reading her thoughts, Andy wrapped her arm around her waist, rolling them to face one another.

Andy played with the hem of Lena's T-shirt. "I'm sorry I didn't tell you I saw them kissing the other day. I hadn't seen you in a few days, and I didn't have your number yet."

Lena tucked her hands under her cheek and Andy tangled their feet together. The most sublime warmth spread through Lena at the ease and comfort they'd so quickly fallen into with each other. Warm sparkles leaked from her heart.

"And I'm sorry for going radio silent," Lena said. "I needed a little time to process all of this, but I should have told you. I'm not used to anyone wondering where I am or why. But I needed to absorb what we've been doing, and now this thing with our dads is blowing my mind. I saw my dad here sometimes when we were little. But I was only interested in seeing you. It's not like I know my dad, anyway."

"What does that mean?"

"Just that. I don't really know him. It's not that interesting." Andy brushed Lena's hair back and Lena closed her eyes as Andy played with her hair. "That feels nice," she said.

Andy kissed her. "I love how we get to do this."

"Good. Because it's one of my favorite things." Lena kissed her back, lingering. Andy was the best kisser.

After a few minutes of kissing, they pulled away and just looked into each other's eyes, while she combed her fingers though Andy's long dark hair. She was so gorgeous.

"Is there a reason you don't want me to know about you and your dad?"

"It makes me look pathetic." She paused, her eyes flicking from one of Andy's eyes to the other, looking for a response. Andy looked interested, but nothing to indicate she felt sorry for her.

"You'll never look pathetic to me, Lena. You're one of the strongest people I've ever known. Maybe too strong." Andy took her hand, holding it to her lips.

She sighed. If she couldn't tell Andy, who could she tell? And that little bit of introspection was surprising. She'd thought she'd never have someone to confide in since she'd lost Andy.

"I've never known him. He's always been peripheral. I adored him when I was little, but when I realized he chose to be absent from my life, it changed. I'm pretty sure he lives in his office at the store, which is more like a small apartment. He and my mother don't talk or interact."

"Are your parents divorced?"

"I wish. I'm not sure what it would change, but it couldn't make things worse."

"That sounds awful," Andy said.

"See? It's pathetic." Lena turned her face into the pillow her head rested upon.

"Lena, it's not. You aren't your parents. Their actions don't reflect on you." Andy tightened her hold around her pulling her closer. Lena slid her arm around Andy's waist, pressing her face into Andy's chest.

"I've hated him for most of my life, Andy. Seriously hated him. I'm more neutral now." She heard her own voice, and she sounded disconnected now. Like she was telling a story about someone else. "I hate talking about this."

"I'm here whenever you need me," Andy whispered against the top of her head. "This has been an emotional night for you. Do you need a break?"

"I'm just tired of talking about my dysfunctional family."

Andy rolled onto her back, pulling Lena into the arc of her arm. Resting her head on Andy's shoulder was a kind of comfort she'd never imagined.

Chapter Twenty-one

Several minutes of listening to Andy's heartbeat and Lena couldn't help it. She had so many questions, and she was tired of feeling ashamed. If she couldn't talk to Andy, who could she? Right?

"I'm glad I didn't know about our fathers when we were kids. I'm already fucked up. Not that it's all about me, but it scares me to wonder how much more fucked up I'd be now."

"Why's that? Do you think it would have changed the way things went for us?"

Lena was absolutely certain it would have. There were so many ways things could have gone down, from never having become friends to having been born enemies. But the one thing she knew without a doubt was, none of them would have resulted in them being friends. As hard as life after the breakup of their friendship had been, she would rather have gone through it, than never to have had Andy as a friend. Andy was the best thing in her life. As soon as she thought it, the guilt washed over her, as predictable as Old Faithful. Most of the time, she could keep from crying about it but not this time. Not with her head resting on Andy's chest. She'd been so cruel to her. God, she was a mess tonight.

Andy shifted to see her face and wiped away some tears. "Hey. I'm sorry. I shouldn't have asked. We can't change the past. We all have our demons." Andy squeezed her. "But I don't want you to blame yourself for any of it. You had reasons. I didn't respond well. It's okay. We're okay." Andy wrapped both arms around her and kissed her face.

"We'll agree to disagree. Obviously, you've figured out my parents weren't..." Loving. Caring. Engaged. She took a deep breath. "Like other parents. They didn't..." Love me. Talk to me. Notice me. The old fear of Andy knowing how fucked up she was had receded, but the pain and shame hadn't.

So far, Andy hadn't been horrified about what a terrible person she was. At least she didn't show it. She rolled to her back, her side remaining tightly pressed against Andy's. She pulled their clasped hands onto her chest and imagined Andy's strength flowing into her.

"My mom's a fucking bitch," Lena said.

It felt good to say it, regardless of the sticky grossness that came with it. She wasn't sure if it was about the subject matter or about finally acknowledging the abscessed pocket of anger and hurt in her heart her mother had put there. Who knew not feeling all the pressure of hiding it would make her want to talk about it?

Andy, patient and unrelentingly supportive, squeezed her hand giving Lena time. Lena squeezed back, not sure how to express something she hadn't ever talked about, except in fragments with short-lived therapists.

She rolled to face Andy again, and Andy mirrored her pose. Lena pulled Andy's arm around her. It was comforting and safe and intimate. She'd always considered herself a non-cuddler. She'd just never had a person in her bed, let alone life, long enough to relax. With Andy it felt natural.

"Do you want to talk about it? Or did you just need a release?"

Andy's expression displayed nothing but care and curiosity. Lena fought the instant feeling of not deserving it. Andy was just being nice. She shouldn't take up Andy's time. Rejection. All that shit.

Andy gently ran her fingers down the side of her face. Lena couldn't look away from her gentle brown eyes. She'd rather disappear into them than wallow in the childhood pain she should have discarded years ago. After a moment, Andy cupped her jaw.

"You don't have to."

"I…I…" Christ. Was she about to cry again? And why was it so hard? She'd just acknowledged that talking about this wasn't as scary as it once was.

Andy pushed Lena's hair back and traced the outside ridges of her ear. "It's okay. We can just hang out."

Lena took in a shaky breath. "My mother's a bitch." She held her breath for a moment. "She knows about our dads. I didn't realize it until now, but she's hinted about it for as long as I can remember. When she saw us leave for the coffee shop yesterday it set her off." *The apple doesn't fall far from the tree*. "She told me I shouldn't hang out with you, that people would think things. If it continued, she'd come talk to you."

"She's aware we're adults, right?" Andy seemed genuinely curious. Not scared. Not defensive. Scared and defensive were her own instinctive responses. "Tell her she can talk to me. It won't change anything." Andy looked confident, not judgy or critical. Not even angry.

"She's unhinged. I'm thirty years old and I'm still reacting to every word she says, every look she gives me, every look and word she doesn't. She's capable of anything, Andy. She doesn't care about me. She doesn't even see me unless she needs something." Like a can of artichoke hearts or an emotional punching bag. "When she does, I want to hide. It's stupid. And when she says she'll talk to my friends—" She couldn't finish.

"What could she say, though?"

"It's not what she would say, but what people would know when she does."

"Know what?" Andy's voice was gentle.

Lena squeezed her eyes shut, not wanting to be seen. It's Andy, she reminded herself. Andy ran her fingers along her arm. She'd always felt like home, even though Lena had never had a home that felt like this. She pressed closer. "I don't know." Why did she lie? Because saying it aloud was different than thinking it. Saying things planted them in people's minds. Andy said she knew the truth, but what if the truth was what her mother had been saying all along?

"Is it because you never came out to her?" Andy asked.

Lena laughed for the first time in a while. Would this emotional roller coaster ever stop? "That's the least of my worries." *I saw how she was all over you when you were sleeping.* "I used to have nightmares about her going off in front you. But when she said she would do it to you, I panicked. Even as an adult, all she has to do is look at me like she did today. I couldn't bear it if she did it to you."

"She did it today? And you were worried about me?" Andy held her and she melted into it. "No wonder you were upset earlier."

"It was the last thing I ever wanted you to know." Lena should have been supporting Andy. She'd acted heartless, bullied her, and made her life miserable. But Andy held her closer.

Andy gently placed her fingers under Lena's chin, guiding Lena to look at her, before kissing her and wiping away her tears.

It was probably the most inappropriate of times, but Lena wanted her so badly. Her inner voice asked if it was really desire, or her body's stress response subconsciously trying to distract her. Probably both. Either way, she wanted her. She rolled onto her back to clear her head. She held Andy's hand, pulling it to her chest, needing the physical connection.

Andy stared fixedly at her. "Nothing she could tell me could change what I know about you. Nothing."

So much time wasted. "But it's like her eyes paralyze you. You can't think. All you can do is try to not set her off or make it worse." Lena felt stupid admitting to it.

Andy's brow was furrowed like so many times in their past when Lena caught her watching her from a distance. As if Andy was trying to predict the next move.

"What sets her off?"

Lena tried not to squirm. Andy still read her better than anyone she knew. Sometimes she saw things Lena didn't even see herself. She didn't have to answer. Andy would never force her. But Andy wasn't going to walk away when her ugly showed. "I have no idea most of the time. She's usually already mad when she comes into my room. Probably because she has no one else to take it out on. She tells me how I ruin everything. Wishes I didn't exist. How unlovable I am. I push my dad away. That's my biggest crime. At least it's the one she falls to the most." She paused. "It's embarrassing to hear myself say all that. I know she's just trying to hurt me. I tell myself I should be numb to it by now. But I'm not. Today, I just stood there while she…I just stood there."

She had a hard time watching the parade of expressions that washed across Andy's face.

"Those things you listed? She's listing her own faults, you know. They aren't yours. You make things better. You're a bright star in this universe. You're an amazing human, Lena. You aren't any of those things your mother says."

She wanted to believe she was the person Andy thought she was. "But, Andy. I am."

Andy shook her head. "No."

"Believe me. I wish I was. Most of the time I think I am. But I ruined us. I worry I might do it again. I don't want to. But I still worry. Maybe I'm subconsciously doing it now, by telling you all this." She paused, unable to get a full breath. She shook like she was cold. But she wasn't. "I can't maintain friendships and don't get me started on dating. I've run from every job I've had, and any woman who wanted more than sex." God, had she really said that? "My mother wishes I didn't exist. It's true, she does. My dad might have thought differently at one time, but he avoids me now. At best, I'm a reminder of all the things they couldn't have. Which makes me unlovable. They…they don't love me." Why did her voice have to crack right then? And was she going to cry? Again? Fuck. "I pushed my dad away. I did. I told him I hated him, and he stopped coming home. I go years without talking to him. Tonight was the third time I've seen him since I've been here. I'm all the things she says I am." She struggled to catch her breath. "What happens when you eventually see it? I mean, the things I did to you. I didn't want her to hurt you, so I did it instead. I was mean. I turned my back on you. I pushed you away. I made your life miserable for years. My mother was at least partially right. She accused me of doing things she did. But I did some of them, too. I'm just like her. Maybe I don't corner little kids and traumatize them, but I inflict my traumas on other people. So, tell me. How am I any different?"

"But—"

Lena shook her head. She had to say it all. She probably wouldn't be able to later. "Even worse, I told myself I was protecting you when I was protecting myself." Lena wanted to throw up. "Her words get into my head. I try to fight them, but sometimes I can't hold them back."

"You were just a kid, Lena." Andy sounded so earnest. "She's the one to blame."

"I know what she does is abusive and wrong. I might have been ten, but I knew what I was doing, Andy." Her entire body turned rigid in anticipation of Andy withdrawing. It made every muscle ache.

"Do you think you'd do the same thing now?" Andy asked.

Lena searched Andy's eyes, looking for the recrimination. "I don't have the strength to push you away. I'm telling you who I really am because I'm a coward. You'll see I don't deserve you. You'll do it to me."

"I mean this is in the nicest of ways, Lena, but you need to do something about that rectal cranial inversion problem of yours."

What did that mean? It was so random, she couldn't even understand the words.

"What?"

Andy sat up, so Lena did, too. "You don't deserve someone like me? Isn't that for me to decide? I didn't leave when we were at our worst. Why would I do it now?" Andy sounded angry. Lena hadn't heard that since around junior year. "And I'll remind you again. You were ten years old, for fuck's sake." Andy pronounced each word slowly to make her point. "Ten." Her eyes were intense and dark, and Lena was a little intimidated.

"But—"

"No." Andy shook her head insistently. "You don't get to tell me we went through everything for no reason. It was all your mother." Andy looked like she tasted something rancid. Her eyes glimmered with tears that didn't fall. "Like you said, she's unhinged." She huffed. The action so like the younger Andy, Lena's chest ached. "I wish I'd known." Andy said the last almost to herself.

"But I'm just like her." Lena needed Andy to see it.

Andy rolled her eyes. Lena didn't know you could do it angrily. "You were just a kid, Lena. I don't have to be a psychologist to know that at ten years old your behavior is influenced by the adults around you. Do you see? She indoctrinated you with lies about yourself. She controlled you by fear. A ten-year-old wouldn't think they had a choice. No one deserves that." Andy shook her head. "You were brainwashed. It wasn't your decision."

"But I did it because I didn't want her to tell you who I really am."

"Self-preservation isn't a bad thing, Lena. In fact, most people couldn't consider anything beyond that. You did. And let's not forget you said it yourself. At the time, you thought you were protecting me. It wasn't until later that you saw how it may have been to protect yourself, too. You can think two things at the same time, Lena. I didn't stick with us because you were mean. I stuck with us because I knew you weren't. I couldn't have left if I wanted to."

"Maybe—"

"Lena, no. You're trying to hurt yourself for some reason. I won't let you. Earlier tonight, when we were walking, you asked me questions about dating. Do you remember?"

The question was a strange transition. She nodded slowly. "I do."

"You'd just put together that I've never seen the same person more than once before you."

"I remember," she said.

"You paused when I answered. I was afraid you'd just realized how broken I am and not want to deal with it. Or you'd think I was a player or something. Either way, I thought I'd triggered some sort of threshold for you, and you were about to stop things between us."

"What threshold?"

"It was irrational, I know. But you kissed me to shut me up, and you stopped the spiral."

Lena wasn't convinced that Andy's logic was accurate, but she wanted to believe her.

"The thing was, when I thought you were getting ready to cut things off, I had the uncontrollable urge to do it first."

"No." She didn't think before it erupted from her.

Andy looked at her. "No?"

Lena searched Andy's eyes. "Yeah. No. I won't and you can't."

Andy exhaled. "The thing is, I know it wasn't rational, but the fear was real." Andy took her hand. "Tonight I very nearly did what you did in fifth grade. It was a kneejerk reaction. I'm an adult and I nearly did it. You were just a kid, with no one in your corner."

"I had you."

Andy nodded. "And your mom made it so I couldn't be there for you. The path was set for you, and you couldn't see it. Because you were a kid."

She had no illusions of this being the last of this, but she finally saw why her therapists had told her to give herself grace. Having Andy on her side changed things, too.

❖

Andy pulled the blanket over them. They'd talked about a lot this evening. It seemed every day with Lena was an obstacle course, with an onslaught of emotions being launched at them while they navigated the terrain of what came next. After their talk, neither of them had much energy, and Andy had shifted them under the covers, where exhaustion fell over them. It covered her like a weighted blanket, both comfortable and restrictive, reminding her of how she'd felt after purging her emotions into her journals as a kid.

They still wore the clothes from the day, and they clung to each other, tangled. She'd never felt closer or more connected to another person than she did right now. She kissed the top of Lena's head, closing her eyes, and breathing in her scent.

"I love you, Lena Grace Holmes. I always have and I always will," she whispered into her hair.

For the first time in as long as she could remember, Andy didn't have dreams about longing for something she couldn't find.

Chapter Twenty-two

Moonlight filtered in through the blinds when Lena returned to Andy's bed after a visit to the bathroom. She gently lifted Andy's arm to reclaim the space she'd occupied for the first half of the night. Her entire body relaxed into Andy, and she wondered how she ever fell asleep without her beside her.

"I missed you," Andy mumbled as she pulled her close. She couldn't remember a time in her life when she'd been held like this. Like she mattered. Like she was wanted. She floated in the deep contentment of being wrapped in Andy's arms, overcome by an emotion she was afraid to name. It filled a space deep inside herself she'd always known was empty, giving her a sense of wholeness she hadn't known was possible. The barest sliver of anxiety slipped in knowing that now that she knew what it felt to have it, she'd be devastated if she lost it. But she refused to let the threat of something that hadn't happened yet ruin the perfect moment. Instead, she savored the moment.

Andy shifted slightly, further entwining their legs, and in the process, positioning her thigh more firmly against her center. The low thrum of arousal she always felt when she touched Andy intensified, coursing through her. Andy's lips rested against her forehead, her soft breaths warming her skin. Gentle fingers traced circles on her back. The two of them lying comfortably together like they'd done it a million times. Lena could easily get used to this. When the voice in the dark corners of her mind tried to tell her their time together was temporary, she shushed it, and it receded so quickly she could almost believe it was gone.

"Hey you." Andy's voice was quiet. Her lips against Lena's forehead barely moved, as if she didn't want to disturb anything. They sent a delicious tingle through every nerve ending in Lena's body. She shifted the arm she had resting across Andy's waist to slide her hand under Andy's T-shirt, laying it flat on the soft, warm skin of her back.

"Hey back," she whispered against Andy's chest. Memories of the night before drifted through her mind. She'd confessed her darkest secrets and Andy hadn't pulled away, healing something inside her.

Fully awake now, she propped herself on her elbow. Moving Andy's thick hair back and over her shoulder, she nestled her hand on the soft curve below Andy's ear, brushing a brief, soft kiss upon her lips. When she pulled back, she met Andy's eyes, half-lidded and dark in the soft glow of the moonlight. The pulse in Andy's neck beat rapidly against her palm. Lena took in the soft contours of her beautiful face, openly admiring her, no longer self-conscious about her appreciation. She lowered her lips again to Andy's, this time taking their kiss deeper, savoring the dreamy soft warmth of Andy's body. She took her time enjoying the gentle pleasure running through her. There had been a few times in the last few days when she'd wondered if it was just a dream, being allowed to kiss Andy in ways she'd only ever fantasized about, and in some ways, she'd never imagined. The thought made electric sparks skip across every nerve, leaving her breathless and wanting.

Lena paused the kiss, raising to find Andy's expressive eyes already on her. She fell into them, her desire mixed with tenderness. She wanted Andy completely. Not just her body, mind, and heart. She wanted her future. The admission slammed into her. The voice returned. *The winds are coming. Run before you give your heart away.*

Instead of pushing the voice away or giving in to the panic, she acknowledged that she'd already given her heart to Andy. If she ran now, she'd leave it behind. The sound of the wind never came, and the voice again retreated, taking with it the accompanying fear. She wanted this. She wanted Andy. Her next kiss would be a promise. She swung her leg over Andy, straddled her hips, and paused to make sure Andy knew the significance of the promise she was about to give. When their lips met again, Lena absorbed the power of Andy's response. Andy wrapped her arms around her, pulling her into a possessive embrace. Lena's body, her very essence, felt their connection, eternal and unbreakable.

❖

When a narrow beam of sunlight moved over Lena's closed eyes, waking her from a peaceful sleep, she threw an arm over her face, grinning. She knew exactly where she was, and it was where she was meant to be. She'd woken up at Andy's house many times before, but this was different. The bed was much smaller with their grownup bodies lying in it, and she was naked. Her body was also tired and sore, having shared another night of emotionally charged sex. She reached for Andy, but found herself alone.

Confused, she slowly sat up, sitting on the edge of the bed.

On the bedside table, a piece of paper was tented with a note scrawled in Andy's barely legible handwriting saying she'd left to teach a swim class, and she'd be back at seven forty-five. How did Andy have the energy after the night they'd had? Remembering, Lena smiled.

It was seven forty, and she'd have been long gone by now. But this wasn't a hookup. She picked up her bra. Memories of Andy humming with pleasure when Lena had taken it off shot desire through her. Andy's tender kisses, her whispered endearments, and the reverence in which she touched her, were so much more than what she'd limited herself to with other women. This was something she'd invested her heart in nearly twenty-five years ago. She felt the opposite of wanting to leave.

She tossed her clothing onto the desk chair and glanced in the long mirror hanging on the back of the bedroom door. Her hair was a mess, and she wouldn't be caught dead in front of a camera, but other than that, she didn't think she looked too bad. Despite the very little sleep they'd had, she looked energized and happy. She ran her fingers through her hair. Her body thrummed with anticipation despite how many times Andy had sated it. And still, she wanted more.

After straightening the dislodged and messy bedding, she turned when the door opened. True to her word, down to the exact minute, Andy was back, along with a travel tray with two coffees and a white bag with the Seaside Café logo on it. Lena would kiss her if it held a twice-baked croissant. Who was she kidding? She'd kiss her even if it wasn't. She'd do a lot more for the smile Andy was already giving her.

Hair still damp, Andy glowed with post-exercise energy. She was gorgeous. But then again, she always had been. Lena's stomach flipped.

"I had ideas of kissing you awake. But this defies words." Andy's gaze roamed Lena's naked body, her voice low and breathy. "No words." She stepped closer, leaving the distance of one drink tray between them.

The stomach flipping thing was a new occurrence for Lena, and Andy caused it often. Lena's heart raced and lightness infused her. Part of it was waking up at Andy's, but she knew some of it was the talk the night before which seemed to have slayed a few demons.

She took the tray, set it aside, and closed the distance between them. She put her hands on Andy's waist. She slipped her hands under the back hem of her T-shirt and flattened them on the warm, soft skin underneath. Her palms absorbed the energy that always flowed between them. She'd never get tired of the way it rose through her arms, radiating through her body.

Pressing close, she slid her nose along Andy's neck. Not kissing her yet but letting her know she planned to. "You're a little overdressed," she said next to her ear, lifting the T-shirt over Andy's head. As soon as Andy was naked, she pulled her close, craving the slide of their skin together while she kissed her. She went slowly at first, but faster as her desire grew. Unable to wait any longer, she spun them around and gently pushed Andy onto the bed. Lena used her knee to open Andy's legs, needing to see more of her.

"Impatient?" Andy asked, spreading her legs wider.

"Shhh, I need to focus," Lena said, pressing a finger to Andy's lips, before drawing it slowly, intentionally down her body as she dropped to her knees on the floor between Andy's legs. Both of Lena's hands rested on her stomach now. Andy's breaths came faster against her palms, and Lena lingered there for a moment enjoying the power of her touch. Sliding her hands apart she reached up, cupping Andy's breasts, stopping to tease her nipples, which elicited a hiss from Andy. She slid her hands slowly down Andy's body, enjoying the way Andy's stomach tensed at every move. When Lena's palms reached the slightly rounded area below Andy's belly button, she diverted their paths, gliding them over each hip to continue the journey down Andy's thighs.

Lena looked up to see Andy propped on her elbows, her eyes dark and intense, watching every move she made. Lena's center clenched. She leaned into Andy, pressing her breasts into Andy's wet center. A moan escaped her and elicited an intake of breath from Andy. She dipped her head, placing delicate kisses on Andy's lower body, causing Andy to press into her. The heat and softness turned her on more than she ever would have imagined, and she rubbed against her, while drawing her hands down Andy's thighs, until they came to a rest on her knees. She slid her hands to the underside of Andy's thighs and gently stroked the back of Andy's knees, an area she'd learned increased Andy's arousal. To prove her point, Andy released a quiet hum. Lena continued to draw abstract lines under Andy's thighs as she pressed her cheek against

Lena's abdomen, nuzzling into the velvety smoothness, before she lifted her head, shaking her head gently, causing her hair to hang with the ends barely touching Andy's skin. Watching Andy's eyes, she trailed her cheek along Andy's abdomen, enjoying her quiet moans. Until Andy, Lena's body had never responded to the sounds of a woman simply enjoying touch, but the rolling pulses deep inside her grew stronger with each sound Andy uttered.

"God, that feels good. You're killing me," Andy whispered hoarsely.

She licked a trail along the top of Andy's trimmed hair. "I don't want to kill you, Andy. But I do want to make you see God," she said against the skin. She kissed a path toward her glistening folds, stopping centimeters away, nipping and licking the sensitive skin at the crease of her thighs.

"Lena." Andy moaned.

The temptation to finally taste Andy was almost overpowering. Andy's hips rose while Lena slid her tongue toward where Andy wanted her. When Lena caught Andy's gaze, the sight of Andy propped on one elbow, caused Lena to moan. She pulled Andy's legs onto her shoulders, then lowered her head and ran her tongue up Andy.

"You taste so good," Lena said. "I knew you would."

Andy rolled her lips into her mouth, uttering a long "mmmm…" while Lena held Andy's gaze, watching a progression of raw passion, vulnerability, and pleasure cross her beautiful face. She licked up one side of her opening and then the other, dipping her tongue in, watching Andy intently. When she gently sucked on her folds, Andy dropped her head back.

"Yes." Andy dragged out the word. Lena repeated what she'd done, only slower, exploring to discover what Andy liked.

The view from where Lena knelt took her breath away. Andy's beautiful body, the underside of her defined jaw, watching her breasts heave at every deep breath, the planes of her stomach rippling, all of it caused a powerful pulse to sweep through Lena's core. She coated Lena's lips and chin, spiraling her desire. Andy's legs trembled while Lena explored every inch around Andy's opening without touching her clit. Lena's arms encircled Andy's legs, holding Andy's hips down to keep her mouth, especially her tongue, where she wanted it.

"Lena. Please." Andy's voice was strained.

Lena pulled back, needing to see Andy's face.

"Who's impatient, now?" She dipped her head back to Andy's swollen and pulsing center. Excitement expanded in her stomach knowing Andy would soon fall over the edge into explosive pleasure. She made a long swipe up Andy's pulsing folds, taking it longer and slower to feel Andy's rise toward orgasm. She stopped just before she got to Andy's clit, where she applied more pressure with her tongue, sliding slowly, teasingly toward it.

"God, yes," Andy whispered hoarsely. "I—I want—"

Lena licked with a pointed tongue around it in a circle. Once. Twice. Three times.

"God, that's good, Lena. I'm so ready. Don't make me beg."

Lena raised her eyebrows but didn't give Andy what she wanted yet. Instead, she slid her tongue down and flattened it before dragging it slowly up Andy's dripping heat once again.

"Fuck. Lena. I need you." Andy spoke through clenched teeth, and Lena had to fight to keep Andy's hips from bucking as she teased her. "Please," Andy begged, but Lena continued up, dipping deeper into Andy's heat along the way, and just as she was almost at Andy's clit, she brought her hand around, slipping two fingers into Andy as she placed her tongue directly on it and pursed her lips, alternately sucking and flicking her tongue.

"Lena. That's...I'm...yes..." Andy's eyebrows lifted, and she held Lena's gaze as she bit her lower lip and shuddered against Lena's face. Her hips were too strong to hold down, and Lena worked to keep her mouth where Andy needed it, while keeping the rhythm of her fingers inside her. She rode Andy's orgasm until Andy finally closed her eyes, breathing hard, and falling back onto the bed. Lena stilled her mouth and fingers, relishing the waning pulses. When Andy's breaths became steadier, she lifted her head, gently withdrawing her fingers. She kissed Andy's inner thighs and carefully lowered her legs.

"Oh, my fucking God, Lena. What did you just do to me?"

Reluctantly leaving her position between Andy's legs, Lena wiped her mouth and chin with her hand before standing up. She'd always thought the mouth wiping thing was a comedic gesture, but now she knew differently. She crawled onto the bed and snuggled against Andy, trailing her hand over Andy's body.

"Whatever do you mean?" she asked innocently, batting her lashes.

"I'm pretty sure you made me astral project."

Lena glowed at the compliment. "Astral projection is unlikely, but a wormhole maybe?"

"Either way, I can't feel my legs."

"Is that a good thing or a bad thing?" Lena asked.

"A very, very good thing." Andy pulled her close and kissed her deeply. "I should have asked you to do that days ago."

"Not bad for a beginner, I guess." Lena kissed her hoping it would distract her from her admission. It almost worked, but Andy stopped mid-kiss.

"What did you say about being a beginner?"

Lena buried her face into Andy's neck. "I've never done that before."

"Make someone astral project?" Andy tried to get her to raise her head, but she kept her face pressed into the angle of Andy's shoulder and neck.

"Go down on someone," Lena mumbled, heat blasting from her face.

"That's a lie."

"It's one hundred percent true." When Andy didn't answer, she pulled back seeing the disbelief on Andy's face. Maybe she shouldn't have said anything. "It's so intimate. I never knew anyone well enough to want to."

"But you let me..." Andy didn't finish.

"I'd do anything with you, Andy. I love everything you do to me, and I've been dying to do it to you." Lena watched Andy's pupils dilate. Her stomach flipped thinking about Andy's mouth on her.

Andy studied Lena's face, pushing a strand of hair behind her ear before she gave her a gentle kiss. "I'd do anything with you, too. To you. By you. With you. So much. I don't want to do any of it with anyone else." She paused. "With you, I feel things I've never felt before."

Lena's throat was tight. She swallowed hard. "No one else has affected me like you. I thought I'd never feel it again." She wished she'd said this last night. Andy had described herself as broken. She could have told her she wasn't alone. "You're not the only one who's felt broken, like a piece was missing. I've felt it since fifth grade." Lena tried to smile, but she wanted to cry. She was caught between two very strong emotions, and her face didn't know how to respond. Andy cradled it and Lena kissed her palms.

"Lena, why…"

"There have been no sleepovers. I can't bring myself to kiss anyone. I've tried to want them. But I don't. I go out sometimes. But I usually go home alone. If I go out looking at it as a hookup, that it's only about the orgasm, I can disconnect and if it makes it to the bedroom, I can usually get there. But afterward, I feel so lonely. I can count on one hand how many people I've been with and not one has even really touched me. Not in a way that counts. I don't even think about them when we're in bed. It's why it doesn't bother me how many women you've been with. You haven't given your heart to anyone, which is the only thing I care about. Not that I have any right to claim it."

"You don't have to. It's always been yours." Andy's eyes were unbelievably soft. "And for the record, I don't think about the women I'm with either. I don't think most of them are thinking about me either."

"What do you think about?" Lena wished she hadn't asked. She didn't want Andy to ask her either.

Andy searched her eyes. "Would you be disappointed if I said it wasn't you?"

Surprised by her relief, Lena shook her head. "I can't stand to have someone else touch me while I think of you. By myself, there's no one else but you. Most of the time I can't bear that, either. I try not to think about you at all. It's too confusing and painful."

"Same." Andy sounded sad.

Lena ran the tips of her fingers along Andy's high cheekbone, before tracing her lips.

"You know what, though?"

When Andy shook her head, Lena leaned in. "I fucking love that I get to think about you in either situation now."

Andy's eyes lit up and her hands ran up and down Lena's sides, making her shiver. "Both situations?"

"When I'm having sex with you or by myself." She closed her eyes and moaned softly.

Andy pressed against her, rolling her onto her back, her body covering Lena's. "Do you know how much I love the way you taste when you come?"

Lena's arousal flared at Andy's words. "I know you taste like sunshine when you do," she said quietly.

Andy's brow raised. "What does sunshine taste like?"

"Like sparks and wild honey."

"Wild honey?"

Lena sighed contentedly. "You'd know it if you tasted it."

Andy dropped to her elbows, one on each side of Lena's head, her long hair curtaining their faces. She kissed her deeply while she slowly rubbed herself against Lena's leg.

"Mmm. I taste like the pool," Andy said against her lips before she went in for another kiss. "And desire." She kissed her again. "Your mouth." Another kiss. "And impatience." Her mouth was like fire on Lena's lips. Andy pushed her onto her back. "I'm ready to taste your sunshine now."

Lena's sex clenched. She already imagined Andy's mouth on her, enjoying Andy's hot center sliding along her thigh. "Don't take your time. You guessed that impatience part correctly. I want you to make me come so I can do it to you again."

"I like that plan," Andy said as she kissed a trail down Lena's body. "I wasn't just saying it, you know."

"Saying what?" Lena was confused, but the trail of fire Andy left with her mouth was leaving her in a daze.

Andy looked up at her from between her legs. "You've always had my heart."

Lena's breath left her at Andy's words.

Being able to see into someone's soul had never been an idiom Lena had ascribed to. She accepted it as an overly sentimental, sappy poet kind of thing, but not real life. Oh, but she was wrong. Andy's eyes showed her the deepest parts of her when she looked at her like that.

Chapter Twenty-three

Stroking Billie sleeping in her lap, Andy gazed out over the beach from a table at Seaside. It was her favorite place in Oceanside, aside from her bed when Lena was in it. It reminded her of them. Today, she barely registered any of it.

Feelings for Lena consumed Andy, growing stronger by the day. Everything in her wanted to tell Lena how she felt, how she couldn't imagine a day without her. How she'd gone from a life she'd thought was happy and mostly full, to one that made it seem flat and colorless in comparison. Since she'd told Lena she'd always had her heart, she felt it beating in both their chests, steady and strong. Happiness had her floating through her days, and Lena was right there with her, beautiful and irresistible, spending most of her time at Andy's, where they parked out at the table near the pool while she worked remotely for the lab and Lena recorded and edited content for her channels.

Yet a hitchhiker of anxiety sat shotgun next to Andy's euphoria.

Every day, and against her better judgment, she fell deeper and deeper for Lena. She'd loved her most of her life, even when she'd sworn she'd hated her. But she never thought she'd see her again, so she'd tossed away the defenses she'd built during their war, thinking she wouldn't need them anymore. But Lena had breached her walls and was now living in her heart. Not only did she not want to make her leave, but she also wanted to make plans. Her feet hadn't felt firmly planted on the ground since Lena reentered her life and she loved it. But did Lena?

They had no plans and hadn't brought up the future. Hope was a heartbreak waiting to happen and Andy had long ago learned not to hope. Instead, she turned to science where control was the baseline. Hope had no place there. She researched probabilities, predicted outcomes, and followed guidance. Regarding Lena Holmes, probabilities had always been stacked against them leaving few positive outcomes. There was no guidance to follow and introducing hope into it would skew the results. All of it held true today.

It was hard to remain optimistic, but she reminded herself of the things that were going favorably, like how her dad was healing quickly. And her request to transfer to San Diego had been approved. Knowing her dad wasn't living a solitary bachelor life made her unaccountably happy.

She'd brought some of this up with Lena the day before when they'd taken their coffee down to the beach and she'd mentioned how happy their dads seemed. When Lena's eyes had welled up, she'd been confused.

"Why are you sad about our gay fathers being happy together?" she'd joked to lighten her mood.

Lena had smirked. "You know they'd be horrified to hear you say that."

"Would they? They seem happy, but since they don't talk about anything personal, I can only guess."

"Are we any different?" Lena asked, unaware that Andy had been asking herself the same thing since she'd discovered the depth of her emotions for Lena.

She tossed her head, ignoring the weight of the question. "Don't conflate my pettiness with actual evidence. I'm having a moment over here."

Lena had snuggled into her. "I just wish my dad didn't have to hide. My mother's a monster to make him stay. She loves Lourdes more than him. Or me." Her bitterness showed up any time she mentioned her mother, and Andy had silently seethed at what her mother had put Lena through.

"Who's Lourdes?" Lena asked.

"I haven't mentioned her?" Lena looked curious. "She's my mother's dog. Seven pounds of pure terror, but we've developed a bond. Unfortunately, I think my mother's punishing her for it. I haven't seen her holding Lourdes the few times I've been there lately. I'm going to miss her when I leave. Lourdes, not my mother." Lena was quick to add the last.

The reminder that Lena would eventually leave had been sobering. She didn't ask about it, and Lena didn't bring it up. She knew Lena was looking for jobs, but she didn't know where. It was this huge gaping hole in the middle of the road, and she was pedal to the metal, singing along with the radio, holding her hands over her eyes.

She'd purposely avoided thinking about Lena leaving, but ignoring it wasn't a solution. She didn't even know what Lena wanted, and she was afraid to ask, telling herself she didn't want to pressure her. It wasn't altruistic, either. It was selfish. Pressure was a trigger for Lena. Pressure from her mother had caused her to end their friendship, and pressure to run came from the derecho when things grew uncomfortable. Andy didn't want to be the cause that triggered Lena to withdraw.

On top of everything, their history had left them both with scars. They hadn't been tested yet. How could either of them feel confident that one or the other had what it took to stick through a rough patch? The odds leaned heavily against them.

Arms wrapped around her from behind, interrupting her gloomy thoughts. The electric happiness she felt when Lena touched her sizzled through her. Holding Lena's hands to her, she swiveled to give her a kiss before standing for a proper hug. After their first time together, Lena had started holding on longer and adding a kiss that always made Andy's blood race.

"I swear Billie sleeps more than Rip VanWinkle," Lena said, sitting and looking under the table at the sleeping dog. When she sat back, her eyes traveled over Andy as she reached for the coffee Andy had already ordered. Andy loved how Lena always seemed to take her in after any time apart.

"She was awake for a good half hour this morning. Being my dad's watchdog is exhausting."

"I think those two have fallen in love," Lena said.

Andy wanted to ask if the same applied to them. The idea both terrified and electrified her, because she knew where her heart stood but had no idea how Lena felt.

Resting her arms on the table, Lena cradled her cup in both hands. "I have news."

"Is it the reason for your effervescence?" Andy couldn't wait to tell Lena her news, too. Transferring to San Diego didn't mean a lot with Lena almost certain to leave, but even if Lena was offered a job today, they'd likely have a few weeks. Not nearly long enough, but she could start preparing for the inevitable.

Lena tilted her head. "First, no one has ever called me that, and second, the cause of my effervescence is sitting across from me."

Andy felt her own effervescence dance in her stomach. "I like knowing I'm your first and the cause of at least a part of your visible happiness."

Lena maintained her head tilt and added a soft smile. Andy loved when she looked at her like that. "You've been my first in a lot of ways," Lena said.

The breath Andy had just taken hitched, and all the feelings she couldn't express hung from her lips. Before they fell out, she mirrored Lena's head tilt. "What's your news?"

"My old producer offered my job back."

Andy's stomach lurched, while she struggled to maintain her smile. All the bubbles went flat. "Is that what you want?"

Lena waved her hand. "I needed the ego boost, to be honest. Turns out they got rid of that asshole Lance. It's more money, plus they'd sponsor my streaming channels."

"You seem happy about it, which makes me happy." It wasn't completely true, but she wouldn't dampen Lena's excitement.

Lena played with the top of her coffee cup. "I think I need to move on, though."

Andy hoped she meant from her old job. "Are you going to turn it down and wait for a better offer?"

Lena gave her a wide smile. "I already have one. Well, an interview, but that's as good as an offer in my experience. I fly to Denver tomorrow for an interview."

Shame washed over Andy at the anger that flared in her. Irrationally, she'd envisioned they'd have more time before this was supposed to be a thing. Her stomach rejected the coffee. She wasn't ready. She was never going to be ready. Tears stung the back of her eyes.

"That soon?" The words felt like dry cotton in her throat. She couldn't hear if her voice was normal over the rushing of blood in her ears, so she reinforced her smile. This had to be a relief for Lena. She just wished she didn't seem so enthusiastic. "I'll keep my fingers crossed for you."

"My agent said they were talking like I already had it."

"Why wouldn't they? You're the total package."

"I think you might be biased." Lena intertwined their fingers. Andy didn't know how much she needed the touch. Why did it feel like Lena was already boarding the plane?

"One hundred percent biased." Andy's cheeks were tired from making her face smile.

"Know what I'm gonna miss?" Lena paused, searching Andy's eyes.

Me, Andy said silently. Say me. Andy tried to ignore the dejection swamping her, focusing, instead, on Lena's good fortune. "Ecuadorian drip coffee from here, of course."

"That, too." Lena nodded, looking very serious. "But I love your little bed," she said just as seriously. "We've made some amazing memories in it. Never get rid of it."

"Wanna go make some more?" Andy asked. Her news could wait. She needed to be close to Lena. To feel their connection. Her heart was breaking, and she needed to feel it beating in Lena's chest before Lena took it with her again.

Lena stood up so quickly she nearly spilled their coffee. "That's the best offer I've had all day." Lena held out her hand.

"You need to get over this indecisiveness of yours," Andy said, gathering up Billie. Every minute counted right now.

❖

Lying in her favorite lounger next to her parents' pool, Lena thought for the hundredth time about how close she'd come to telling Andy she loved her this morning. All casual and glib, too, when there was nothing casual nor glib about what she felt for Andy. Her feelings ran as hot as a supernova, more expansive than a universe, and more beautiful than a nebula. There was a song in there, she was sure. She recalled the pop and thump she'd felt when she first saw her again, in front of her father's store. Looking back, she knew it was the love she'd always had for Andy escaping the vault she'd stored it in.

Although she'd been forced to hide it for most of her life, it was the one thing she could count on. It sustained her when it seemed she had nothing else. In the moments when she was afraid it would show itself, she'd been at her worst. Acting just like her mother, she thought, looking for chinks in Andy's armor to drive her snide comments in like daggers of dangerous truths turned against her. She still carried the shame of it. Sometimes, she wondered how Andy had been able to remain mostly unreactive in those moments. The time she'd tripped her in the cafeteria was probably the worst thing she'd ever done. It was also the only time their feud had gotten physical. Immediately regretting it, she'd flown to Andy, screaming for help. Her behavior had sent Andy to the emergency room, yet Andy had never told anyone. She'd told everybody she'd tripped. Lena cringed in self-hatred just thinking about it.

The thing was, Andy had loved her when Lena didn't think anyone could. Andy had never told her, but she'd shown her in countless ways, despite her parents proving time and again, that she didn't deserve it. Andy had been relentless, though. She'd shown it in her restraint at reacting to Lena's actions toward her and she'd demonstrated it by respecting Lena's boundaries yet never quite leaving her orbit. Even when Lena had been at her worst. And for a long time, she'd agreed with her mother and had actively tried to force Andy away. But deep down, she suspected it wasn't because her mother was right, but because she didn't love herself. It was only when Andy had come back into her life, and Lena had seen that Andy truly believed that her unhinged mother was wrong about her being unlovable, that she'd been open to explore the possibility that she wasn't as horrible as she'd been told. Lena knew Andy loved her even if she hadn't told her. Lena had always been able to read Andy. She wondered if Andy could read her, too. Did she know she loved her just as much?

It was because she could read Andy that she knew she was just being supportive about the interview. As excited as she was at the job prospect, Lena was torn. She didn't want to end this thing between her and Andy. She'd known they'd eventually have to go back to their lives, but she'd pushed it to the side, refusing to acknowledge it. And while it was in no way a done deal, she had a pretty good chance of being offered the Denver job. She hadn't prepared herself. How could she? And it was killing her. Her lungs burned when she thought about drowning in the tears sure to come. But what options did they have? Andy had to go back to Monterey, and she had to move to where the job was. Aside from ending things, it came down to two possibilities: either they attempted a long-distance thing or Andy asked her to stay. She would do either if it meant keeping Andy in her life. She wasn't sure the first was sustainable, but she'd try. And Andy hadn't asked. The only thing she knew for certain was she wouldn't run.

Chapter Twenty-four

Hey, Dad." Lena thought she'd misread the caller ID when she picked up her phone. Had something happened?

"Hey, daughter. How's Denver treating you? Settling in okay?" He sounded normal, but did she know what his normal was?

Was five days enough time to settle in? She was still in company lodging and hadn't had time to start looking for something more permanent. Living in a hotel room had its perks, but it was already starting to get old.

Her agent had told her she basically had the job when they invited her to Denver, that the interview was just a formality. But she hadn't expected the offer the same day. Or that they'd need her to start immediately. Or that she'd be doing the work of two anchors at first because two jobs had opened up when the morning and evening weather anchors had been fired after a video of them having relations on the news desk between broadcasts went viral on a prominent pay-to-play video site. They'd worn masks, but the set was distinctive, and they hadn't changed wardrobe from what they'd worn on air that day. She'd been assured the Denver 5280 news and weather sets had been completely revamped.

She'd had no idea that she'd be torn in two when she'd told her agent she didn't care where her next job was. That was when she'd pulled out of the station parking lot in Phoenix several weeks ago.

She kicked herself daily for not having the courage to tell Andy she'd move to Monterey with her if she asked. Now she wondered when she'd stop crying herself to sleep every night, thinking how she should have memorized every detail of their last night, their last touch, and their last kiss. Because she didn't know when she'd see Andy next. But the worst thing of all was how her heart hurt every second of every day, knowing Andy had been committed to being outwardly supportive, while obviously dying inside all the way until they said goodbye at the airport. Lena was an expert at watching Andy hold in her pain over the years, attempting to appear disaffected as Lena inflicted cut after cut. She wondered if Andy could see her breaking, too.

"As settled as I can be, I guess. I'm at the hotel trying to decide if I want to order dinner or just have a glass of wine before bed."

"Why not both?"

"Good point." Small talk with her dad was still so weird.

"I'll bet you miss your girl." The statement shocked her.

"Yeah." She could barely get it out. "She says she's working too much."

"I meant Lourdes. I was over to change filters today and she's moping around. But Andy's mopey, too."

If small talk was weird with him, real talk was even weirder. "I miss Lourdes, too. But I miss Andy more."

"I figured. It's obvious how you feel about each other."

"Yeah." Lena sighed. She didn't know what else to say.

"Well, I just wanted to tell you I'm proud of you. I wish…" His voice was strained, and he let the sentence hang before he continued. "Well, you probably want to get off the phone."

"Are you okay?" It was tempting to ring off, but he sounded down.

"Everything's status quo."

"That's good. Right?"

There was an awkward pause, and her dad cleared his throat. "I wish I'd tried to see more of you when you were here. I wanted to." She pictured him with his hand on the back of his neck looking uncertain. "I just thought you'd be here a little longer so I could build up the nerve. I should have asked."

It was a lot to take in. How did she respond? Like a real dad? Or maybe, "You should have." Or maybe, "I'd have liked that." All of it was true.

"You deserve to be happy, Dad." Where the fuck had that come from? The pause was so long, she hoped he'd hung up, so they didn't have to talk about it.

He cleared his throat. "I suppose we have a lot to talk about."

But she didn't want to. She already had enough baggage in storage. "You don't have to right now. Ever, if you don't want to. Your life is yours to live."

"I want to…" His voice trailed off, and he cleared his throat once again. "We can talk soon, okay?"

She'd given him the out, but when he took it, she was angry. Really angry. She hadn't meant it as a test, but he'd just failed. How could he call her, get them both emotional, and then bail? Just like he'd done when she was a kid. Jesus. She wasn't going to tell him, though. He didn't deserve to see her pain. And she sure as hell wasn't going to be like her mother. That fear had too much power over her already. "I guess that's up to you," she said, trying to sound neutral, but she was anything but. He had to do the work. It wasn't her job.

"You're right," he said, unexpectedly. "I find myself unable to find words at the moment, though." He laughed self-consciously, and she almost excused herself with renewed anger.

"Is this why you called?" she asked. She heard the steel in her voice. It used to be a frequent seasoning to her words. Not long ago, either. Not since Andy part two, though. She'd forgotten what it sounded like. She hated it.

"Glenn suggested I check in when I told him I wished I'd spent more time with you."

"Glenn?" Seriously? Irritation and disappointment fell like a corroded metal ball into her stomach. Did he have to be told to do everything? Couldn't he act like a dad for once in his life? "Maybe he should have called then." This time she wasn't couching her response or worrying about channeling her mother. She was speaking up for her ten-year-old self. The shadow-girl hoping he'd spend time with her if she didn't cause trouble, or speak, or breathe. How fucked up was that? Yet, the one time she'd spoken her mind, he'd stopped visiting.

"I deserve that. I can't jump to casual conversation when I barely—" He sounded defeated. Anger made heat crackle across her skin. He had no right to share his troubles with her. None. He should feel bad for her, not himself. "I should have been a part of your life. I was a coward."

So, he had known. At least there was that. He swallowed so hard, she heard it across the line, the self-reproach dragging after it. *He's a coward.* Her mother's acidic accusation had been repeated endlessly in her diatribes.

She hadn't been the only casualty. He'd done what he'd been expected to do, trained to do, told to do. It didn't make it right, though. Just because she knew he was also a victim didn't mean she had to be okay with it. And she sure as hell didn't want to be his therapist. She needed a father.

She took a shaky breath. "Is that what you want? A casual conversation with me?"

She heard his breath hitch. "Yes. At least someday. I want to be part of your life. I can't change the past, and I'll understand if you don't want it, but I'd like to do better going forward."

It was uncomfortable to hear him talk this way. Basically, a stranger to her and he was showing her his ass. It was embarrassing. Why should she even care? Feeling guilty, she reminded herself he was her father, and flawed or not, it should mean something, right?

Why should I care?

She was reminded of something one of her therapists had told her about how a child's relationship with a parent doesn't continue to evolve after the parent leaves, and if they reunite, they start back up where they left off. The therapist had gone on to explain there were different ways to desert a child, and it didn't always mean physically. That meant she and her father would essentially be starting at zero if she agreed. It was the same for her mother, except hers were in triple digit negative numbers. Did she have an obligation to try with either of them?

"Did Glenn tell you to say that, too?" The snarky words came out sounding tired, but at least she could justify her childish responses as her being an infant in their relationship. Put that way, she was acting mature for her age.

"It was one of the things I told him when he asked what I was going to do."

"You had a conversation about me?" She was back at the coffee shop when Andy had made the off-handed remark that their dads probably exchanged information about her, which had sliced right through her heart because she knew they hadn't.

"I'm not sure I'd call it a conversation. He let me know what a terrible father I've been. Along with other gems. None of it was new information to me, but when I claimed reasons, he pointed out that they were excuses. And he was right. So, he gave me an ultimatum. It forced me to open my eyes, and what I saw was devastating." His breath hitched again.

"What kind of ultimatum?"

"To stop letting fear keep me from the one thing I ever did right in this life." She heard a faint sniffle. This time she didn't feel embarrassed for him, because she was crying, too. She had a lot of feelings about it, but anger wasn't the top of the list anymore. She waited for him to tell her the "or" part of the ultimatum, but he didn't share. What would Glenn do if her dad didn't? Neither of them said anything for a few moments.

"So. That's why you called, then."

"It's not your responsibility to tell me how to do it." It appeared that he understood more than she gave him credit for. "I'm going to figure it out. If you don't like it, or if I overstep, you can ignore me or tell me to stop or fuck off. I just want to try. I'm not letting fear make my decisions anymore."

She'd always thought they were so different because he could leave, and she couldn't. But they were more alike than she'd known.

"Okay." Her throat was tight, and it physically hurt to say it.

"Thank you."

"Hey, Dad? I have to go."

"Can I call you tomorrow? If you don't answer. I'll try again later. Sound good?"

"Yeah," was all she could get out. She hung up and all she wanted was Andy.

Hey, she typed before she could stop herself. Why would she want to stop herself? It was a habit she needed to work on.

Hey back. Andy's text was almost immediate. Lena texted her every day when she got back to the room after work.

I'm at the hotel. I got here a little while ago, but my dad called.

You okay? She always knew.

I'm processing, Lena sent.

I'm here to talk.

You always are.

It's a lot to deal with, Andy texted.

That's an understatement.

We still on for later?

Nothing could keep me away.

Can't wait, Andy told her.

Andy knew exactly how to be supportive without pushing. God, she adored her. She gave the thumbs up and a heart emoji. She second-guessed the heart as soon as she sent it.

She felt better when Andy sent one in response.

I miss you. Lena sent back.

I miss you, too. They don't know how lucky they are.

Lena relied on Andy's support to fight off the loneliness and homesickness. But she longed for her to ask her to come back or at least tell her she was having a hard time. As much as she hated the memory of Andy trying to hide her feelings when she'd dropped her off at the airport, she'd love to see a little of it now.

What would she do if Andy did?

❖

The unsent texts were like a meditation. Andy would never send them, but it was comforting to see the words that dominated her thoughts spelled out like they could possibly make it happen.

Please come back. <delete> *Please come back.* <delete> *Please come back.* <delete>

Chapter Twenty-five

I wish I was there," Lena said almost every time they spoke. Please come back. "You'll be back soon," Andy said. She hadn't expected not to see Lena for over two weeks the morning she'd dropped her off at the airport. But they were more than halfway through it and Lena had a long weekend coming up. If they could see each other every other weekend, she could make it work. Probably.

"Five more days." Lena sounded tired, but Andy thought she looked as beautiful as ever over FaceTime. Lena would have been in San Diego this weekend, but she'd had to change plans to go to Phoenix to get some paperwork she needed to complete her hiring package. As disappointed as Andy had been when Lena had explained, she understood. "I should have labeled these boxes better. I have five boxes labeled 'office.'" Lena retaped the box she'd just gone through.

"You don't put any clue on them at all?" Andy sat forward, kind of amazed Lena wasn't more methodical. Andy created inventories to track every item when she packed. She was already creating lists for the move from Monterey.

"The moving companies usually do. This is the first time I've packed things myself. It just didn't occur to me to indicate anything other than the room. Lesson learned."

Andy sat back, blowing out a breath. "That could have been a deal-breaker."

Lena looked up from the box in front of her, a serious expression on her face. "Deal-breaker?"

Although intended as a joke, Andy heard it. She'd inferred them packing for a move together. The look on Lena's face indicated she had, too. Andy shrugged, pretending to not notice. If she did anything else, it might have broken her. "They say moving is one of the most stressful events for a family. It's like squeezing the toothpaste. Some people push from the bottom, and some are animals and squeeze in the middle. Divorces have occurred for less."

Lena nodded, going back to her task. "I'm a bottom squeezer. I agree. Only monsters squeeze from anywhere else."

The indication of compatibility should have made her happy.

"So, you like this pack-and-store method?"

"I should have had someone do it all for me. But, for this move? Yeah, I like it. No guessing the right sized truck when you can just order another container. No trying to predict pickups or deliveries. Pack it up, let them hold on to it until you're ready for it, and they'll unpack it on the other end." She gave a half-laugh as she moved her phone to a different location to check out another box. "I should have my agent talk to them about a brand deal for that endorsement."

"Is not having me underfoot still working in the new content department?" Andy asked.

Lena looked up from what she was doing. "I never said that."

"'I fill my free time with making content. They let me use the set sometimes, too.'" Andy recited with a smirk. "Same thing."

Lena pointed through the camera at her. "Please note the absence of 'you,' or 'under my feet' as key elements in the list of objective observations regarding my free time to content production correlation."

"It's hot when you get all research Lena on me." Andy wiggled her body for emphasis. It was fun to banter like this, but she always felt lonely when they turned off the video and the room grew quiet again.

Lena smiled and lifted a small stack of what looked like frames from the box she'd just opened. "Wanna see something?" When Andy gave her a crooked smile, she laughed. "Get your mind out of the gutter."

"But you didn't specify what it was. Leaving it open-ended infers I have a choice. And my choice will always involve seeing you naked." Andy spoke in a dreamy voice, resting her chin on her fist.

Lena moved closer to the phone she'd propped up so she could use both hands. "Maybe later when I'm somewhere more private." She winked and Andy felt it low in her body. God, she missed her. "Not as salacious, but check these out." She turned the frame. "Remember this?"

Remember it? It was a cornerstone of their childhood. "We were lying on the floor in my room. Remember how we'd lie side-by-side and hook our legs while we drew? It was a rainy day," Andy added. She remembered having the excuse to just be close to Lena, drawing Lena's favorite animal from memory. She'd been so proud of the giraffe. But her real joy came from how touched Lena had been when Andy had framed it for her birthday.

"Your mom made cookies, and we watched *Star Wars* for the gazillionth time."

"You spent the night." Andy remembered how Lena would cuddle with her. She still did. "Who would have known we'd be doing sleepovers twenty years later?"

Andy thought she saw a glimmer of tears before Lena looked down at the small pile of frames with a wistful expression. Andy's heart ached. Lena turned the next drawing toward the phone. The picture Andy had drawn of the wave house and had also given to Lena for her eighth birthday. She remembered because of the snowman she'd made out of the eight in the message on the back of it in honor of Lena having been born on Christmas day. It hadn't been as well-executed as the giraffe, but the love Andy had put into it was the same. Before she had a chance to mention it, Lena showed her the pictures of the solar system and a horse she'd drawn for Andy. Andy had never understood why she chose to be so publicly dramatic, but the day after Lena had given her the note, she'd packed a box of things Lena had given her or had left at her house, and left it on Lena's desk. Including the pictures. Lena and the box had been absent from class after first recess and the remaining two days of the week. Adult Lena put the pictures in the box she was packing to take back to Denver.

Andy cleared her tight throat. "How are things going with your dad?" Lena had told her about their daily calls.

Lena sighed. "I can't seem to stop asking about things I know are going to be hard to hear."

Andy watched Lena push her hands through her hair. She missed the smell of her hair. The softness of it.

"Anything in particular?" she asked.

"Why my mother hates me, for one." Lena continued to sort through the box, seemingly unaffected.

Andy couldn't fathom her pain. "A nice safe topic."

"Why they regretted having me, was another." Lena's unemotional delivery hit like a series of punches. Andy hadn't known this one.

"God, Lena."

Lena moved around the space as if she hadn't just revealed what Andy knew was deeply held pain. A breakdown would have been easier to watch.

"When I told him she blamed me for ruining the family and that she would have given me up if she could, he started crying."

What the fuck? Given her up? How had Andy not seen this? What kind of mother says that to their kid? Still projecting stoicism, Lena paused before continuing. Andy yearned to comfort her. To hold her. To tell her she loved her. That she loved her so much she couldn't breathe from holding it in.

"Oh, Lena…"

"As far as he knew, my mother focused all her anger on him. He thought she was a loving mother. It was her who kept him away. She told him he was a bad influence in every way." Lena's voice cracked, breaking Andy's heart. "She forbade him from seeing me after he started sleeping at his office."

"How are you dealing with all of this? I wish I was there." Andy didn't care if Lena saw her tears.

"I know. It's pathetic." Lena brusquely wiped her eyes, not looking at the phone, but not hiding her face either. Andy wished she didn't think she always had to be strong. "It doesn't excuse him for abandoning me. He even said that. Called himself a coward. And he's right." Lena's voice had more emotion in it, but it was obvious to Andy that she was still holding back. "But talking to him fills in some of the gaps. His parents forced him to marry if he wanted the business. They couldn't have a gay son. What would people think?"

"He told you?"

"Not all of it directly, but it's easy to infer and he doesn't say otherwise. They know we know."

Andy sighed. "My dad hasn't said anything." She hoped he would. Not having to feign ignorance would be so much easier.

"He calls your dad and him 'more than friends,'" Lena said.

Lena continued to sort and told Andy what her father had told her, connecting some of the dots her dad didn't say outright. It was a surprise to find out that all their parents had known each other most of their lives, and they were in the same friend group as they grew up. Robert and Glenn were very close and he made it seem like it was an open secret they were together. At one point, Robert's parents started hinting that he needed to start a family before they would make him the manager of the family pool business. Lena's mother, who'd always known about Robert and Glenn, suggested she and Robert get married to make his parents happy. She didn't care if they weren't in love and just wanted to be a wife and mother. Glenn and Robert drifted apart after that, and Andy's parents fell in love and got married soon after Lena's parents did.

Lena's mother grew bitter when he didn't eventually fall in love with her, because she saw Glenn and Paula so happy together. Robert said he kept hoping she'd get over the disappointment, but she just became more bitter, and then he was stuck. She convinced him he'd ruined her life by saddling her with a baby and reducing her chances of ever finding a husband who'd love her. She made him feel guilty, saying he owed it to her. As soon as he started blaming himself, she used that to make him do what she wanted.

"And here we are." Lena shrugged. "Like a fucking soap opera."

"Did he answer your questions?"

"Some. When I told him what she used to scream at me, about him not wanting me, and not loving me, and ruining their marriage. He said none of what she said was true. He said he wanted to be in my life and didn't know she was like that to me. According to her, she was a perfect mother. He berated himself for believing her. And, you know, it wasn't okay for him to make it about his feelings. I was the kid. He needed to apologize to me. Not fucking feel sorry for himself." As she spoke, her voice grew angrier and angrier, and Andy was relieved she seemed to be allowing herself to feel it, even as she hated to see Lena hurting.

"Do you think he really didn't know?"

"I think I do. It was hard to hear, though. It's really easy for him to be mad now. He just accepted what she said. He should have…" She shook her head. "The way he described it, he shut down when your parents fell in love. Our dads didn't see each other even as friends for a few years after that, while my parents' marriage crumbled and my mother became meaner. I don't think it makes any of it okay, but it explains why she hates your family."

Andy wanted so badly to be there to comfort her. "I know it can't be easy. I'm here if you need anything. You know that, right?"

Lena blew out a slow breath, looking at her wistfully through the screen. "I do. It's all that gets me through the day most days."

"What does this mean about you and your dad?"

"Maybe we can be comfortable in each other's presence someday. At least I don't dread his calls anymore." Lena rested her elbows on the stack of boxes where she'd propped her phone, resting her chin on her hands. This close, her eyes were a vivid blue, and as usual, Andy got lost in them. God, she had it bad for her.

"Do you think you'll ever have that with your mother?"

"No." Her answer was immediate. "She's a horrible person."

"Is she why you took the job in Denver?" She hadn't meant to ask it, although it had been on her mind. Was Lena's mother still keeping them apart?

Lena's answer was immediate. "No. I hate being so far away from you. I won't let my mother do that to us again. I'd still be there if I could find a job where you are."

Andy hadn't known she needed to hear that. It made her feel like they'd find their way back to one another.

❖

Six weeks was a long time, especially when all Lena could think about was how much she missed Andy. In some ways, it had flown by with so much to learn, she'd had little free time in which to wallow in her sadness. In other ways, time had crept by so slowly, Lena was almost convinced that the altitude might be messing with the fabric of time and space, stretching time so that every real time second seemed three seconds long.

On a positive note, Lena had hit her stride. She felt like a valued member of the evening news team, which had made her feel more welcome and at home than any previous station had. As far as market share went, the Denver audience seemed to like her from the spike in digital subscribers, her personal channels, and the traditional market share. Overall, the Denver job had been a good move, but all that good stuff didn't come close to making up for the loss of Andy in her life.

She hadn't been back since she flew out for the interview. The long weekend they'd planned had been canceled because the scheduled stand-in had fallen during a pickleball tournament, sustaining a concussion, and all the backups to the backup were either on vacation or otherwise unavailable.

The following four weeks hadn't been any better. Summer schedules were hard to fill with vacations, and the niche aspect of being an anchor/meteorologist made it hard to find suitable stand-ins. And while the market loved her, she was still the new kid at the station. Lena was on the verge of going AWOL, knowing Andy couldn't leave her dad to come visit her.

Andy hadn't wavered in her support, and Lena joked she should start a side gig as a life coach. But Lena missed her with every cell in her body. They spoke every day, sometimes multiple times, and video-called often, usually just before bedtime. None of it eased the ache of not being able to touch her. Sometimes, the frequent exchanges made it more difficult, reminding her of everything she missed.

Finally, though, Lena had the whole weekend off, and planned to surprise Andy. She hadn't told her because she didn't want to get her hopes up and have it canceled again. But, she'd already booked three nights and four days at a condo on the beach near their café. Although, she wasn't sure she'd let Andy out of bed, even for the Ecuadorian drip. At this point, Lena would go without food and water to satisfy her need for Andy. She'd even arranged for her dad to stay with Glenn so she could breeze in and sweep her away.

Lena's stomach fluttered thinking that this would be the first time they'd be truly alone. With no one and nothing to distract them or hear them, her mind continuously sent her previews of what she planned to do to Andy when she had her to herself.

Nearly delirious with her fantasies, Lena floated through the unnaturally quiet hallway at the station on her way for a coffee refill, which she dearly needed. The research aspect of her job was one of her favorite things, but she found she couldn't keep her eyes open today. She wasn't complaining, though. She and Andy had stayed up later than usual on their video call the night before. As if picking up on her fantasies, Andy asked her what she wanted to do first when they were together again. Lena, having spent a lot of time thinking about this, wasted no time telling Andy she wanted her on her back, legs around her neck, and her mouth between her thighs. She'd sustained herself with that fantasy for six weeks, and she described it in vivid detail. Andy responded by showing Lena how much that turned her on, and it had escalated from there. The next thing she knew, it was a few hours past her bedtime, but well worth the lack of sleep. Now, while Lena wore a wide smile, her eyes still wanted to shutter. She needed coffee stat.

Pouring coffee, wishing it was the Ecuadorean drip from Seaside, the phone in her back pocket buzzed. It was almost time for Andy's afternoon call, and the breakroom was empty, so she tapped her ear bud, answering immediately. The corporate suits who usually kept the breakroom in business, had been at an off-site meeting all week and Lena enjoyed the quiet.

"Hey, hot stuff," she said in a sultry voice.

"Hey, my gorgeous friend who owes me a Spicy Margarita Monday at Rose's," Claire responded in the same sultry voice.

Lena laughed. "Are you going to bring that up every time we talk? I've already begged your forgiveness. What will it take? My first born?"

"God, no. I already have my allotted number of children." Claire giggled. "How's the job going?"

"So far, it's all sunshine and clear skies for the short- and long-term forecasts."

"I take it you like it there, then?"

"You sound disappointed," Lena said.

Claire sighed dramatically. "I guess you probably aren't interested in an interview at *Totally San Diego* next Friday at two p.m., then."

"Wait." Lena's heart rate skyrocketed. "I thought I heard you say," Lena lowered her voice to just above a whisper. "Interview with *Totally San Diego*?"

"I pretty much said those exact words."

Something was doing cartwheels in Lena's stomach. "Say more."

"Josh has a buddy at the police station, whose wife is the sister of the weekend events anchor."

"And how did this interview come about?"

"Josh and his buddy got drunk last weekend at a retirement party for their captain. His buddy's brother-in-law called to see if he knew someone to be a fourth for their team at a golf tournament at Torrey Pines that *Totally San Diego* sponsored. Yadda, yadda, yadda. And Josh gets paired with Paulo Costa." Claire paused as if that would answer Lena's question.

"So, Paulo Costa is leaving *Totally San Diego*? Is this an interview for an events anchor? Because I—"

"Do the weather." Claire finished the sentence. "I am aware. I stream your meteorology channels. I loved it before, but now? Girl, you're killing it."

Lena loved hearing it, but she needed to hear about the possible job in San Diego. "Is the opening for a weather anchor or a meteorologist? I'll do either to get back to San Diego, but I prefer meteorologist because that's what—"

"You have your doctorate in." Claire finished for her again. "I am aware. The position isn't technically open. It's hush-hush but Shanks Timm is going on a quote-unquote sabbatical which is code for rehab. They intend to bring in a quote-unquote temporary weekday meteorologist during his quote-unquote sabbatical, who will just stay on until people are so used to them, they won't even remember you're supposed to be quote-unquote temporary."

Lena didn't miss the use of "you're." "I have questions, but I go on air in half an hour. Just bare facts. Okay?"

"Yes."

"If it's hush-hush, why did Paulo tell you?"

"Paulo is a notorious blabbermouth. He told Josh, who told me."

"Who set up the interview?" She needed to get her agent on this.

"Me."

"Who should my agent get in touch with?"

Claire had already texted the info to her.

"How many applicants are there?"

"It's hush-hush, remember?"

"Okay."

"That's why it's only you."

"I'm the only applicant?" Lena put her hand on her stomach as if it would calm it down.

"Yes. When Josh told me, I made an appointment with the station manager, who was surprisingly not interested in seeing me. So, I asked Josh's buddy to ask Paulo to happy hour at Poseidon yesterday evening and Josh and I just happened to come in and Paulo—"

"Remember bare facts, Claire."

"Oh yeah. I'm just so excited." Claire took a deep breath. "I showed them videos from what you're doing now, your streaming channels, and even one from when you used to be in video tech in high school. So, I think you have the job in the bag unless you purposely screw it up or decide to go on a bender which would be in seriously bad taste."

"Don't worry. No benders for me. You did all that for me? Or is it for Spicy Margarita Monday?" Lena tried not to get her hopes up, but she had her hopes up.

"Both, of course. I look out for my besties and I'm a junkie for Spicy Margarita Monday."

"But you've never been."

"Don't underestimate the power of a jalapeño-infused tequila blanco, blended with orange liquor and lime juice, served on the rocks in a long-stemmed glass with a salted rim."

"You've definitely ascended from the trashcan jungle juice, my friend."

"What can I say? I'm fancy now." Lena could almost hear the shrug in her voice.

They chatted for a few more minutes and made plans, which included Spicy Margarita Monday, and Lena had an interview lined up for next Friday. The only way it could have been better would have been if Claire had a one degree of separation connection from a station manager somewhere close to Monterey. Despite her history of leaving without notice, it wasn't in her nature to leave without cause, so she didn't like leaving just weeks after starting the job. But she'd do anything to be closer to Andy, even temporarily. She couldn't wait to tell her. It would have to be after the interview, though, so she didn't ruin the surprise getaway. Nearly trembling with excitement, she went back to her office with the coffee she didn't need now. Depending on how much longer Andy's dad needed her, they'd have a little more time together before Andy had to move back to Monterey. After that? Well, they'd figure it out when it happened.

They'd find their way back to each other. They'd done it before.

Chapter Twenty-six

The cool glass felt good against Lena's forehead as she leaned against the floor to ceiling window on the twenty-fifth floor of the hotel that had been her home for over six weeks. She'd be happy if she never saw another hotel again, and it looked like she'd be granted her wish soon. Everyone from Claire to the station manager told her she had the job, and the interview was just a formality, but she was trying not to be too confident until she knew for sure. But, God, she wanted it. More than anything, she wanted to breathe the same air as Andy, and this was going to make it happen if she was offered the job. Good thing she'd dragged her feet on finding a place to live in Denver. All she had to do was zip up her suitcase and get on the next plane to San Diego. Bless Claire and her ability to wish a thing and make it happen. She made everything seem effortless, and maybe it was for her. She had a way of seeing opportunities in everyday occurrences, and when she wanted something, she knew how to navigate the paths to make it happen.

With all of that in the works, Lena should be floating on clouds about how easily things were falling into place, especially the part where she would be able to see Andy in less than three days. Her stomach broke into flutters every time she thought about knocking on Andy's door, seeing her surprised expression, then flinging herself into her arms. However, for the last forty-five minutes, she'd been looking out one of the windows of the hotel's exclusive Diamond Lounge, barely taking in the world outside. A complimentary glass of wine dangled at her side by her fingers, all but forgotten, while she stared at the Rocky Mountains with her mind almost a thousand miles west of here. Normally, her meteorologist mind would have been gleefully observing the formation of tall cumulonimbus clouds building over the foothills, creating a storm line that would become the dynamic afternoon rainstorms accompanied by thunder and lightning she'd predicted and reported on earlier that morning. Denver came with an amazing array of weather, and she'd miss it if she got the new job. It wasn't unusual for a hailstorm to be pounding a neighborhood, while the neighborhood adjacent enjoyed clear skies overhead and snow fell in the nearby mountains. It wasn't hyperbole when the locals said if you didn't like the weather, just wait five minutes, it would probably change.

With her mood as chaotic as the storm brewing, she barely saw it, let alone felt any glee, as she mulled over the amazing opportunity Claire had dropped into her lap yesterday. She tried to understand the dark mood she'd woken up with that morning. The job in San Diego was exactly what she wanted. She'd be with Andy, in a top market, doing the work she loved. It was a dream come true. Yesterday, the excitement over it had her planning the move, envisioning how excited Andy would be about the news. She'd called her agent as soon as she'd finished talking with Claire.

The news had been hard to keep from Andy when she'd talked to her last night, especially when Andy had asked her why she seemed distracted during their nightly FaceTime. Lena had passed it off as workload, but when she suspected Andy wasn't fully convinced, she'd come close to telling her all about it. Especially since Andy seemed a little down and she knew it would make her happy. But she'd kept her secret, feeling a buzz of anticipation tingling across her skin.

Later. Sometime around two a.m., she woke from a fitful sleep with a heavy sensation in her stomach and uncertainty about whether San Diego was the right decision. But why? She was on the brink of getting what she'd longed for. Instead, she felt like she was on a cliff, getting ready to jump, even though she was terrified of heights. When all she could think about was getting to see Andy, why would anxiety be the thing that woke her up in the middle of the night? It should be joy. She lay awake envisioning going to work each day, doing the work she loved, and coming home to wrap herself around Andy. They would exchange details about their days, while they did everyday things like make dinner together, take walks with the dogs, and make love before falling asleep each night. She couldn't wait to sleep in the bliss of Andy's arms, something she longed for every night when she went to bed. She would do anything to have an everyday life with Andy. Anything.

What about Andy, a little voice whispered in her ear. Would she do anything?

She realized that question was the source of her anxiety, the heaviness she felt, and the reason she woke in the night with her stomach full of worry and fear. Was Andy ready to fight for the same things? Or had Lena mistaken the pain she'd seen Andy covering up when she'd dropped her off at the airport for something else? Could it be fear instead? A fear that had been growing over the weeks they'd been apart. Had Andy been building her defenses, getting ready for what she might see as the inevitable end of their relationship? Or, worse, had she grown tired of anticipating the possible challenges, and decided it wasn't worth it?

Maybe it was simply that Andy looked forward to moving back to Monterey. Back to her life. She'd never mentioned wanting to do anything else. But she'd told Lena she dreaded when it came. But they hadn't talked about what came next. Andy hadn't suggested that Lena come to Monterey, or that Andy could stay in San Diego or move to Denver with her. Could returning to Monterey on her own have been her intention all along?

Just when she had the San Diego job nearly in her hands, they only had weeks until Andy's dad was on his feet again, and

Andy would leave, leaving them in the same spot they were in now. A long-distance relationship that started to crumble when they couldn't see each other for weeks at a time.

With time to think, the interview now hung like a pendulum with a blade on it over their relationship, swinging lower and lower. Was San Diego the right decision? Aside from staying in Denver or returning to Phoenix, were there any other choices? Her agent had been looking all over the country and hadn't found any in the top markets. But, then again, his search was in top markets exclusively. She hadn't considered broadening the search. Were there stations with smaller markets closer to Monterey? The simple thought gave her a slice of hope.

Without overthinking it, she texted her agent. Within ten minutes, she had a response with a short list of opportunities at smaller stations closer to Monterey. All were for weather anchors, not meteorologists. She didn't care. It didn't mean she couldn't forecast, it just meant it wouldn't be official. She knew this route would be a huge step backward, and she'd be lying if she said it didn't disappoint her. However, if it meant being with Andy, she'd do anything. She'd made a mistake by not fighting for her once. She wasn't going to do it again. Even if Andy hadn't asked her. When it came to Andy, fear wasn't going to influence her decisions ever again.

She just needed to make a call.

She bit her lip as the phone rang, nervous about the reaction. She thought about hanging up and calling the station instead, when her call was picked up.

"Hey, Claire. Please don't hate me."

"Why would I hate you, Lena?"

Lena explained what she'd been thinking about and waited for Claire to respond. She'd been worried that hearing it out loud would show her what a fool she was being. Instead, it just made her more certain that this was what she needed to do. She owed Claire so much. She'd gone to so much trouble and Lena owed her the decency of giving her at least the high-level explanation about what she planned to do. Minus the details about Andy. She still had things to work out, and she didn't want to bring her into it before she knew more.

After a long pause in which Lena grew increasingly more anxious, Claire responded. "It's about time, girl."

What? She felt like she'd missed something.

"Time for what?"

"For you to realize that you're in love with Andy and have been since elementary school."

"Wait. You go to all this trouble to get me an interview at one of the most sought-after stations in the country, and that's what you say when I tell you I don't want San Diego, I want Santa Cruz instead? How does that have anything to do with me allegedly being in love with Andy?"

"Oh, come on." Lena heard the flap of Claire's hand in the tone of her voice. "Allegedly? Really? And you're just coincidentally interested in a podunk station in Santa Cruz because why? The hippies? Mini golf at Neptunes? Because surfing on the mainland originated there?"

"You have a suspiciously broad knowledge about Santa Cruz." Lena deflected, even though she was impressed with Claire's power of deduction. Or maybe she'd been way more obvious than she thought. Either way, she wasn't ready to get into it. Maybe one day, but it was a little too raw now.

"What can I say? I'm invested in that spicy margarita. The more I know, the more effective I will be at getting you back to your homeland so you can make good on that promise. So, I did a few googles while you spoke to check the area out. It seems nice. A chiller version of Encinitas or maybe P.B."

"So, you're not mad?"

"More like bummed. I was hoping to hang out with you. You still owe me spicy margaritas at Rose's. Oh, and it looks like *Totally San Diego* and the Santa Cruz station are owned by the same parent company. UC Santa Cruz home of the Banana Slugs? Seriously? Gross. And I just texted Logan. He said he'd work on getting the Santa Cruz interview set up. I gave him your info. He'll call you."

"What are banana slugs? Who's Logan? I'm so lost." Claire's multitasking skills were seriously frightening.

"The GM for *Totally San Diego*. He and I dated before I snagged Josh. I had no idea he worked there, but Josh told me when all of this came up. My husband might be a cop, but he's not just a pretty face in a sexy uniform. He knows things."

"Like someone else I know." Lena laughed.

"And I need to know all the hot sapphic details about you and Andy. I'll start. You and Andy had the hots for each other all through high school, but you pretended to hate each other. All the while you were…Now you go."

❖

Exploring the La Jolla tide pools were Andy's favorite part of her day. Picturesque, with a diversity of species, they were protected from the surf during low tide, making them more accessible for what Andy had come to do, which was looking for new species to introduce to the tide pool at the lab she now worked for. Today, Andy was able to collect several different kinds of anemone. The tide pool at the lab was impressive, but not as diverse as the lab in Monterey, something she was trying to rectify. That morning she'd seen a trio of juvenile California two-spot octopi playing in one of the smaller tide pools. Andy would have collected them for the lab pool, but it wasn't a closed system, and the clever octopi would get out. So, she enjoyed watching them for a few more minutes before she went on with her collection efforts.

When she returned to the lab, she put on her waders to get into the pool where she'd put the anemones after acclimating them. Today was a non-teaching day, which meant she had more time for non-project related specimen analysis. She usually enjoyed this part of her job, but it was less mentally taxing than other aspects, and her mind had a habit of wandering. Without fail it found its way to Lena.

Back to full-time work, and without Lena there to distract her, Andy found herself falling back into working too much. She still took breaks to check on her dad. And she took work home in the evenings. She needed to keep busy to distract herself from missing Lena.

She'd just floated the last bag into the center of the tank for acclimation when her phone rang. In a screwed-up facsimile of déjà vu, she'd left it on the counter and the sound echoed through the room. She cursed under her breath, as she headed out of the pool, berating herself for not remembering to put it on silent. She thought about last time this had happened, and a nugget of anxiety formed in her chest. Her mother, father, and Lena had ring-through privileges. She hoped it wasn't bad news and hoped it was Lena. She could use a little light in her day.

Although she tried to keep it from others, especially Lena, Andy's mood had slowly degraded over the last six weeks. Lena still hadn't been able to get time off. And after their second planned weekend had been canceled just hours before Lena would have flown out, Andy didn't want to invest in the prospect of a next one. If it happened it happened, but she wouldn't let herself get excited just to have another one be unexpectedly derailed. Just thinking about the crushing disappointment she'd felt when she'd received Lena's text, a blanket of despair fell over her. At the same time, Lena hadn't brought up trying to plan another one, and she wondered what that meant.

In the meantime, Andy continued to look forward to their calls, and she genuinely felt happy when they spoke. That hadn't changed. Lena was still everything to her. She'd just resigned herself to the idea that this was their life now. At least she was trying to. It would take some time. She would invest in being happy with what they had. So far, it had worked during the time they spent on the phone. It was when they weren't on the phone that life had lost its shine. She was working on that.

While she'd been taking off the gear she used while in the pool, her phone had stopped ringing. But it started to ring again. Seeing it was her mother, and remembering the last midday call she'd received from her, she picked it up immediately, facing away from the others in the lab.

"Hey, Mom," she said, trying not to sound as if she was mid-flashback.

"Hello, Andrea. I was beginning to think you wouldn't pick up." Some things never changed.

"I was in the tank, so I had to remove my gear."

"Oh, yes. The reef. Can you send pictures?"

Her anxiety eased a bit. Her mother wouldn't waste time if there was an emergency.

"Where are you? Are you near a television?"

"I'm at work. No TVs here."

"Well, I just saw Selena Holmes on the news. Do you remember her? Here in Denver. Can you believe it?" Andy blew out a breath. She'd talked to her mom several times since she and Lena had reconnected, but she hadn't told her mom. First, her mom usually did all the talking and it was hard to bring up new topics. But, while her dad didn't make a big deal about it, she knew her mom would. She wasn't ready for that.

"In fact, I can."

"She's doing the weather report. I thought I saw her doppelganger on a billboard off the 25 for another station a month or so ago but didn't think it was really her. However, I was flipping channels just now, and there she was on a commercial about changing stations, so I googled her, and found she's been here for nearly two months. I know you two had that falling out in school, but I always imagined you two someday picking up where you left off."

Andy was about to respond, when she heard a bell ring in the background.

"Oh damn. Break is over. I have to get off the phone. I'll call you soon. I love you, honey. I hope you look her up. She was such a sweet kid." And then she was gone.

Andy didn't have a chance to process the call with her mom, when her phone rang again.

The display said Lena, and a school of very active octopi frolicked in her stomach.

"Hey," she said, moving into the hallway for privacy.

"Hey, back," Lena said. Everything in Andy relaxed. They'd video-called for over an hour the night before, as they did most nights. "Sorry about calling midday. I just missed you and wanted to see how your day was going."

"Better now." And it was true, but she didn't look forward to when they hung up. Having the gloom descend during her workday wouldn't be optimal.

"How's your dad doing?"

It was always the first thing Lena asked. His disposition had improved a little when the casts had come off but had been short-lived. He was struggling with physical therapy and still confined to bed until his strength returned. Like hers, his mood declined every day. He hardly cheered up when Robert came over these days. He tried to hide it, but it was obviously hard on him. "About the same. We'll know more this afternoon. I hope the doc has good news. I'm not sure I can take much more of his sad eyes."

"I wish I was there to distract you."

"Me, too." Fuck. Lena didn't know how much she wanted it.

"That's the first time you admitted you might need me." Lena sounded amused, but her words hit Andy in a painful way.

"I need you all the time."

"I meant in more than a sexual way."

For one of the first times ever, Andy couldn't manage banter. She leaned against the wall. "I miss you. I miss having coffee with you. I miss lying in bed just talking. I miss how you play with the little hairs on the back of my neck. I miss being the big spoon. Or the small spoon. Just as long as you're the other spoon. I just miss you." She hated how needy all that sounded. The last thing she wanted to do was apply pressure on Lena. She wanted to be the support Lena had never had. Even if it was at her own expense.

"I miss all those things, too." Lena's voice was almost a whisper.

Voices came around the corner. Andy faked a smile for her passing colleagues.

One of them stopped and asked about tide pool time.

"Who was that?" Lena asked after Andy rejoined her.

"Just someone asking about pool time."

"Are you at the rec center?"

Andy laughed. "The tide pool at the lab."

"Lab? Are you in Monterey?"

Andy realized she hadn't told Lena about the transfer. It had seemed insignificant at the time with Lena's new job. After seven weeks it had become background information.

"I'm at the lab at Arliner Young. I transferred here so I can take care of my dad and work full-time. I needed some distraction, and my mind was starting to atrophy, working only part-time on stuff any intern could do."

"Full-time? For how long?"

"Well, full-time for me, which means ten to twelve hours a day. I do a couple of hours of field work in the mornings, six hours in the lab, which is where I am now, and then I work in the evenings from home. It switches up a little when I'm teaching." She didn't mention how it was the only thing keeping her mind off how much she missed her.

"I meant how long will you work there before you go back to Monterey?" Lena sounded serious. Andy didn't know what it meant.

"It's permanent. I know it doesn't help us much. But my dad's here, so there's that." She hoped the mention of distance didn't come off as pressure.

"What does that mean?"

"The airport's closer here."

"No. I meant about your life up north."

"My life is here now."

"Oh."

"You sound pensive," Andy said, wondering if the distance thing had actually bothered her.

"It's just a surprise. I didn't know it was even an option. When did this happen?"

"I applied a couple of days after they told us he'd need full-time care. It took a while to go through, but it was approved about seven weeks ago."

"Was that before or after I got the job here?"

"I found out the day they asked you to come out for the interview. I'm sorry I forgot to tell you. It was during—"

"But we talk—never mind."

Lena sounded strange. Distant. Cold passed down Andy's body. She second-guessed every decision she'd made since the day her supervisor had called to tell her the transfer had gone through.

"Lena, I—"

"I have to go."

"Hey, really quick. My mom saw you on—" She looked at her phone. The call had dropped. She felt like she'd fucked up in a big way but didn't know how. The transfer didn't change anything. She redialed Lena and reached voice mail. The texts she sent next were left on read.

Chapter Twenty-seven

Lena stared at her phone feeling numb, wishing she hadn't ended the call like that. But why hadn't Andy told her? Maybe this was a sign. If forgetting to tell her about the transfer wasn't a big deal, what was? Apparently not her.

No. She hated when she went directly to that old recording. She knew she mattered to Andy. She needed to stop letting fear keep her from the only woman she'd ever loved. Still loved. Couldn't live without.

Well, she had some explaining to do. Claire picked up on the first ring.

"Hey there, bestie!" Ever bubbly Claire. Gotta love her.

"Do you have a few minutes?" A baby started to cry, and Lena was sure Claire would say no, but the line quieted and she heard cute little grunts and satisfied cooing. It occurred to Lena, that for someone whose life was pretty hectic, Claire never seemed to be bothered by much.

"The others are playing and my milk just let down. We have about fifteen minutes per side. I'm all yours."

❖

"Cut!"

Lena held her smile for a count of three before she relaxed.

"Please tell me you got it," she said before stepping off the platform. All she wanted to do was get out of the heels she'd been standing in for the past three hours as she'd shot promotion footage for the new station.

"We'll see in a few, but I think that was the one," Doug or Dan or Dave the director said. "Don't change anything yet. I'll let you know."

"Looked good up there, Lena."

Lena looked toward the voice and smiled. "Logan." She gave him a hug.

"We're good," Doug or Dan or Dave said. She'd need to learn his name since she was working here now. "Thanks for coming in late notice like this."

"She's a life saver, huh, Doug?" Logan said to him before giving Lena a wink. They both watched Doug leave the set.

"Anyone else would have skipped past me after I bailed on the first interview. I should be thanking you." Lena slid out of the uncomfortable heels.

"What? And risk Claire exacting revenge? Yeah, no. She gets what she wants. Remember when she decided to have Lime Green perform at the Spring Festival sophomore year? She rented that billboard and put up that picture from their yearbook of them playing their own high school dance."

"It worked." Lena had forgotten about that. "She does get what she wants."

"And she wanted you back home. You should have seen how sad she was when you turned down *Totally San Diego* in favor of Santa Cruz. Crystal had to take her to the mud baths up in Rainbow to cheer her up."

"I can't believe you married Crystal." Lena shook her head. "I also couldn't believe it when I saw you at the station in Santa Cruz."

"I'd planned to see you when you interviewed here, but when you opted for the spot in Santa Cruz, I had to go up. I mean, Derecho Media is lucky to have you anywhere, but Santa Cruz over San Diego? I had to know why."

Lena shrugged. "There are things more important than market share."

Logan rolled his eyes. "Don't I know it. I never thought I'd have left the movie biz for TV. But Crystal wanted San Diego, and I wanted Crystal. Love, man. Am I right? And you and Andy? I called it in seventh grade, you know."

"You did not."

"Ask Crystal. Anyway, it all worked out. You were the number one pick out of three in Santa Cruz. None close to as good as you, but it was covered when you asked for San Diego. Everyone in corporate wanted you in our biggest market anyway."

She'd wondered how she'd never heard of Derecho Media. But when she'd interviewed in Santa Cruz, she'd found it was the rebranded parent company of the biggest markets in the western United States, including her old station in Phoenix. It felt right, though. The name, the timing, the associated markets. She said she didn't believe in fate and destiny, but whatever it was, it seemed that having the wind at her back wasn't the scary thing it used to be, especially since it had blown her home.

"It all worked out. Most of it anyway," Lena said. "My dad always says, 'It's not what you know, it's who you know.'"

"And having Claire in your corner. Did he say that, too? Because he'd be right." Logan smiled. "You were at Denver 5280 for less than eight weeks?"

She nodded sardonically. "The station merged with an East Coast company featuring a morning chat show format. Not really my thing, but I might have signed on or at least signed a new contract until Denver 5280 went dark. Instead, they started airing commercials like I'd already signed on with the new company. I found out when I saw my image on a billboard. They should have talked to me or at least read my contract." She huffed. "Instead, they had to buy me out, and here I am."

Logan fist-bumped her. "We're lucky to have you, Lena. Welcome home."

❖

Idling her rental car at the intersection, Lena was exhausted on every level, mentally, emotionally, and physically. In the last four days, she'd been in three different states, four different cities, and she'd lost count of how many flights, all while playing the most important chess game of her life. And she didn't even know how to play chess, but that wasn't going to stop her. She was willing to do anything if it meant being with Andy. They'd already lost too many years due to Lena's fear.

She'd never felt as distant from Andy than she did now. At least Andy was still returning her texts, as minimal as they were. Lena wouldn't have blamed Andy if she hadn't answered at all, though. Not after she'd hung up on her and ignored her texts for over six hours. Andy had always shown up. But people had limits. Even Andy.

Lena questioned again if her decision to make the drive to Oceanside was a good one. She should have called Andy to make sure she'd be there. It was a moot point, anyway. She had no choice, terrified or not. Nothing mattered if she didn't have Andy. Lena was prepared to keep trying forever if she had to.

At that thought, and with the exhaustion and loneliness she'd been contending with for so long, Lena could no longer hold back the tears. After one escaped, they all spilled over, and hot despair streamed down her face, splattering like rain onto her dark blue shirt. A sob tore from her, forcing its way out, pressing against the tightness of her throat. She had to pull over when her vision began to blur. When she'd wiped her eyes, she discovered she'd stopped in front of the wave house. It almost seemed cruel, but it actually made sense, no matter how things turned out. The house had been a meaningful part of their friendship. It had been hard to see it falling into ruin the last time she'd been here, and she'd meant it when she said it was fitting because everything fell to shit. But she hoped when she saw Andy, they'd be able to get back on track to what they'd begun to rebuild and maybe that meant leaving the old shit in the past. And if Andy wasn't willing or able to keep trying, her original thought that it was fitting because everything fell to shit would still apply. Either way, it felt like she was here to light a candle in honor of what came next.

Lena didn't care who saw her tear-streaked face when she got out of the car. She was almost looking forward to being in the company of sadness. Instead she was in the company of something else. Someone had put the rock garden back to order, and *The Great Wave* greeted her in its original glory. The weeds and dead plants were also gone, replaced with healthy new ones. When she noticed the *Sold* placard on a newly erected real estate sign, she briefly worried about developers and the almost sure prospect that the lot would be the next in line for a new build. But why go to the trouble of fixing up the garden if the house would just be torn down? Choosing the side of hope, she envisioned a family living there again, happy someone had seen the beauty behind the neglected home and turned the Havisham Garden into Rebecca's Manderley Garden.

❖

For a change of pace, Andy sat at the kitchen table to write up the report she should have submitted the week before. It wasn't healthy to hole herself up in her room all the time like she had been since Lena left. Her dad had stopped watching so much television and had started reading and doing word search puzzles. He'd also started doing the exercises his physical therapist had given him. All things she'd tried to get him to do, but it had taken an argument between him and Robert to make it happen. It came about as a result of her dad's persistent complaints about being stir-crazy, even though he wasn't doing anything to address it. It sounded as if Robert had reached the end of his very patient rope and told him that her dad wasn't allowed to complain to him anymore until he did the bare minimum. It was the way two people in a very close relationship spoke to each other. Until now, she hadn't heard this between them. It stunned her.

A similar thing had happened the day before, when she'd overheard them talking about Robert's calls with Lena. He'd sounded committed to becoming more active in her life, just like Lena had said, and he'd asked her dad for advice. Her dad and Robert had a real conversation, with her dad engaging on a personal level, asking questions and interjecting thoughts.

This morning, her dad asked if she was okay. After hearing him talk to Robert, it had taken her a minute to decide how much she wanted to tell him, before settling on telling him she was just tired. The concern in his eyes told her he didn't believe it. But he'd given her so many indications that he wasn't comfortable talking about personal things. The few times he'd gone there on his own were when Robert had asked him to ask her, or her dad had suggested Robert reach out to Lena. Although Lena had told her about the conversations she'd had with her dad, and that Lena was certain they were aware she and Andy knew about them, she wasn't about to risk making her dad uncomfortable.

It would probably help to talk to someone about Lena, but she didn't have anyone to go to. She'd deliberately not told Talia about them because she hadn't even told her about the kisses or her feelings for Lena in high school. With everything going on, she wasn't sure she had enough emotional energy to soothe Talia for not opening up to her in addition to all the rest. She'd been such a jerk after Lena hung up on her, and she didn't know why. It felt justified, but she couldn't explain it.

To Lena's credit, she kept trying, while Andy could barely manage inconsequential responses, afraid she'd say something to cause Lena even more pain.

Sitting on the porch swing wasn't the most comfortable option at a little past noon on a Saturday in September when the Santa Anas were blowing through. But after Robert left, her dad was back to sitting in a dark room watching TV, and she'd had the choice of sitting next to her grumpy dad, both of them feeling sorry for themselves, or go outside in the heat. Either way, every second of being away from Lena felt like it was puncturing holes in her heart which was breaking into smaller and smaller pieces every day. When her dad started to snore, she opted for the latter, turning off the TV as she headed for the porch swing.

Between her and her dad, they were the king and queen of sad sacks, morose and sullen. Even Billie was done with them. With two laps to choose from, she opted to sleep on the grass in the shade of the ramp.

Her dad's snores issued through the open front windows, making her wish she had her noise-canceling earbuds. She'd never felt so lonely in her life. When her phone vibrated in her pocket, she pulled it out quickly hoping it was Lena. Feeling like an asshole for being disappointed when she saw it was her mother, she decided not to let it roll to voice mail like she had the last two times.

"Hey, Mom," she said, trying not to sound pathetic. "What are you up to?"

"I'm sitting on the back deck, drinking my third cup of coffee, watching hummingbirds, and I thought I'd call my favorite daughter."

"Well, it looks like you get to talk to me instead." Andy managed a small smile. She should have answered the last two calls. She missed her mom, and she could use someone to talk to.

"Your dad told me you're in a funk. What's going on?"

"Dad told you that?" Maybe he'd mentioned it to her when she called to check in with him, like she did each day. Weird though.

"You sound surprised."

"It's just that he's not usually dialed into that kind of thing. But that's changed in the last few days. He asked me if I was okay twice this morning. It kind of threw me for a loop." Maybe her mom had coached him or something.

"What do you mean?"

"He just doesn't talk about personal stuff."

"Hmm."

"I get the feeling you're not in agreement." Andy suspected her mom might have had a different experience with him. Her mom was the best communicator she'd ever met. It would have been hard for him to avoid it when they were married.

"What did you tell him?" her mom asked.

"I told him I was fine. Just tired."

"Are you?" her mom asked.

"Not really."

"Your dad is exceptional at expressing his feelings. He just doesn't initiate it. Do you?" Exceptional but doesn't initiate. She agreed about the initiation part.

"I asked him if he was dating when I visited last time I was here. Before the accident. He gave me a short answer, which had been the norm, so I've tried to honor his comfort. I'm not mad. It's just the way it is."

Her mother paused. Andy didn't get the impression her mom was upset, so she wondered what was on her mind. In the brief silence, broken by lawn mowers, birds, and the distant surf, Andy wondered if she'd given her dad enough ramp for him to engage, the times she'd tested it. It wasn't like she engaged the first time personal things came up, either. Except with Lena when she needed support. Well, that was something to think about.

"It's not about his comfort. He doesn't like to complain or discuss things that bring other people into the conversation who aren't there to join a conversation about them, even if it's tangentially."

She thought about that. He did engage in some conversations he had feelings about, such as Mrs. Norman's passing and later about the travesty in progress, when developers bought her house and erased his memories of her. He'd also had a lot to say about the slow demise of the rec center's importance in the community. But dating would entail talking about whoever he was dating, and his accident was complaining—which apparently, he'd gotten over. Damn. Maybe this was about her not wanting to talk about things that were uncomfortable for her. Something Talia had complained about since fifth grade. She rubbed the center of her chest.

"Remember hearing about how homophobic your grandfather was?" her mom asked. "Your dad relied on other people's discretion, so he made sure he did the same. Lord knows, he helped me and Lydia when we started dating. People like to gossip, especially at schools even if the school policy is okay with it. You might want to get your dad's perspective. You can tell him I said it was okay to bring me and Lydia up."

"Aside from Grandpa, I didn't know any of that. But you and Lydia didn't start dating until I graduated and then we moved to Santa Cruz."

"Lydia and I started dating years before we moved. We waited for our divorces to make it public. Your dad's and mine went quickly, but hers took a lot longer and her husband didn't even know she was gay until we moved. It was a mess. Her husband wasn't at all as understanding as your dad."

"How did I not know this?" Her parents waiting to divorce until she was out of high school was a point of pride she'd often leaned into when trying to express how cool her parents were. Did this new information have that kind of shine? Or did it tarnish it a little?

"We didn't hide it. You were a kid, and kids are understandably focused on themselves. It's hard learning how to be a functioning human. Your dad and I tried to keep your ship steady. I don't know how little Lena managed. Poor thing."

Andy was still processing the information that her parents had been divorced years before she'd thought they had, but the mention of Lena's name pushed everything to the background as every sense came to attention in her.

"I hated it when her mother refused to let Robert participate in her life. And then she told us she'd get a restraining order on our whole family if we tried to see her."

Wait. What? Andy thought Lena's mother convinced Lena to cut off their friendship. But she threatened her mom and dad, too?

"That woman is a piece of work. Using a child to manipulate a man she knew from the start, well, she knew what she was asking for. I wanted to do unthinkable things to her when her bitter ass caused so much pain. Especially to you and her own daughter. I don't know how Lena came out of that house as adjusted as she did. What an effing B.I.T.C.H." Her mom stopped to take a breath. Andy had never heard such vitriol from her mother. And she certainly didn't know what she was going to do with what she'd learned.

"I had no idea," Andy repeated, head spinning.

"Maybe I should have talked with you about it." She sighed. Her tone was mostly back to normal. "But you and Lena seemed over things by high school, and you were both doing so well academically and socially. Neither of you acted out. It seemed a non-sequitur to bring it up even when it became appropriate."

We were too focused on acting out on each other. But Andy didn't want to give her mother more to be angry about. She decided the way her parents had handled everything was more amazing than just waiting until she graduated before changing the configuration of their family, despite the horrible people who'd tried to make things worse. They needed to be commended. And she and Lena really were past it now. Or were they?

"I'm lucky I have you and Dad. You make a great team." A few tears escaped. Andy was glad her mom wasn't there to see. She didn't want to explain. "I should have talked to you earlier."

"What's going on?"

"Well, Dad for one thing. I'll talk to him when I get off the phone, though. Thanks for the insight. But you know when you called to tell me Lena was in Denver? I've been meaning to let you know she was there. We've sort of been mending fences. Dad probably told you, though."

"He didn't. But I'm sure he didn't think it was his place. Oh, Andrea. I'm so happy you're working on your friendship."

"Actually, we've been seeing each other." Flutters erupted in her stomach getting to say it, even as sadness tinged it because it might not be the case anymore.

"I'm even happier. But where does the funk come in?"

"It's complicated. I think I've been waiting for her all this time. But I might have screwed it up." And Andy told her the whole story, glossing over the sex. "I don't want to, but I can't seem to stop pushing her away. I don't know what to do."

"How are you pushing her away?"

"I'm walled off."

"I see. Is it possible you're protecting yourself?"

"There's a little of that, but I'm mostly protecting her. She's had so much pressure from her mother. I don't want to add to it."

"Maybe you've been protecting both of you. Being supportive for her, might be preventing you from telling her how you really feel about not getting to see her and that you didn't want her to leave."

She nodded even though her mom couldn't see it. "It wouldn't be fair. I did it a long time ago. I pestered her, embarrassing myself, and forced her to be awful to me so I'd stop. I don't want her to run away again."

"Has she told you she'll run?"

"Not directly. But she did tell me she runs when things get hard. And things are hard now."

"So, you're doing it to her, instead. Before she can do it to you?" her mother asked.

She was asking great questions. Making her think. And how hadn't she seen it? She'd known she was doing it the night they talked about past relationships. But this wasn't so obvious.

"I'm doing exactly what she did, aren't I?"

"It sounds like it's possible."

"I have patterns I didn't know I had. How can I see it when others do it, but not when I do?"

"That's the million-dollar question that keeps the self-help industry in business."

Chapter Twenty-eight

When Andy ended the call with her mom several minutes later, she had a very different perspective, and her head was swirling with how it changed a lot of what she and Lena had been dealing with. She tried to calm her mind. Like it did anytime she sat on the porch swing, her gaze drifted to the ceramic mosaic her father had installed on the wall adjacent to the front door. Her, Lena, and her mother, had made it two decades or more ago. "Love Resides in This Home," was written in broken tiles in rainbow colors, arcing over the wave in the middle.

She didn't believe in arbitrary signs. But she had to admit waves had been showing up too much to be discounted. They had always been a symbol of her and Lena's connection. But looking at the mosaic now, it occurred to her that their relationship had been like a wave, beautiful in both its smooth power to move so much water, and the turbulence that came from released energy of it before it destroyed everything in front of it. It needed both power and turbulence to be what it was, and without the strength of their connection, the wave would fade. She closed her eyes, leaning her head back against the swing, in her mind seeing the tiny initials she knew were inscribed near the bottom of the mosaic.

Andy's bare toes were tired from keeping the swing in motion, and the tinkle of Billie's collar had drawn her gaze to the white Hyundai Elantra that had just driven by for the second time in the last three minutes. She tracked the car as it inched past the house, stopped, and backed up to where it was now, idling in the middle of the road. She stared at it with a suspicious longing, because it achingly reminded her of a red Mercedes that had once done a similar thing. She'd give anything to see that red car come around again.

When the car pulled to the curb, she sighed in frustration. This developer with their useless cash offer could fuck right off. She glared at the car. Surely, whoever was in that car could feel the angry energy she blasted their way.

Then a cruel mirage got out of the car and walked up to stand in the middle of the lawn. When the delusion began walking toward her, she didn't think twice about reality and fantasy, having Lena in either dimension was better than none at all. The fresh cut bouquet scent of her favorite person surrounded her as Lena melted into her arms, tangible and warm. It was really her. She wanted to laugh and cry when every emotion she knew exploded within her.

❖

"You're here," Andy whispered.

"I'm here," Lena whispered back. She pressed her face into the curve of Andy's neck. "I thought I lost you."

"I wasn't gone. I just had to figure things out." Andy paused. "I found out I just needed you."

"God, Andy. Me too. I'm not going to let fear keep me from the one thing I've ever wanted in my life," Lena said. The time for not telling Andy how she felt was over. She would never leave her again.

"Which is?" Andy pulled back without letting go.

"You," Lena said without hesitation. "I wanted you to ask me to stay. I was afraid to tell you. I made decisions for you once and I hurt us both. I wanted you to have a choice, but I should have said something. Instead, I waited for you to ask."

"Please stay." Andy had never looked so ardent.

Lena nodded, her eyes filling with tears. "I'm staying wherever you are. I'll lay across your feet to prove it." She looked down at Billie, who was doing just that.

"You don't need to prove it." Andy used her thumbs to wipe away Lena's tears, and the back of her hand to wipe away her own. "I should have asked sooner. You've lived your entire life under pressure. I just didn't want the derecho to come."

Lena studied Andy's eyes. She saw fear in them. She wanted more than anything to make that fear go away.

"The derecho did come. It brought me back here. I think it was a guide, rather than a fear. Maybe a mix of both. But it doesn't control me. I do."

"What about your contract?"

"That's a long story. For later?" Lena noticed something while looking into Andy's eyes. "Your eyes just did a thing," she said. Something danced in her stomach. Andy's gorgeous warm eyes sparkled with an internal light.

"What?" Andy asked.

"They let me in." Lena felt like she'd seen the birth of a new star. Awe, wonder, and gratitude shared space within her.

Andy looked confused. "Always. They don't know how not to."

"I thought so, too. Until just now." Lena searched for words. "After watching you keep your guard up for all those years, and seeing you drop it when we found each other again, I assumed it was completely gone." Amazement rocked her. "But just now, I saw it completely disappear. You've let me in."

While Lena spoke, Andy rubbed the center of her chest, nodding slowly, her face a display of dawning understanding. "I feel it. I think I've learned a lot in the past few days helping me see things I was trying not to."

"Maybe we both needed to prove we trusted this. Trusted ourselves, too." Lena's expression softened. "I do, you know. I trust this. I've learned to trust myself. I've always trusted you."

Andy shivered and her eyes glimmered. "Me too," she whispered. She nuzzled Lena's neck. They held each other for several minutes. During that time, Lena breathed her in, having missed the touch and smell of her.

"I've missed this so much." Lena didn't know how to express it, so simple words had to do.

"Lilac, star jasmine, magnolia, roses."

Andy recited Lena's favorite scents. The unique fragrance and memory of their lives together.

"You have a good nose."

"You smell like our childhood," Andy said quietly near Lena's ear giving her a shiver. "I've been meaning to ask about your perfume."

Lena pulled back, wiping away a tear, remembering a time when she didn't know if she could bear the space between them anymore and not knowing how to bridge it. "I had it made a few years ago during one of the times missing us hurt more than usual."

A warm smile infused Andy's face. "Lilac and star jasmine are your favorites."

"Magnolia and roses are yours."

Andy held her tight. "I love how they blend so naturally."

Lena pressed herself into Andy, kissing her for the first time since she'd arrived. It started slowly but quickly became something deeper, something stronger. Time stopped while they made a start at making up for all the kisses they'd missed in the nearly two months they'd been apart. Their lips rested against one another's, and their breathing began to settle. Lena smiled against Andy's mouth.

"I want to wrap around you so badly, I ache. Remember what I told you I wanted to do to you the next time I saw you?" Andy nodded and her eyes went dark. Images floated through Lena's mind thinking about the time she'd told Andy exactly what she wanted to do to her. The deepest parts of her responded when she thought about all of the times she'd brought up images in her mind of Andy on her screen showing her how much her words had turned her on. She'd made herself come countless times thinking about them. Always immediately followed by longing because Andy wasn't really there.

Tingles spread all the way to Lena's toes when Andy's mouth pressed against hers again. Lena didn't waste time before opening her lips and sliding her tongue along Andy's bottom lip, giving Andy free reign to deepen the kiss. She felt incandescent in Andy's arms.

❖

"You two might want to take that inside before you start a brushfire. With these Santa Anas, the whole neighborhood is likely to go up like kindling."

Andy pulled away to see Mrs. Rafferty standing on the driveway with a casserole dish.

"Oh, shit," Lena muttered.

Andy pulled her closer. Lena dropped her head to her shoulder. Her back shaking with silent laughter. Andy couldn't help but smile, although she held back the laughter. After letting go of Lena, she hurried across the lawn to her neighbor.

"Afternoon, Mrs. Rafferty."

She handed Andy the dish and turned away with a flap of her hand. "It's a beautiful thing, young love. And none more exquisite than sapphic love. I can still remember Sinead like it was yesterday. Her hair was red and so very soft. We'd sneak afternoons sunbathing when the beaches weren't so crowded and we'd kiss when no one was around. That's not all we would do, though. My Bruce loved how happy she made me. He'd pack us picnics. So loving. Not an ounce of jealousy. I remember..." The volume of her voice faded as she grew further away. She sounded wistful, lost in her memories. Andy could only stand gaping until Mrs. Rafferty made it to her porch steps.

Andy couldn't wait to tell Lena what she'd heard. When she went back, Lena was on the swing with Billie standing in her lap. With Billie's paws on Lena's chest. They were forehead to forehead, staring deeply into each other's eyes. Andy's heart did a summersault, and she had a vision of the three of them together watching a sunset somewhere, happy and in love. Who knew? Depending on what Lena wanted, there might be another dog or two, maybe a baby or two, too. Hold the phone. Where had all that come from? She gave herself a silent shake. First things first. Get the casserole into the house. She'd tell Lena about Sinead and Mrs. Rafferty later.

At the top of the ramp, Lena and Billie waited by the open door. Her dad's snores were still rumbling through the house. Billie toddled over to her dad, and they put the dish in the refrigerator. When Andy faced Lena again, she knew that look.

"I had plans for you. Remember?" Lena said quietly, draping her arms over Andy's shoulders.

Andy could barely speak, trembling in anticipation. "Vaguely."

"Get me to your room and I'll remind you." Lena's kiss made Andy's toes curl.

Lena tugged Andy's hands, walking backward down the hall. When they passed Andy's room, she gave her a mischievous smile. It set off small quakes in Andy's stomach, and she barely felt her feet as they walked outside and around the pool.

"I used to fantasize about us in the pool house," Lena said.

"When?" Andy's core pulsed.

Lena opened the door and pulled Andy in, pushing her against the wall as soon as the door was closed. She pressed her breasts against Andy's.

"You were the first person I had any sexual thoughts about." Lena drew her hands down the front of Andy's T-shirt before sliding under it. "Those thoughts about you revealed everything to me. It was innocent at first. Kisses. Holding hands. By the time I kissed you in the auditorium, I didn't know exactly how we'd do it, but I'd envisioned touching you everywhere by then, and I was desperate to be naked with you."

Andy couldn't wait. She had Lena's shorts unbuttoned and her hand inside them before Lena hit the cushions of the couch. Andy swiped through her wet heat, her fingertips barely dipping inside. Lena gasped and she hooked a finger on the waist of Andy's soccer shorts, pulling them down impatiently. Andy pushed them the rest of the way off, shivering at the air that touched her wet center. Lena's fingertips went directly to Andy's clit, teasing her before sliding deeply into her. Andy's shiver became a shudder. A pulse surged through her. At the same time, Andy plunged her fingers into the heat between Lena's legs. Their unrestrained moans blended.

"You're so wet," Andy said against Lena's neck, luxuriating in the dripping heat wrapped around her fingers.

"You do it to me. I told you I wanted my mouth on you. I start throbbing before I even touch myself. I come so hard when I think about it. I'm thinking about it now. How you taste, how you feel between my lips, against my tongue."

Lena moved against her. The sounds she made spilled into the room; no need to be quiet out here. The sound alone nearly made Andy come. Lena's hips rose and fell beneath Andy, meeting the thrusts of Andy's fingers. Andy hovered on her knees above Lena, legs spread as wide as the couch allowed. Lena's fingers had stilled inside of her, as if she couldn't concentrate in the throes of pleasure. It didn't matter as Andy rode them with Lena's thumb pressed against her clit.

"Just hold your hand like that," Andy said breathlessly. Delicious rolling began low in her body. Her orgasm was just about to crest when Lena gasped.

"Oh, God, Andy. I'm gonna…"

She savored the throbbing clench around her fingers, as Lena arched beneath her, pushing Lena's twitching fingers deeper inside her. At the same time, Lena's hand wrapped around Andy's wrist holding her hand in place as she ground into it. Their loud cries, one almost a scream, the other a plaintive moan, filled the space around them. Lena's walls clenched, and the pressure and sounds Lena made caused a sustained blast of radiant pleasure to rush through Andy. She rode the tidal wave of ecstasy as Lena rocked beneath her. When she was able to breathe, she looked into Lena's eyes which were intensely focused on her. She experienced her gaze like a physical sensation, piercing and hot. Compelled by the concentration of desire in Lena's expression, she rubbed her thumb over Lena's clit and spread her fingers while they were still inside. Lena's eyes grew wide, her lips parted, and she rolled her head back, lifting her hips. "Oh fuck," Lena whispered hoarsely. Dripping heat clenched around Andy's fingers again, while Lena arched into her, breath held, and finally rushing out in a shaking exhale when Lena's body went limp beneath her.

"Did you?" Andy asked.

"God. Yes." Lena's entire body quaked before she went still again, and Andy worked her through aftershocks, so intense Lena arched and whimpered with each one.

Andy watched as Lena's body relaxed into the couch. "You are so beautiful, Lena. You…I…fuck," Andy whispered hoarsely because she'd slightly strained her vocal cords with her unrestrained vocalizations.

"I didn't know it was even possible." Lena sounded reverent.

Andy slowly removed her fingers and relaxed against her. Lena slid her hands under the back of Andy's T-shirt where she traced haphazard lines before she pulled the shirt over Andy's head. After which, she removed her own shirt and bra. The sensation of the sensitive skin where their breasts met after the heights their bodies had experienced, was sublime. Andy tangled their legs together and held Lena close, their heart rates slowly returning to normal. Andy kissed a trail up Lena's neck before her lips arrived at her mouth, settling into a lingering kiss.

When their kiss slowed, Lena's lips still moved against Andy's, saying something Andy couldn't hear. Andy found Lena looking at her with the softest of eyes. Her lips continued to move against hers, but now a whisper floated between them. It grew louder. “I love you. I love you. I love you,” she repeated, as if it was a chanted prayer. Every new “I love you” increased the joy in Andy’s heart until she couldn’t contain it.

“I love you, too,” she said in sync with Lena’s whispered mantra. Andy felt the smile that accompanied the words Lena continued to whisper against her lips.

Chapter Twenty-nine

Early afternoon the next day, they made their way to the beach in front of the Seaside Café. Andy went in to get coffee while Lena and Billie spread the blanket. Billie did the hard work of holding the blanket down by napping on it, Andy noticed when she rejoined them. Lena accepted her coffee like she'd been deprived. Honestly, Andy couldn't blame her.

Once settled, Andy explained how her transfer had come about, as uninteresting as it had been. And Lena described the chess match that resulted in her taking the job at *Totally San Diego.*

Andy put her hands palm up in front of her, wiggling the fingers on her left hand. "A weather anchor reciting weather feed information at a traditional news station without digital, serving less than five hundred thousand viewers from Santa Cruz." Andy wiggled the fingers on her right hand. "Or an on-air meteorologist at a traditional, digital, satellite, and current events channel, with an audience of twenty-five million, from Santa Barbara down to the tip of Baja California." Andy dramatically dropped her right hand onto the blanket. She squinted with consideration. "Hard to call."

"You forgot to include being with the woman I love." Lena leaned in to within an inch of space between their mouths. "Nothing would tip the scales the other way," she said. "Nothing."

A murmuration of starlings swooped through Andy's stomach as Lena kissed her. "Good answer. Have I mentioned I love you?"

Andy asked when she ended the kiss before they went too far in a public place.

"Several times," Lena assured her. "Not to call favorites, but the one you screamed when you came in my mouth the first time yesterday, was probably the most memorable."

Andy didn't miss the way Lena's eyes shifted almost imperceptibly. She placed her hand on Lena's cheek, tracing her cheekbone with her thumb. "I've loved you for nearly twenty-five years. And I'll keep telling you." It had torn Andy's heart when Lena confessed no one had ever said those words to her. Not even her parents. Andy would say them until Lena could hear them without her mother's lies saying she didn't deserve it. And she'd keep saying them until her last breath.

"I love you, too," Lena said, turning her head to kiss Andy's palm. "You'll never know how much."

"I know every time you look at me."

Lena playfully pushed her shoulder. "You're such a sap."

"Me? Yeah. I admit I am, just for you," Andy said. They were quiet for a few moments. "Come here." Andy indicated she wanted her to sit with her back against Andy's front. Lena moved into place with a happy sigh. "Almost sunset time," Andy said, kissing Lena's neck.

Lena sank into the kiss. "What made you drop your guard yesterday?"

Andy rested her chin on Lena's shoulder.

"I've been thinking—"

"Big surprise there."

Andy blew a raspberry against Lena's neck, drawing a shriek from her.

"I guess you don't want to know." How had she ever lived without this?

Still laughing Lena wiped her neck. "I honestly do."

"I don't think the reason will be as earth-shattering as you might think."

"Try me." Lena traced her fingertips along Andy's arms. Andy added how Lena touched her to the things she loved list.

"You know when you said you needed to fix the mess you made of things, and I told you both of us participated in it?" Andy asked.

"Yes."

Andy wished they were facing each other so she could see Lena's face.

"And you said you'd do whatever it takes for us to be together?"

"I will. Anything." Lena took one of Andy's hands and threaded their fingers together. "I have a lot to make up for."

Every time Lena berated herself for her actions when she was a child sent an arrow of pain directly to Andy's heart. She scooted around so Lena could see her.

"I don't blame you," she said. "I wish you wouldn't, either. We both have things to work through. If one of them comes up, we should talk about it. Telling each other what's on our minds will help us support each other. I realized I didn't need to do any of this on my own. That's what I was thinking about."

Lena turned to fully face Andy. Tears filled her eyes.

"First, you need to stop making me cry. Second, you don't have to do anything on your own. That's a big part of why I came back. You showed me your pain. You've never done that before. I've seen it sometimes underneath your courage, but you showed me. I had to be here for you."

"I tried not to pressure you. You had enough from your—when you were little. I wanted you to have a choice."

"You've always had to be the solid one. You were always there, even in the hardest days. Always. I want to be there for you, to be the solidest part of your life. You've always been my home. I leaned on you for so long, and it helped me get through the hardest parts of my life, Andy, whether you knew it or not. I want to be your home, too." Lena's eyes were both earnest and intense, searching Andy's. Always searching. "You kept our connection through all our crap. When I couldn't feel it, you had it. Let me do that for you when you need it."

Andy felt Lena's words settle into her. "I want that, too. You were there for me these last weeks. When I began to lose hold of our connection and thought I was drifting away, you kept texting me. Giving me space, showing you were there. You kept our connection solid. I used to think I couldn't hope. I just waited. That's changed this week. I have a lot of hope. So much."

"I want to know what you hope for, Andy. I want us to weave our hope together."

They were quiet for a while. Lena wound her arms around Andy's waist and rested her head on her chest. Andy wanted to live in this moment forever. At the same time, she couldn't wait for what was next for them.

"Do you ever think about stardust?" Andy finally said.

Lena chuckled. "Random. But I spend an inordinate amount of time thinking about it, actually."

"The cosmic or romantic kind?"

Lena pulled back and looked at her, looking amused. "I thought I was the only one who thought of stardust as two separate things. But, to answer your question, I used to only think about the cosmic kind, the stuff we're all made of. Recently I've expanded my ponderings to the romantic kind. Why?"

"It just popped into my head. You and your solar systems and whatnot." Andy waved a hand breezily. "I spend an inordinate amount of time thinking about sand."

"Yeah. You and your reefs and whatnot." Lena flapped her own teasing hand.

Andy caught it and kissed it. "Sand and stardust. They seem like two very different things. But sand is silica, created by stars, and dispersed by supernovae. So, sand is stardust. We're sand and stardust. You and me. Eternally bound together in body and heart. I believe that."

Lena's eyes were soft, her smile loving. She pushed Andy's shoulder. "You're such a sap. A science-y sap, but still a sap."

"Just for you." Andy gave her a tender kiss, trying to express everything she felt. When she gently ended it, she fell into Lena's eyes. It was a habit she'd gotten into, and she didn't plan to break it.

Lena leaned in, nuzzling their noses together. "Just the way I like it."

Maybe this was the right time to tell her the news. "Hey, so I have a surprise followed by a question."

Lena squinted warily at her. "Typically, when people feel the need to warn someone about a surprise, they're worried it won't be received well."

Well, that part hadn't gone the best. She'd forgotten how Lena didn't like surprises.

"You're not wrong. Let's see how this goes, then." She sat up straighter, rocking to get comfortable, which was impossible. "You brought up being each other's home. I want it. So much." Andy had never been so nervous. She didn't know if she could survive it if Lena didn't like her surprise. But why wouldn't she? She would. She knew it. "I know we've only been"—she waved her hand between them.—"for a few months, and most of it was apart. But we've known each other most of our lives. Again, most of it apart." She laughed, but Lena didn't. So, that had fallen flat. "Let me start over."

"Okay." Lena dragged the word out. Her stillness a sign she was overwhelmed.

"So, I don't think it's rushing into things. Not really." Andy couldn't look at her. She'd been so excited to tell her when the stars had seemed to align. And then things had gone sideways for a minute. Now she was thinking this was something she should have talked to her about before doing. She'd made assumptions. Fuck. When she looked up Lena looked scared. "You look…oh crap." She'd done it all wrong. She had to lighten up the mood. "I'm not going to ask you to marry me. If that's what you think," Andy joked. Was that disappointment? What? Not because…but she wasn't…Oh. Christ. This was getting worse by the second. "I mean, unless…I think…I probably will. Just not now? I just need to stop talking."

"Hey." Lena reached for Andy's hand. "I've never been good with surprises. I haven't had many and the ones I have, well. I'm not good at them. You were just so serious. I think I was just reacting to your energy." Lena laughed nervously. "I'm sorry. Please continue."

"I bought a house." Andy just blurted it. "If you don't already have plans, you're welcome to stay with me." That wasn't what she wanted to say. Not at all. "What I really meant was, will you live with me? I need to be better at telling you what I want. I can't keep waiting for you to tell me. I mean, if you have other plans, we can talk about it. But I wanted you to know. So, if you are so inclined, I would like to begin building our home." Her heart was beating like a jackhammer, but she'd done it. Lena seemed to have taken it well. She was smiling. Now they had to discuss it.

"I'd love to."

"Really?" So, she wasn't going to get an award for eloquence. But she'd gotten the girl, which was better.

"I was planning to keep doing sleepovers on your little bed. This is better. So, yes, yes, yes." Lena grabbed her face and peppered it with little giddy kisses. "I can't wait," she whispered and paused. "And yes, to the thing you said you probably will too. If you're so inclined. Just not now."

Lena stared deeply into Andy's eyes before giving her a long, deep kiss that held so much promise. Andy was floating when they parted.

"Probabilities and outcomes are your daily job. They're my way of making the best decision about what to hope for. I think things are leaning in our favor." Andy kissed her. "We'll have to continue doing sleepovers on my little bed for a couple more weeks while some work gets completed. I would really love to not be the only one making decisions about how we upgrade our house."

"Our house." Lena pressed her forehead to Andy's. "I like the sound of that."

Andy tipped her head. "It's always been our house. What else would I call it?"

Lena pulled back. "Our house? You bought the wave house?"

Andy dropped her head to Lena's shoulder. "I forgot to tell you the surprise part," she groaned.

Lena bounced excitedly. "Oh my God! We're going to live in the wave house." She turned to face Andy again. "Kiss me."

Andy leaned in, stopping just before their lips met. "Do you remember what you said to me right before you kissed me that very first time?" she asked.

Lena's eyes glimmered in the gloaming. "I only meant half of it."

"You may have only meant half of it. But your eyes said all of what you meant."

Lena nodded slowly while she leaned forward. "I hate you. Now kiss me."

Andy had never known what it meant to swoon, but she did now. When Lena's lips met hers, she felt transformed. It was a new kind of kiss, a promise to protect the bond they'd always shared, and to celebrate the hope they shared for their future.

"You don't hate me," Andy said when they came up for air.

"I never have. I love you so much it astounds me."

"I love you. Now kiss me." Andy slowly closed the distance between them again, loving that any distance they had to close now was just a kiss away.

"Much better," Lena said right before their lips met again, and she continued to press in, getting as close as she could. Which meant pushing Andy onto her back and deepening the kiss.

They missed the sunset on account of that kiss. But they didn't care. They'd have a lot more sunsets to watch together.

Epilogue

Two Years Later

Relaxing near the siderail of the boat, Lena rested her chin on her stacked fists, watching the fading sunlight dance over the calm water. Catalina Island rose out of the horizon in the distance, and the prickling heat of the sun had dropped to a comfortable temperature. The gentle rocking of the boat, coaxed her into a pleasant lethargy.

Bubbles rising to the surface at the back of the boat roused her, and she rose to attend to her deckhand duties. A mask-covered face with a familiar smile greeted her at the ladder. Lena attended to the specimen samples and scuba gear Andy placed on the deck. An errant set of swells rocked the boat, knocking Lena off balance. She squeal-laughed, grabbing the edge of the livewell tank. When the boat stopped rocking, she continued to place the live specimens into the tank.

"Careful there, Captain. Precious cargo," Andy called as she started up the ladder.

Lena scoffed. "Telling me to be careful? I'm not the one who fell into the drink attempting to jump from the dock directly onto the boat."

"That was years ago, and I was showing off for my girlfriend."

"That was a year ago, and your wife will tease you about it for the rest of your life."

Andy unzipped her wetsuit, rolling the top down to her waist, exposing her bikini top. Lena ran her fingers over her bare abdomen. "I turn you on. Admit it."

Lena kissed her neck. It was cool and salty from the water. "Always."

Andy's hands slipped around her, resting just above her ass. Lena shivered as Andy's cold-from-the-sea body pressed against her while her fingertips teased under the top of her bikini bottoms. Lena loved the way Andy looked at her when she touched her. She always felt the most beautiful when Andy looked at her like this. Every inch of her body responded to the promise of what would come next. But when Andy pulled her closer, her baby belly prevented their bodies from molding together, and she missed the feeling of Andy's skin against hers from thigh to breasts. It took her a bit out of the sexy zone.

"Wanna see more?" Andy asked.

"You just spent forty-five minutes gathering samples. You must be tired."

"I wouldn't call diving thirty-five feet physically demanding. I'd like to expend a little energy with you right now." Andy kissed her slowly, intentionally, purposefully.

When they came up for air, she nipped at Andy's lips. "Let's go below deck."

Andy untied her bikini top. "How about here, in the open air and the breeze to cool us? Besides, Billie and Lourdes are down there. We don't want to disturb their beauty sleep." Lena took in Andy's perfect breasts as she dropped her top to the deck and reached around to untie Lena's.

Lena hooked her thumbs into Andy's wetsuit, her mouth already watering, thinking about the rest of Andy's skin she'd get to taste. She always loved to make love to Andy after she'd been swimming, whether it was in a pool, with the heady smell of chlorine or the taste of the salty ocean. Especially now, when she was so sensitive. One of Andy's hands moved between them, cupping one of Lena's breasts, lightly tracing around her nipple.

Lena felt the touch like Andy was tracing her clit. Fuck. A pulse pushed through her lower body and a flash of electric heat followed. She was so ready.

"I love how sensitive you are." Andy took a step away, her hungry eyes scanning Lena's body. Lena felt a wave of heat at the way Andy looked at her. She shivered in anticipation while Andy pulled the cushions from the bench seats and situated them on the deck, draping a large beach blanket over them. Lena removed the rest of her suit. Andy approached her, sweeping her hands down her arms, her hips, her stomach. "God, you're beautiful." Andy took her hands, lowering her to the bed she'd just created. "I could look at you all day."

"You can when we're finished. I don't want slow, Andy."

"Fast and hard. Got it," Andy said, kneeling between her legs.

The sky was a cloudless blue behind Andy, framing her gorgeous face. Her features looked dark and serious as she drew lines up and down Lena's inner thighs. They were bent and spread, ready for her. Lena could feel the moisture pooling between them. Andy wouldn't have to ease into her. The reaction she had to Andy's touch was visceral.

Andy drew two fingers through her folds, barely dipping in. "You're already so wet." Her voice was awestruck. Lena had to admit the speed of her response to Andy was worthy of awe. Andy never failed to turn her on, but it was at lightspeed lately. Andy's response to it turned her on even more.

"I need you inside. Make me come."

Andy smiled her beautiful smile, before she lowered herself. Lena closed her eyes as Andy's soft mouth descended. She had such a talented tongue. And her fingers. God, her fingers. They slid inside, and Lena couldn't think anymore. She craved the way Andy made her fall apart. Lena couldn't help the sounds she made when Andy's fingers fucked her fast while her tongue worked magic on her clit. She loved the flare of tingles flashing over the sensitive places on her skin and the throbbing in her center as Andy drove her insane with her mouth.

Andy's ass rose and fell with her concentration, as if she was sliding a cock into her. An image of Andy standing in their harness, with her favorite toy already in place sent a riot of sensation coursing through her. She rose. She lived in the stratosphere now. Her back arched. She emitted a long moan as the pressure built, filling her with a luminescent pleasure. It radiated out of her like the long arm of a solar flare. Indescribably hot. Her stomach caught in a freefall as her pleasure crested. She fell headfirst, downward, crashing through brilliant colors in a show she wished Andy could see. Finally, Andy caught her and cradled her in bliss.

When she caught her breath, Andy was beside her and in the slowest way possible, removing her fingers. She trailed them up, gently grazing her clit, and Lena twitched, ready to go again.

"I love you more, each passing day," Andy whispered against her lips.

Lena smiled. "I've never doubted it."

Andy smiled back, their lips still touching, sharing breath. "It's because of the atomic orgasms I give you. Admit it."

"Those make me lust after you. It's this," she said, looking down her body. Andy's hand rested on her stomach, rubbing circles around it. "When I'm feeling self-conscious, you know how to make it go away. You've always done that for me."

Andy smirked. "So, it is the orgasms."

"I'm being serious, you jerk."

"I know. I can't stand for you to feel like that. Fuck your mom for telling you to say goodbye to your looks when you told her we were pregnant. You're beautiful and I want to blow away the clouds that float across the gorgeous blue-green skies of your eyes."

"You show me every day. You kept your cool when I thought you were going to go full nuclear on her."

"She got the point. I wasn't about to let her minimize you winning an Emmy for the coverage of the floods. Limiting contact with her helps. Going to her wedding was enough for a while," Andy said with a frown.

Lena's heart filled with so much love for her wife, who never failed to support her, who always had her back. A tear fell from the corner of her eye farthest from Andy. She hoped Andy didn't notice. Fuck. Was she getting emotional now?

"I still can't believe she was having an affair with the facility manager at the country club," Lena said. "For years. And everyone knew. They deserve each other. Lourdes won't stop growling at him. It says a lot. She's so much happier with us." Lena shook her head, watching Andy's hand caressing her round baby belly. "Enough about your evil mother-in-law. I want to focus on you, my goddess. Always there for me, protecting me from others and, sometimes, myself. Today it was my insecurity."

"With a mind-shattering orgasm," Andy said. Her tone inferring the "duh." "Does that make me your Aphrodite?"

Lena rolled her eyes.

"I recognize that look. Don't go all high school Lena on me." Andy kissed her as if to remind Lena they weren't those kids anymore. "I know what you mean."

Lena pulled Andy back in but stopped their mouths from meeting only millimeters away. "You're the best thing in my life, Andy Phillips. I knew it when I was high school Lena. It just took twelve years for me to admit it." Another tear fell. Andy saw it this time and she licked it away. Lena's whole chest filled with warmth.

Andy rubbed her belly. "I knew it when we were five and you sat next to me during story time. You'll be back to secure in no time, Lena Phillips."

"Who knows how long my baby body will last."

"I'll love you just as much. I'll always be here to tell you how sexy you are. How much I want you. How fucking happy I am that you're carrying our baby. You will always be beautiful, and I will tell you every day for the rest of my life." Andy kissed her again. "I won't lie, though. I can't wait to see your face when I look up from between your legs."

"How do you feel about looking at it from between your legs? I miss tasting you when you've been in the ocean. Think you can balance with the rocking of the boat?"

Andy's eyes darkened and Lena could almost feel the contours of Andy's center on her tongue. "I'm willing to give it a try."

"You did just fine last night," Lena said, enjoying the view as Andy straddled her face.

Epilogue

Two More Years Later

Preparing for her dive, Andy looked out over the pools at the rec center, admiring the work of P&H Pools and Landscaping. Her dad and Robert had done a great job on the first commercial job they had done after they'd merged their companies. It made sense, given they'd spent most of their time together in the four years since her dad's accident. Especially now that they were married. Her dad had recovered better than the doctors had expected, but he still walked with a limp and couldn't lift as much weight. Her dad called it old age, but she called it an excuse to keep Robert nearby. And Robert was the first person to say that's where he wanted to be, second only to being with his grandbabies. Her dad and Robert were the perfect grandpas.

It was like night and day how they were now. Almost immediately after the divorce was final, Robert was the same kind person, but it seemed as if a weight had lifted. It affected her dad, too. The two of them were always laughing and on the move. Andy had never seen either of them as happy and joyful. Her mom and Lydia had even commented on it when their dads got married.

The remodeled swim center was now four times as large, with a lap pool and separate diving and recreational pools, one of which was a saltwater pool. All the new features had reinvigorated the community's interest in the rec center, returning it to the hub of activity it used to be with Danny still at the helm. It had been a sad day for Andy and Lena when Danny retired, but he was living it up in Ensenada now, teaching tourists to surf.

Andy had a forty-five-minute break between Saturday morning swim lessons and swim team practices, and she usually spent the time diving. She still loved the feeling of flinging herself from a high place and piercing the water with little to no splash.

With open swim in full swing, kids and adults were enjoying the pools on a hotter than usual July day. Andy was on the diving platform getting ready to execute the dive she'd been working on, a forward one-and-a-half somersault in pike position. Only a medium difficulty dive, it frustrated her because she couldn't stop over-rotating. Although she'd nailed the same dive in the tucked position in high school.

She went through the movements in her head, blocking out the sounds of the other swimmers. Diving was just geometry and physics. Running start, left foot power spring, legs straight and together, all she needed to do was let her body remember the rest and keep her eyes on the landing point.

After going through the motions in her head three times, she was about to begin the approach, when an adolescent voice broke her concentration. "Are you gonna jump or what?"

Andy was transported to over a decade and a half earlier.

The bottoms of her feet, raw from walking barefooted on the skid tape Danny had gone overboard with. Mitch was standing at the base of the ladder. His voice was playful, yet he'd broken her concentration. The bustling activity not enough to mute her acute awareness of Lena, who sat on the bleachers watching her, but pretending she wasn't. She had to nail the dive.

Fast-forward, sixteen years later. Again, hyperaware of Lena watching from the bleachers, she didn't bother going through the steps in her head. Using body memory only, she took the four running steps to the edge of the platform and leapt off. Her body moved through the steps effortlessly. She hit the water as if a hole had appeared, letting her through without a trace. Beneath the surface, she flipped as she blew her breath out, kicked off from the bottom, and followed the bubbles up. A couple of confident strokes to the ladder, and she was rising out of the water, adjusting her suit bottom. She was squeezing the water from her hair as a voice called out.

"Show off!" Lena stood, wearing a teasing smile. She held a hand over their month-old son's exposed ear, seemingly unaware of his surroundings as he slept in her arms.

Two-year-old Justice, hair still wet from swim lessons, played with a toy whale. Andy approached with a flutter in her stomach. God, Lena was beautiful. When she focused on her, Andy always felt like the luckiest person in the universe. Heat, not at all caused by shame, like all those years ago, spiked through her as she picked up her towel, slinging it over her shoulders.

"That was amazing, babe," Lena said. Pride joined the heat in Andy's body. "You need to work on that entry, though. Massive splash." Lena shook her head as if disappointed. There was a time when Andy both dreaded and craved Lena's taunting, but now she drank it in.

"Oh yeah?"

"Huge splash. Drenched the deck. Almost hit the baby." Lena's eyes sparkled in amusement.

Andy looked toward the pool. The only water on the deck was her own footprints. She shook her head and stepped closer to her.

"Our dads just got here. You want to see if they'll watch the kids for a few minutes while I show you something in the locker room?"

"Is it the same thing as last Saturday?" Lena asked.

Her eyes had gone vibrant blue, but her irises were thinning as her pupils dilated.

Andy grinned. "Yeah. But I've been practicing. I think I'm close to nailing it."

Pink tinged Lena's skin and Andy wanted to see how far under her T-shirt it went.

"You have, indeed, already nailed it. Several times. I can attest to it."

Andy stepped closer. "I guess I need to start learning a new one with a higher degree of difficulty. You know. To impress the judges."

Lena groaned. "Judge. Just one. Me. And I'm already impressed." She leaned toward Andy. "I hate you, now kiss me," Lena said.

"You love me." Andy leaned in, careful not to get the baby wet.

"True, now kiss me," Lena said.

Andy melted, and without a word, she did.

About the Author

Kimberly Cooper Griffin lives in Denver, Colorado, and is probably, at this very moment, writing while sipping a spicy chai latte. She believes in love at first sight, happily ever afters, that not every story needs a third-act breakup, and most books aren't complete without a four-legged companion. Her novels explore the complexities of building relationships, good communication, and finding balance when life has other ideas.

KimberlyCooperGriffin.com

Books Available from Bold Strokes Books

A Million Dollar Marriage by Margo Glynn. Their marriage ended months ago, but with an inheritance on the line, Elsie and Petra will fake it until they cash in, or until their true feelings catch up. (978-1-63679-961-2)

Changing The Game by Lissandra Rowe. Two former college basketball rivals turned lovers are reunited at a luxury resort, where hot days, sultry nights, and undeniable chemistry ignite a second chance at forever. (978-1-63679-998-8)

I Hate You, Now Kiss Me by Kimberly Cooper Griffin. When family brings them home, childhood enemies Lena and Andy are surprised to discover not only are they civil, but they find the missing parts of themselves in each other. (978-1-63679-996-4)

Musical Theatre Mondays by Marie Incontrera. A messy, musical queer romcom about falling in love, falling apart, and rewriting your second act. (979-8-90035-014-1)

Shot Through the Heart by Claire Donniere. When a Secret Service agent goes undercover to protect a senator, she falls for the woman she's meant to investigate and must choose between breaking the rules or breaking her own heart. (978-1-63679-985-8)

The Girl Next Door by Georgia Beers. A witty, heartwarming enemies to lovers romance about falling for the girl next door that proves the best stories are the ones with endings we never see coming. (978-1-63679-933-9)

Experts Only by Kel McCord. Torn between comforting solitude and the irresistible pull of connection, Michelle and Cas begin to wonder if the life they thought they wanted is enough. (979-8-9003507-0-7)

Never Say Die by Meredith Doench. Detective Rory Scott's personal and professional lives converge as she races against time to find the connection between two crimes and bring a killer to justice. (978-1-63679-793-9)

Swept Away by Radclyffe. When ER physician Sloane Marshall is called in as a last-minute replacement for a federal outreach mission in the remote mountain town of Coulter's Gap, she doesn't expect to fall in love with a sharp-edged helicopter pilot. (979-8-90035-008-0)

When Hearts Collide by Renee Roman. A car accident isn't a likely way to meet the love of your life, but when Harlen's and Annie's hearts collide, they may not have a choice. (978-1-63679-923-0)

Yes, Honey by Claudia Parr. Four sexy couples break stereotypes about committed sex to explore lust and love when the honeymoon is over. (978-1-63679-992-6)

Hurricane Season Hustle by Greg Herren. Scotty must catch the killer to protect his nearest and dearest, before they strike again. (978-1-63679-882-0)

Royal Rush: 75 Days to Fall in Love by Lissandra Rowe. When a royal matchmaking scheme leads to a chance encounter with Isabella Acosta-Ramon, a slow burn sparks that neither can deny. (978-1-63679-965-0)

The Moon to Me by Ana Hartnett. Sometimes it takes traveling thousands of miles to discover what's been yours all along. (978-1-63679-918-6)

To Love Violets for Their Thorns by Rachel Sullivan. Forced to face the heartbreak they never quite got over, Elly and Sonia must decide: breathe fresh life into an old love or try again with someone new? (978-1-63679-928-5)

Virtually Perfect by Melissa Sky. If your AI flirts better, listens harder, and never ghosts you...does that count as love? (979-8-90035-005-9)

Brooke Takes Queen by Alaina Erdell. Brooke Staley faces personal and professional upheaval when Elizabeth Bettancourt, the emotionally scarred new owner of the resort she works for, considers selling. (978-1-63679-886-8)

Coda by Anna Gram. Parker is intriguing, magnetic, impossible to ignore—and completely wrong for Hannah. But sometimes love's melody refuses to end. (978-1-63679-926-1)

Secrets Under the Junipers by Suzie Clarke. Who killed Hallie Lynn Peeples? Cecilia McConnel needs to know. Bitsy Hanover holds the key. Can love uncover secrets? (978-1-63679-845-5)

The Debutante Dilemma by Jane Walsh. Two debutantes are engaged to wealthy and titled brothers...but discover they only have eyes for each other. (978-1-63679-896-7)

The Love Book by Gun Brooke. When literary agent Rowan Cross receives an anonymous manuscript that deeply resonates with her, Verity realizes she has accidentally sent her own manuscript, complete with her very real feelings for her boss! (978-1-63679-850-9)

Traveling Toward Forever by Erin Dutton. When almost-strangers take a road trip through America's national parks, love may be the final destination. (978-1-63679-894-3)

Beautiful Things by Emma L McGeown. A warmhearted romance of missed chances, undeniable chemistry, and a stubborn love that maybe, just maybe, can find its way back. (978-1-63679-934-6)

Love Takes a Village by Karis Walsh. As Lena Preiss struggles to manage a busy restaurant in the Bavarian Christmas village of Leavenworth, Washington, chocolatier Devin Meyer brings an unexpected richness into her life, along with her delicious desserts. (978-1-63679-902-5)

Secrets of the Heart by Jenny Frame. When a beautiful stranger starts asking questions about Nikki Sharkey, head of an infamous crime syndicate, Nikki will stop at nothing to protect her daughter Isla. (978-1-63679-653-6)

Talon and the Songbird by Julia Underwood. In a world where survival depends on strategic alliances, Makayla and Talon must navigate not only complex politics but also the dangerous territory of their hearts. (978-1-63679-970-4)

The Great Popcorn Romance by Georgia Beers. Opposites attract, and Riley Shaw stands no chance of resisting Hannah Kramer's magnetic pull. But opposites know just how to drive each other crazy… (978-1-63679-910-0)

Three Blissful Days by Dena Blake. Kendall Jackson attempts to make her ex regret dumping her by announcing she's dating beautiful park ranger Ivy Patterson. But there's nothing fake about how attracted Ivy is to Kendall. (978-1-63679-707-6)

Chasing Her Scent by MJ Williamz. When Sheridan Rousseau walks into Lisette Mouton's charming little bookstore in Quebec City, she unknowingly holds the key to a mysterious box hidden in a secret room. (978-1-63679-900-1)

Heart's Run by D. Jackson Leigh. Hoping to recover an escaped racing mare, stock transporter Tobie Mason locks horns with local wild horse advocate Maggie Wilkes. (978-1-63679-825-7)

Scandalous by Kris Bryant. When a Hollywood actress trades places with her twin sister, everyone's in an uproar about getting duped, but Lindsay's more concerned about finding out which twin she made out with. (978-1-63679-874-5)

The Art of Love by Ali Vali. When Mimi and Bianca both set their sights on Jolly, sparks fly, loyalties are tested, and hearts collide as they navigate the unpredictable nature of their hearts (978-1-63679-719-9)

The Other Side of Forever by Kel McCord. Will Kenzie and Rachel be able to make love work when Rachel's cozy suburban dream feels like Kenzie's worst nightmare? (978-1-63679-812-7)

The Secrets of Rhydian Hill by Ronica Black. A doctor in need of a new start. A woman running from a killer. A love story that could end in tragedy. (978-1-63679-880-6)

www.ingramcontent.com/pod-product-compliance
Ingram Content Group UK Ltd.
Pitfield, Milton Keynes, MK11 3LW, UK
UKHW040742160426
11895UKWH00002B/230

9 781636 799957